The Boat at the End Of Lover's Lane

Robert P. Barsanti

Copyright © 2012 Robert P. Barsanti

All rights reserved.

ISBN:9798324882525

DEDICATION

To my Sweetie

ACKNOWLEDGMENTS

Thanks to Charlie Britton, Meri Lepore, Rourke, and his Mom
For reading

Cover art by Alondra Barragan,
Nantucket High School, class of 2024

CHAPTER ONE

At six in the morning, Miss J.T. Palmer lay on the floor of her kitchen. In the other room, Valerie Bertinelli was making some delicious s'mores popcorn on the Food Network. Miss Palmer wore sweatpants and a Nantucket Whalers sweatshirt. A wine glass had broken in the fall and the wine had spilled. It had since evaporated. Half of her face didn't move. The other half was gasping.

Detective Danny Abraham had a battering ram ready to break in the front door, but his partner had slipped around the back and rolled open a sliding glass door which led to her vegetable garden. He walked past the former history teacher, former principal, former school superintendent, and the woman for whom the high school gym had been named, turned off the TV, then opened the front door.

"Danny, call the E.M.T.'s."

The sergeant brought the battering ram back to the trunk, then called dispatch from the front seat.

Inspector Henry Coffin squatted near her face. One eye was darting around, but not focussing. She was trying to make a noise, but it only sounded as if she were trying to clear her throat.

Henry stroked her hair.

She stopped making noise.

The silence saddened him.

We had not seen her at Sunday Mass. Then, she didn't come to Tuesday morning coffee, so, on Thursday, we called the police and asked for a wellness check. So it could have been as short as five days, or as long as…

Well.

Henry stood so as to put the house to rights, somewhat. Pick up the broken glass, put the wine bottle away, something like that. But she starting hacking again, so he returned to his haunches and stroked her hair.

When the E.M.T.'s came, they lifted her onto the stretcher, belted her down, then carried her out of her house for the final time.

Coffin waved off his partner in the early dawn, then sat in the back of the ambulance. It wasn't his first ride.

Pidge had spent two straight nights on the night shift. Roberta, the head nurse, was happy to put her on the schedule and she was happy to accept it. Her fiancé, Brian could take the nights by himself. Third shift was quiet. No administrators, no doctors, and no visitors. Just patients who were trying to sleep.

When she worked the third shift, she shared the nurse's station with Gabriella. Gabby had come to nursing on the easy path. She knew what she wanted to be in high school, went to a nursing school, did her hours at Mass General in Boston, partied in the Fenway, slept when she could, and came to Nantucket as one of the last steps on her career climb. She was 27.

Pidge had taken the hard way, thanks to her father. Pre-med at Colby ended right after Dad walked away into the Casco Bay fog and left her with a sheriff, a bankruptcy, and an auction. After, there were a series of community colleges, evening classes, bartending, waitressing, and less flattering work to pay through Organic Chemistry, tests, and nursing rounds in order to wind up on Nantucket at 33. Gabby looked bright and shining, Pidge was stick-whipped and gasping. But here they were.

Most of the time, the work was easy. You walked around, checked the vitals, cleaned up from dinner, and went back to the desk. In the great digital world of modern medicine, you really didn't need to get up from the desk. It was all spread out before you on four flashing screens.

Not so much in the emergency room.

The nurses had got the call from the ambulance right after the E.M.T.'s had loaded the old woman into the back. They would let Doctor Tupper sleep for this one, but they called Pidge down.

At this hour of the morning, coming from Easton Street in town, the ambulance would run the lights, but not the siren. This was no longer an emergency.

The ambulance backed into the parking slot, the doors slid open, the boys pulled the stretcher out, extended the legs, then wheeled it in. Its passenger was getting oxygen from a mask and fluids from a saline drip.

Mrs. Stein, the head nurse in the emergency room, received her with Pidge at her side.

Henry Coffin, in a gray flannel shirt and green khaki pants, walked along. Pidge looked at the older and native nurse, then at Coffin.

Pidge stopped him. "I'm sorry sir. Family has to wait out here while we get her cleaned up."

Stein didn't look up from the form she was filling out. "He's not family, are you Henry?"

"No, I'm afraid not," he said. "But I will stay for a bit, if you don't mind."

"Suit yourself."

At a nod from the head nurse, the two of them shifted the passenger over onto a hospital gurney. Pidge pushed her past the desk into Examining Room One. She replaced the mask and the line, then made a note of it on her chart. Normally, she might start prepping, but Pidge suspected she should wait. Stein came in almost immediately.

"Pidge, can you do this?"

"Of course."

"She was my high school history teacher. I can't clean her up."

At this point, both women noted that Miss Palmer didn't smell as ripe as she might have had someone found her earlier.

"Sure," she said. "Who is the guy?"

Stein smiled. "That's Henry Coffin. Rather, Inspector Henry Coffin. He's a cop. They found her on a wellness call."

"Doesn't look like a cop."

"Doesn't act like one, either," she said.

Stein, like Coffin, took a moment to stroke the old woman's hair.

Pidge smiled. It was an odd island.

Stein noted it. "He's a good person. He says he is a Quaker and that keeps him from guns, uniforms, and the rest. And he has the right last name."

"How is that?"

"If you work down here with us long enough, you'll soon see why."

Stein continued to stroke the older woman's hair and cheek.

"Miss Palmer is a nice person. Be good to her."

"Absolutely."

We like our hospital. It is one of the things we need to live out thirty miles out to sea. We don't want to go to the mainland if we don't need to. And if we fall off a ladder or get hit by a drunk driver or have a heart attack on the seventh hole at Miacomet, we want to be seen by someone who knows our name.

In particular, we want our children to be born on island. The maternity ward is in one of the corners of the second floor, with windows visible from the streets. Island mothers can see those lights, learn who the woman in there is, and can wish her luck. If we did it, someone else can too. And when we are going to die, we would like to die out here as well.

Miss J. T. Palmer was in Room 22.

It was a waiting room. Generally, if we make it to Room 22, we aren't going to stay long.

Room 22 was decorated as if it was a hotel room. On one wall, a print of Great Point Light flashed in the darkness. On another wall, a painting showed a fishing boat heading out. The painting was titled "Outward Bound."

Otherwise, the walls had been papered with a subtle green and white stripe, table and standing lamps illuminated the room, and four folding chairs were ready in the closet.

Inspector Coffin came to visit Miss Palmer two evenings later. He wore the same green pants, although he had changed his shirt. He got off the elevator at five o'clock and walked down to Room 22. None of the other nurses stopped him. Pidge watched them, understood that her shift was ending, and that there were a lot of things she needed to learn about Nantucket.

The stroke had left Miss Palmer without speech and partially blind. Her mind was skipping from groove to groove and the medication helped, but sundown came every day. And with sundown, came panic, and anger, and the frog sounds that she still could make.

Inspector Henry Coffin held her hand. With his other hand, he smoothed her sweaty hair.

She calmed.

Pidge stood in the door.

"Did you know her?"

"I do," he said, without turning. "She doesn't like me much."

"Were you lovers?"

He snorted. For Henry, it might be the first laugh he had in a while.

"No. I didn't arrest people and put them in jail as fast as she would like. Especially speeders."

"Oh."

He stroked her hand.

"Her house is on Easton Street, just up from Brant Point. Five feet from the street, practically right outside, the drivers would accelerate from one stop sign to the next."

"Scofflaws."

"She wanted one of those automatic signs posted outside her house that flashed the speed limit."

"You guys didn't do that."

"Nope," he said.

She watched the care the old man took.

"It's nice that you are here. For her."

He nodded.

"How is she doing?"

"You know I can't tell you. HIPAA and all that."

"Okay."

She resettled. "Her heart and lungs are strong. We will probably transfer her in a day."

He nodded. "Off island?"

"Probably."

"It will be the first time she went off island in fifty years."

Coffin turned slightly so he could see Pidge. The nurse was young, it seemed, with blond hair and pink scrubs. Around her neck, she had a series of lanyards and badges.

She had a very shiny ring on her left hand.

"That's quite a ring."

She put her hand over it. "I probably shouldn't wear it here."

"It's fine."

"I don't want it to get caught on things."

"I'm sure you are careful. Who gave it to you? Anyone on island?"

"Brian Swain."

Coffin cast his mind back and got an image of the realtor.

"He's a nice guy."

"Yeah," she says. "I suppose he is."

"He is. I knew him when he was a kid."

"Well, I think he still is a kid."

"Do you have a date?"

"Not yet."

"Don't rush."

"I won't."

Coffin knew of Brian. He had come back after college, he had married, he had two kids. Then, he was single. He knew Brian's father, Big Jim, in a professional way.

Coffin smiled. "Where are you from?"

"Boston."

"Before that?"

"Maine, if you go all the way back," she said. Pidge stepped forward and check the saline drip. In that moment, she measured Miss Palmer's vitals.

"I'm Henry Coffin."

"I was told."

"Good."

"I'm Pidge Hamill. Most of the time I will be in the Opiate Clinic."

"We need that."

"The state thinks so."

"Sometimes, they aren't wrong."

On the next morning, Miss Palmer did not wake up. The nurse on duty thought that the machine that administered morphine might have been set too high. These things happened.

Inspector Coffin visited at the end of his shift and found Room 22 empty. He sat in the chair for a moment and listened for the chains of history.

CHAPTER TWO

At eleven in the evening, Orion was climbing over the Nantucket's eastern horizon. Sergeant Danny Abraham had finished the novel he had brought out on patrol. He sat silently behind the wheel. Inspector Henry Coffin, too, was silent. September air built up on the windshield.

Coffin was silent because he was asleep.

Unlike his partner, Inspector Coffin did not wear a uniform, carry a badge, or have a gun. The habit of the Quakers settled on his shoulders easily and he felt no need to shrug it off. He hadn't put the cuffs on anyone in at least ten years and hadn't even raised his voice.

Coffin could be silent for the entire night…or even for a week. He lived in silence without expectation. Danny believed that, on any given day, Coffin might say a total of ten words and all of them were addressed to him.

But, we knew Henry. He was one of us, whether he liked it or not. He was an islander, though not by birth. His family stretched back to the first white man to cut a deal out here. But he was born and grew up in Connecticut, had the rich kid background, went to the rich kid schools. Then. at twenty five, he moved into the house of one of the whaler ancestors, Zenas Coffin.

Twenty summers ago, there had been a young wife and a younger son in the old family mansion on Main Street. Lisbeth played the cello; her music washed out the second floor music room window and flowed up the street. Tourists on the brick sidewalks, by the cobblestones, would look up and have feelings. The boy, Pete, played in rooms decorated with Chinese lacquer and British porcelain, underneath paintings of whalers and their boats. The boy had toys, videotapes, and loving parents who gated off the stairs and cut his grapes in half.

Then, on the Fourth of July, mother and son walked down to South Wharf to welcome her parents for a week of vacation and grand-parenting. In the summer time crowd, the little boy had slipped out of his mother's hand on Straight Wharf. Her parents were waving from the deck of the Gray Lady as it backed into the pier. Pete had run to them, leapt off the end of the dock, and disappeared.

In spite of a full Coast Guard search including divers, draggers, and a helicopter, he wasn't found for three days. Finally, his body washed ashore across the harbor at Monomoy and was found by a golden retriever on the beach.

We didn't want to know, but we learned. Gravity brought us to the ground.

So.

Inspector Coffin had been farmed out to the night shift. Pacifists have very few friends in police departments. In fact, the Chief had offered him a no-show job several times. If he wanted to drink himself to death each and every night, the Chief would happily clock him in and clock him out. Coffin had smiled at that.

We knew the man was haunted. And one of the few bits of self preservation Coffin did every night was to get out of the house. Danny could imagine why.

Who would want to spend the night in a house hearing those footsteps?

Who would want to stay?

He did.

So, Danny rode with Henry Coffin on the third shift. We knew why. We understood. Better to spend the night working than listening for the footsteps.

At two in the morning, he woke up.

"Let's get coffee."

"It's Friday night."

"So?"

"Do you think that we should be out here preventing drunks from hitting trees?"

"We are only getting coffee."

"No, we aren't."

But Danny put the squad car into gear and pulled out of the parking lot.

The Chicken Box was monument to the unimportant people of Nantucket. Back in its youth, it sold fried chicken to the workers, the sailors, the farmers, the house cleaners. Then, with the winking acceptance of a liquor license, it became the dance floor and dive bar for the rich and the poor.

At two o'clock, on a Friday morning, the Box was bright and shining. A horseshoe bar sat in the middle of the room, between a dark dance floor and a well lit, but equally empty, pool tables. Two men lazily pushed brooms around the floor. The bar, however, had six people sitting around it, all in blue t-shirts, while the Red Sox make a mess of the Angels on twelve televisions. The six people had money drawers in front of them, stacks of cash, and a long string of register tape.

Danny knocked and walked in first, but no one looked up at a black man in a blue uniform. Coffin followed and led his partner to a corner of the bar, away from the bartenders.

The owner, Jon-Jon Duarte, came over to shake hands. He was over six feet tall, rail thin, and darker than Africa. He wore thick gold chains around his neck and his wrists. In his youth, Henry had rescued him from a dark mob with the help of headlights and a camera. They never spoke of it.

"Inspector! How can I help?"

"Coffee for the two of us."

"Sure."

A pot of coffee had been warming for the last five hours. Jon-Jon poured two cups of coffee then began talking to one of the bartenders. While he was talking and one hand was gesturing, the other dripped a shot of Jim Beam into the old man's mug.

Danny didn't understand why he bothered with the sleight of hand.

Jon-Jon slid the two mugs over and returned to his bartender and the Red Sox. The old man dumped two containers of cream into his coffee. Danny took his black.

The Chicken Box bartenders were slow to ring out their registers for obvious reasons. Last call, in all island bars, came at one. But if you were downtown at the Club Car, that last call might really have happened a lot earlier, when the last of the rich and respectable were getting shoved out the door and the crew was deep in clean-up. By one-thirty, the Club Car doors were dark and locked; the younger waitresses and bussers headed out to the beach party, or the moors, or some house. They had pockets full of tips, the night was young, and fun was breaking. We know how it is. The older ones, the cooks, the bartenders, and some of the waitstaff slipped off for one final drink. At the Chicken Box. We know how that is, too.

By the time Coffin finished his first cup and was onto his second, twenty men and women, in black and white, had stepped in the doors. The bartenders had finished with the drawers and counting the tips. One of them had slipped into the back and returned with a sheet cake from Stop and Shop with "See You Later" written on the frosting. Labor Day had passed four days before.

Jon Jon returned to the two police men.

"Sorry to hear about Miss Palmer."

"She fail you as well?" Coffin smiled.

"She would say that I failed."

"Of course she would," Henry said. "In the end, though, there was no pain."

Jon-Jon, with a beer bottle in his hand, raised it. Coffin met him and they toasted.

"It's the best we can wish for." Jon-Jon said.

"Spoken true." Coffin answered.

Sergeant Danny Abraham watched the crowd and ignored his partner's second drink.

"Did you go to the wake?"

"No wake." The Inspector answered.

"No?"

"Families don't want that anymore. They can't get everyone here."

"There will be a service?"

"Tomorrow. But at Lewis'."

"Wasn't she Catholic?"

"She was." Henry added, "But it's wedding season and they don't have any time at the church tomorrow. And the family can't be here too long."

"You're going?"

The old man nodded.

"I'll try." Jon-Jon nodded.

"Noon."

With the ending of this conversation, and the ending of the Inspector's mug, Danny lifted him off the stool. Coffin stood on his own feet, waved good bye, and walked out on his own to the door.

Outside, the September air remained warm and wet. Danny had parked the car in a nearby parking lot, although he wasn't sure why he did that either. We all knew where they were.

They had crossed the street when they heard footsteps approaching from behind them. Danny Abraham, late of the Boston Police Department, turned and put his hand on his gun.

"Inspector!" A voice shouted.

Now the old man stopped along the far side of the street.

He turned, "How are you, brother?"

The speaker was heavy, with chef pants with blue checks, a white tunic shirt stained with food and a baseball hat. Like most of the island cooks, he was hispanic.

He huffed to a stop, "Been better."

"Busy night?" Coffin asked.

"Labor Day doesn't end."

"No."

Coffin had no idea who the man was.

"I am Henry Coffin." The old man introduced himself.

"I heard," he responded. "Juan Collonne. I cook at the Atlantic Cafe."

"Sure."

"Are you a cop?"

It was an understandable question. Henry Coffin was out of uniform and looked out of sorts. Probably a little bit buzzed, truth be told.

"He is," Danny chimed in.

Juan looked into the dark of the parking lot. "You're not a Fed, or an undercover, or anything like that?"

"Just a guy with a job," Coffin added.

"You don't have ID, do you?"

Coffin glowed with impatience. "How can I help you?"

"Look, the waitresses, they say that you are the guy to ask, but I don't know."

Coffin smiled at him.

"What did the waitresses say?"

"They said that you handle things unofficially."

"That depends."

"Sure."

Juan looked back into the darkness. "I don't have money for this."

Coffin smiled, "No money needed."

The chef nodded.

"What's the problem, my brother?"

"We are missing one of our waitresses."

"What do you mean by 'missing'?"

"She has missed her last three shifts."

"And…"

"She lives in a house with the other girls. And they are worried."

"It is Labor Day. People move on after Labor Day."

"She left all of her stuff. ALL of her stuff."

The implication was not lost on the old man.

"Where do they live?"

"Off Lover's Lane."

Coffin looked at him. Lover's Lane was a dirt road that paralleled the state forest.

"They are staying in a boat," he added.

"What is her name?"

"Caroline."
"What is her last name?"
"I don't know."
Coffin nodded.

CHAPTER THREE

So, when dawn came, they went to Lover's Lane.

The plutocrats did not live on Lover's Lane. The road had been laid out and built in a time when the need for housing was more important than the need for roads. One side of the road was dark with the ordered pines of the State Forest. The other side was dark with houses. Most of the houses had eight or more cars parked in the yard. Near the end of the road, when the dirt, sand, and water converted to pavement, one final single story house had been tucked into the woods. A peeling and gray cabin cruiser was propped up next to it: "The Sea Breeze."

And a ladder.

"Don't wake them up." Danny cautioned.

"I won't."

Coffin opened the car door and stepped out. Danny took the moment to ease the big car up onto the pavement fifty yards ahead. In the pool of light that surrounded his cruiser, Coffin could see the water dripping from the car's undercarriage.

He crossed the road and slipped into the driveway.

An old dark house.

A driveway that had been shells and pebbles that had devolved into weeds.

Four cars. One without a license plate.

And a cabin cruiser on a rack.

So.

We know how it is. Everyone has to work.

The girls didn't have money. And they may not, strictly speaking, be legal. They were bartenders and waitresses; they got paid cash and spent it. When the morning came, someone would come down the ladder and slip into a waiting car and clean houses for the day or they would work at another restaurant or they would work in other ways. Their bed cost a couple hundred a week. In a grounded boat.

We know how you start out. It isn't pretty.

The Inspector knew other things. He knew that the owners of the Atlantic Cafe did not want the Inspector to look too carefully into their employees, their payments, the other jobs they worked, or the housing arrangements. And he knew the women in that boat were worried. They didn't speak to the old man themselves, but they sent an emissary. And if they were worried, they didn't think that Caroline had gone to Florida to get a start on her winter work or that she eloped with the son of a hedge fund magnate.

A light went on in the cabin of the boat.

Coffin backed into the shadows and walked to the waiting patrol car.

Another car was making its way down the rutted dirt road.

Coffin raised his hand to Danny. The sergeant left his hand on the keys and waited.

Pink's Cab, a white minivan with a glowing sign on top, bounced into the driveway. Three women, carrying their high heels, left the cab and walked towards the boat.

Pink looked over at the police car.

He waved.

In Coffin's mind, a penny fell.

Henry Coffin, for a moment, thought of talking to the women carrying their shoes. But history and prudence suggested that Pink might know something about the women he was dropping off so early in the morning.

They let Pink reverse and head back to the Boulevard. Then, Coffin nudged his partner and they followed.

Halfway down the empty street, Pink pulled over. Danny pulled in behind him. Coffin walked out of the car.

Lewis Pinkham resembled a defrocked priest. He was a good fifty pounds overweight, middle aged, and should be sitting in a parish somewhere, wearing a roman collar, drinking tea and eating sugar cookies out of a tin. He had been born on the island to a long time fisherman and woman who sold "antiques," left for UMass and then Suffolk Law, before returning to the island for the last of his father's illness.

Pink kept his cab clean and well organized. He was a lover of jazz, mostly from the bebop era, but his tastes could go back to New Orleans and Kansas City and advance into the music of Sun Ra. He kept stacks of brochures for the whaling museum and the deep sea fishermen on the front seat. He also kept his iPod, his cell-phone, and a 24 ounce, insulated mug of coffee. Were you a New Yorker coming from the airport, you would find that the seats were clean, the windows transparent, and the conversation sociable. And if you happened to need an eight ball, or were looking for some friendly female company, he could help you out with that as well.

Coffin straightened himself and approached the driver's side.

"What can I help you with, Inspector?"

Pink put both hands on the wheel and looked forward.

"Your last fare. Where did you pick the three of them up?"

"They were at the ferry."

"They were?"

"Yup." He looked straight ahead.

"So if I go in there and ask them, that's what they will say?"

"I have no idea what they will say."

"But they were at the ferry dock six hours after the last boat arrived?"

"I don't ask personal questions."

"Let me ask you another question. Have you picked up anyone named Caroline?"

"No."

"No?"

"No." He said. "I don't ask those questions. I don't care about their names."

"Even on a credit card?"

"No Caroline." He said. "Not at all." He glanced at the Inspector. "Can I go now?"

Coffin backed away. "Always helpful, Pink. Always helpful."

CHAPTER FOUR

Pip waited for the Inspector. Today, he had a woman's size four ballerina slipper in his mouth. When the door opened, he started barking, running in circles, and chewing on the slipper.

"Oh, Pip." Coffin closed the door behind him. With the slipper firm in his mouth, the dog walked between the Inspector's legs and waited for a butt scratch. After a long moment of relief, the dog circled around and sat in front of the old man.

Henry had learned not to try to pull the slipper from the dog's mouth. That was the sign that playtime was ready to begin. Playtime was always ready to begin.

Instead, Coffin fastened the collar around the dog, clicked the leash, and turned around for the morning constitutional. Pip dropped the slipper. Henry had no idea where his ex-wife, Lisbeth, had left this, but he suspected she wouldn't need it anymore.

Outside and on the bricks, the dog bounced up to an elm and took attendance for all of the other dogs who had stopped there.

Pip was new to the Inspector. Six weeks prior, house cleaners had called for help from Animal Control. Since Animal Control didn't start answering the phone until nine in the morning, the call went to the Inspector and Sergeant Abraham on the night shift. When they arrived at the house in Madaket, a squad of Guatemalan women stayed in their little Ford while the house reverberated with barks. Nobody knew how long it had been inside.

Henry had grown up with dogs, although smaller ones. His parents had liked beagles and terriers; his mother had wanted a dog to sit on her lap. On the other hand, Danny had not grown up with dogs. In his words, the only dogs he knew were the ones that chased him. So, Coffin was selected to deal with the door.

Just as now, the barking increased as he approached the door. When he unlocked it (with the maid's keys) the dog came sprinting out. It ran circles around both cars, barking all the time, then ran around the house four times.

Danny had not finished his ham sandwich. Coffin took it and placed it on the ground near the front of the car. The dog inhaled it.

Inside the house, the cleaners would have their work to do. The dog had been locked in here for a week or so. Henry found a soup bowl, filled it with water, and brought it outside.

The dog slurped that all up.

Then he sat in front of the Inspector.

Danny clapped his hands from behind the windscreen.

Coffin found out who had rented the house and he called. There was no answer for a week.

So, now he had a dog. He named him Pip.

This morning, like all mornings, Henry walked him up Main Street to the corner of Pleasant Street. September had robbed the street of the idle traffic and the most of the walking tourists. The plumbers and electricians rocked their vans back and forth on the cobblestones, but the traffic had gone home for the year. The Hadwen house had pride of place at that corner, with four Corinthian columns and a long white bench.

Man and dog, they visited the gardens behind the house, with great relief, then turned down Summer Street, past the Summer Street church, up an alley alongside the Barnacle Inn, and then down Fair Street, back to the cobblestones on Main and a brief stroll back to the house. Pip walked straight to his dish and looked up. A tired and annoyed Henry Coffin filled the dish with kibble, and, because he could, he doused it with beef broth. At a word, Pip dug in.

Coffin was asleep before the dog finished.

His house on Main Street was, like almost all older houses in town, pushed right up onto the sidewalk, but his bedroom was in the back on the second floor, with a door that walked out onto an open porch over the kitchen. The kitchen had been built for his then-wife, Lisbeth, as had the porch.

After she had left, things remained as they had been. Lisbeth had emptied her music room of all but a stand. Friends had packed up Petey's room into boxes and trash bags. That which could be re-used, went to a church. That which couldn't, moved into the basement. Thomas the Tank Engine had been silent in that dark for fifteen years.

Henry had added heavy curtains to his room, at least, and paid two Jamaican women to come through the house, clean his messes, and leave him some barbecue every week. Danny sent them by and Henry paid them, in cash, tucked into an envelope on the stairs.

The centuries sat on the sofa. His family built the house back in the last days of whaling. Inside, many of the treasures remained, be they ivory, malacca, or gold. Zenas Coffin, he of the whaling fortune and father of eight, looked down on the main hall and coat rack. Perhaps, he was thirsty for one last glass of punch from the famous punchbowl that had filled with dust in a cupboard.

While Inspector Coffin slept, the last of the tourists biked by, the contractors drove their trucks home, and the rabbits hopped over his yard and left chocolate drops. They would dissolve in the evenings rain and get spread in the next visit from the landscaper.

Pip wandered the house. He lay on the sofa in the sitting room, then he padded through the downstairs before finally coming into the master bedroom. A pile of dirty laundry sat at the foot of the bed. Pip lay there as well. At noon, he started licking Henry's hand and poking him with his nose. Coffin opened an eye. Pip wagged his tail. Then he poked him again.

"Okay."

And the old man was shoved into another day.

Today, he showered and put on the fresh clothes that had been folded and placed into one of the drawers. Downstairs, he had a cup of orange juice and a piece of toast, Then he laced his sneakers on, found a Whaler hat, stuck his phone in his pocket, and put Pip on a leash. He did not lock the door.

The path to the Dickie Lewis's Funeral Home led him through the center of Nantucket. In the early afternoon of a school day, the streets were quiet. The bicyclists were all honeymooners; either the couple was young and giggly or they were middle aged, grim, and moving on with the rest of their lives. Henry was careful with the people on the white bicycles. The rumors were that the bicycle rental shops handed the white ones out to the people who looked least capable of pedaling over the cobblestones and amid the narrow streets.

Pip liked everyone. Even the ones on white bicycles.

We nodded to Henry. We waved at him and we stared at him and his dog. Coffin had been on island long enough to know, remember, and bury many late night residents of angry and drunken houses. He had met the fathers, he had met the sons, he had sat with folded hands, while they explained that this simply could not have happened the way that it did. It couldn't have.

So we waved at him. Good to be on friendly terms.

Lewis's Funeral Home was tucked at the end of Union Street; the road started off as a very expensive street downtown and wound up as the last step before you come to Poverty Point. The houses at the far end of the Union Street should never have been built. Their basements were beneath the high tide line and only plastic and cement kept the gray

Atlantic from filling them twice a day. Poor people had made it work when they had to. Today, the new hedge funders hoped the technology and a good sump pump could keep their investment dry until they flipped it.

Dickie took over the business from his Dad. His Dad took over the business from someone else. His house had been a barn, then it was refurbished into its current form. It remained as plain as most of the people who had made their last stops there. From Rickie's, you didn't have to drive far to get to the church, and it wasn't much further for the cemetery. He stood tall, but he didn't want to. He was tall enough to knock his head in most of the doorways, so he stooped and shuffled. He shook hands, said the right things, and tried to be worthy of the grief that flickered in his front room. He knew he wasn't worthy of it, but he could put on a good try. We appreciated it.

Not many had come for J.T. Palmer's Memorial Service.

Dickie shook Henry's hand as the old man walked in. They had met many times. Coffin knew the undertaker's son in a professional capacity. Both of them hoped the Marines would help.

Dickie put his hand out and scratched the dog's head and back. Pip endured it with a wag. Then, Rickie reached into his pocket, found a treat and asked who was a good boy? Both men were self aware enough to know that they didn't qualify. Pip sat with a wagging thump and was rewarded.

Habitually, when the Inspector came to Rickie's for a memorial service, he sat in the back row, in the corner, so that anyone who might want to talk to him had to clear many hurdles to do so.

No one was surprised by the presence of a dog at a wake. Pip, who felt he truly was a "good boy," lay down at Coffin's feet.

Today, he was the sixth one in the room. He was joined by the chair of the school committee, the current superintendent, and a blue haired Math teacher. A young couple, unknown, sat in the first row. And Herman Lamb, the lawyer for that generation, had his briefcase beside him.

In the front of the room was a low table with two bouquets of flowers on either end, two pictures of Miss Palmer, one as a teacher, one as a principal. In the middle, a black box waited for the bell to take attendance.

After ten minutes Father Nunes eased in the back door.

Dickie took the moment to head backstage and have a conversation, then both men came out. Father Nunes carried himself as an Archbishop. He wasn't going to allow anyone to kiss the ring, but he beamed his personal holiness into all before him. He shook hands with her niece and her husband, had a quiet word with the chairman and the current principal, then he eyed the Quaker with his dog in the back row.

Father Nunes turned and headed back behind the door. He would prepare for this, as he did for all services, as if he was in a cathedral. Outside of holy sanctuary, he could not offer the bread of Christ, nor could he perform the miracle of water and wine, but he could say a few sanctified and holy words for a parishioner. It was the least he could do.

The six of them resettled as they waited for the ceremony to start. Jon-Jon joined the group, but ducked into the back and sat next to Coffin.

When Father Nunes returned in gold and finery, Rickie asked everyone to rise.

And everyone did, save one.

Nunes shot an eye at the Quaker, but he remained unmoved and seated.

Afterward, the niece carried the box with her, She had a few words with the lawyer, smiled, and stepped away with her husband. And with that, the school teacher for two generations of natives left the island forever.

In the Atlantic Cafe, three couples had late lunches in the tables near the windows. Two older men, known to Henry professionally, sat together at the bar, nursing warm Budweisers. Coffin sat at the stool next to the server's station. Pip, with a few crackers to remind him that he was, truly, the Good Boy, lay down at the foot of the stool. The bartender stared at him, discretely, in the mirror over the back of the bar.

The Atlantic Cafe was in an older building that had once been another restaurant and, before that, it could have been a workshop for catboats. In the rafters overhead, an inverted canoe, with wicker seats and paddles rested. A set of windows ran along the front of the restaurant and looked out on the town. Inside, the decor was brass, ferns, and pictures of old fishermen looming over the buffalo wings and mozzarella sticks.

Today's special was fried clams.

The bartender slid over.

"We can't have dogs in here."

"Is he bothering anyone?"

"Doesn't matter."

A large man looked out the door of the kitchen. He gave the bartender a wave. She reset herself.

"Can I get you a menu?"

"Don't need one."

"Okay then," she produced an order pad.

"How about a Deep Fried Chicken Sandwich and …" He looked at the brown liquor in bottles, but thought that might be counter-productive. "And a Bud."

She slid away, drew him a draft, and placed it back in front of him. Coffin had taken out his phone, but he turned it over when she placed the beer on the coaster.

"Can I ask you a question?"

"Maybe."

"Did you know someone named Caroline. She worked here."

"Yes," she said. "And you are?"

"My name is Henry Coffin, I work with the police."

"You are police."

Coffin smiled, "Are you Atlantic Cafe, or are you someone who works here?"

She looked at him. This guy.

"You're the Inspector. You're the guy who doesn't arrest people."

"I am," he said and sipped. "And Caroline?"

"What do you want to know?"

"Her last name."

"Bird."

"Okay."

"She started here in April. Came up with a bunch of folks from off-island. She's staying out on Lover's Lane."

"In the boat."

She shrugged.

"Do you stay in the boat?"

"No. I am with my boyfriend."

A large bellied man came out of the kitchen doors. He had on chef's pants and golf shirt. Henry recognized him, vaguely, but positively, from the winter.

Pasquale.

He had been passed out on the floor of his house, with his wife and two children on the sofa, while the EMT's shot Narcan up his nose. He had woken, coughed out a two ounce phlegm ball, sat up, looked into the terrified faces of his family, and asked what the fuck cops were doing in his kitchen.

The bartender immediately drifted over to the other side of the bar. Pasquale plodded over.

"Inspector."

"My brother."

"To what do we owe the honor?"

The cook pulled a chicken finger from his pocket. Pip sat up, like a Good Boy, and hung out his tongue. The chef fed him from his hand.

Coffin took a moment to drink a mouthful of beer. Then he set the glass onto the coaster.

"I understand that you are missing a waitress."

"Which one?"

"Caroline Bird."

"Okay."

"Do you know her?"

"I remember the name. She is in the front of the house, though," He said, "I think she got her last paycheck."

"Did she pick up it up?"

"Last Friday," he said. "Is there anything else?"

"I wonder if I could talk to anyone else about her?"

"No."

"No?"

"They will be working. It will be a busy night."

"Maybe I'll just sit here and wait."

"You could, or you could see them after work."

"At the boat."

"What boat?"

"The boat that they live in."

"I don't know where they live."

"They aren't renting beds from you?"

"I don't think so."

Coffin smiled at him. "Okay, Danny and I will come by at midnight. We will park right in the handicap space outside with the lights on."

"Do what you want. Inspector…"

Coffin looked at him. Pasquale relaxed and came closer. He realized that there was no point in being petty.

"It's mid-September in a tourist town. I am sure she is headed back to St. Petersburg, Key Biscayne, or Miami for the winter. I don't know where she is, but she wouldn't be the first waitress to give us the Irish goodbye."

Around him, the bartender and a small, light haired, elfin waitress watched him.

Coffin took note.

"My sister?" He looked at the waitress.

Her eyes widened.

Pasquale turned around. She started to back into the kitchen.

"Come on out, Moira. It's okay." Pasquale spoke.

She slipped out and stood with her hands behind her back.

While we had employed our share of white college kids and Jamaicans in the past, in recent years we have turned to Bulgarians, Lithuanians, and Slovaks. And the Irish, always the Irish.

"Moira, my sister?" Henry said.

She nodded.

"Would you come out here for a second?"

She nodded.

She took a few steps and stood in front of Henry, as if she was taking an order. The bartender had slipped out and come back with his chicken sandwich.

Pip sat up in case she knew that he was still a "Good Boy." Even the "Best Boy."

"Moira, did you know Caroline?'

She nodded.

"Do you know where she is?"

She shook her head.

"Would you show me her bed and her stuff at the boat?'

She nodded.

"How about tomorrow, around three?"

She nodded.

Coffin looked up at Pasquale. "That okay with you?"

"Sure," he said. "Caroline's gone."

Coffin looked at him, "Let's hope just to Florida."

CHAPTER FIVE

While Inspector Henry Coffin and his dog were downtown annoying the Roman Catholic clergy and the chef at the Atlantic Cafe, his partner slept. Working the night shift requires certain alterations to a normal person's life. For example, you bought and installed blackout curtains. You left for work as your wife and daughter went to bed. You returned as they went to work or school. After a few years, you either adjusted or gave it up.

But it allowed him a luxury.

He could wake up in the afternoon, put on his civilian outfit, and watch his little girl play soccer.

This year there had been a small squabble that he had tried to avoid, but he stomped into like a five year old in a puddle. Hadley had thought about joining an elementary school cheer team. The Bellas, Briannas and the Brooklyns, and their mothers, had wanted her to join. They got to wear their skirts and cheer gear in school. They had fun little cupcake parties. They wanted, in Danny's words, some chocolate in the marshmallows.

Both daughter and mother told him he was wrong. They were good kids from good families. And the girls were just having fun. Why couldn't he just accept things for what they were?

But he wasn't wrong. And he won.

He didn't win because of any warm sense of racial justice. He won because his daughter, like her Dad, liked to hit people. In soccer, Hadley could tackle, she could elbow, she could muck it up; she was so aggressive that her coaches would smile and place her in front of the goal. There, they thought, she wouldn't hurt anyone.

When she learned about the rules of the box, she enjoyed goalie even more than she enjoyed defense. After some tears and blood, the coaches moved Hadley out of the box and back to defense, where there were rules and yellow cards. Jackie, Jennifer, and Julianne had to be ready for the black girl.

Dad couldn't be more proud.

This afternoon, in jeans and a "Let's Go Whalers!!" sweatshirt, he drove the minivan to Delta fields (out by the airport) to watch the nine year old pride of his life take on the eleven and twelve year old team. Pickup trucks, Suburbans, Jeeps, Subarus, and one very dinged Volvo station wagon waited, like dogs, for their families.

For mid September, it wasn't warm. In the shoulder season, a warm, sunny, windless day would settle you back into the month of August, but another morning, when the wind came out of the northeast and the clouds arose from the sea and the moors, the month of November dropped by to get the house ready for the winter.

Danny made his way across the various empty fields to the busy one tucked against the scrub oak and pines at the far end. Not cold yet, but not warm in the wind, he joined the huddle of fathers and mothers with their arms wrapped around themselves. The five men had left job sites with tools in their belts and saw dust in their hair. The mothers were in various uniforms, ranging from nursing and teaching, to Lane Bryant realtor. Sherrie was stuck in meetings with the insurance representatives at the hospital. So he was the only black person there.

Puberty had tilted the pitch; the Pixies were playing the Paulas. Hadley and her team seem to be giving up twenty pounds per player, but they still had the breathless speed of recess. So, they could run ahead and keep out of reach of the pounding power. Until they couldn't and went ass over tea kettle.

Hadley roamed the middle like a bat. She darted around their legs and hips, knocked the ball loose and left her opponents staggering over their ankles. If only she had someone to pass to.

Danny clapped at another theft as two girls went down. There were looks among the parents..

After fifteen minutes of turnovers, futile passes, and fevered claps, play stopped for a crying player. In the pause, another adult arrived late to the game. Pidge, in her green scrubs and with a big purse, jogged over the idle fields towards the game. When she came to the field, she considered crossing the white lines, before she circled the far goal post.

One of the mothers waved and two of the girls eyed her movements. Their mother, Wendy, had been married to Brian Swain, the realtor. Pidge was replacing her.

Or joining her, we thought

There were smiles and apologies. There was a hug. The two of them opened up their phones and tapped something into the screens. They smiled and nodded at each other. Wendy came up to the younger woman's shoulders. She was dressed in a her realtor's best, with a cashmere coat, a scarf, and corduroy pants. The two women walked to the huddle of parents while the time out ended. Two girls on the field watched the two women in particular.

Wendy folded up her chair, waved to the girls, and walked purposefully to her Yukon. She left a pink and white L.L. Bean bag with sweaters and snacks. Clients were waiting.

Five minutes later, the game continued. Pidge stood in her scrubs and Crocs, wrapping her arms around her self. Danny took off his "Go Whalers" sweatshirt, walked over and presented it to her.

"Here, put this on," he offered.

"I couldn't," she said.

"Is it because I am black?" He smiled at her.

She took the sweatshirt, but just held it.

"Do I know you?"

"You might remember. You know my partner., the Inspector."

She looked at him.

"I have to put this on now, don't I?"

"If you don't, it will be a hate crime."

She brought it over her head then dropped the sweater onto her self. It fell over her butt. She pushed the sleeves up.

"Do you have one of those?" She gestured at the girls.

Danny smiled, "Five bucks if you can pick her out."

Pidge glanced over. "Okay," She said. "That's a fair shot."

Danny patted her on the back. "We are both on the same side."

"Which side is that?"

"The Pixies, of course," he smiled. "And this crazy island."

"This place is nuts."

"Turtles, all the way down."

She nodded.

"It's nice that you and Wendy seem to be getting on."

"She is being very patient."

Danny continued to smile. "Patient isn't the word I always associate with first wives."

"And mothers."

"Yes."

"Have you been divorced?" Pidge asked.

"Not as of today. Can't speak for tomorrow."

Pidge tried to interpret that. Danny helped.

"I brought my wife and daughter to this white island. Every day is an adventure."

"Or a hate crime."

"Watch my daughter play soccer, She seems capable."

"It takes an adjustment. For everyone," she said.

"I'm sure."

"Well," Pidge showed him a massive engagement ring on her left hand. "Divorce does not have the same meaning out here that it has off-island. And I am, truly grateful, to Wendy because we are becoming sister-wives. I get the bedroom, while she still has the rest of the house."

"It's not that bad."

"No," she smiled. "But you did see us coordinate our schedules there?"

"Yes."

"And you don't see Brian?"

"I assume he is selling some multi-million dollar property?"

"He is. We are celebrating tonight," she said. "But this requires sending the kids to his first wife's house," she said. "For the whole night."

"Oh."

"Quite," Pidge answered. "As I said, she is being very patient with me. I appreciate her willingness to suffer. Can we please change the subject?"

"Of course."

"Is your partner for real, or do you just pick him up and let him ride along with you so that he doesn't drown in Johnny Walker?"

"Can I say both?"

"Of course."

Danny sighed. "He is a cop. He does have the rank of Inspector. And, believe it or not, he is very good at his job."

"I'm told that he doesn't arrest anyone."

"True."

"I'm told that his little boy died in the harbor on the Fourth of July."

"True."

The two of them took a moment to watch the little girls chase a soccer ball and feel the chill of the ocean.

"He's the real thing. Fifteen years ago, the police chief, just before he retired, promoted Henry. Now, he can't be fired without a massive amount of paperwork and the approval of the entire select board."

"I see."

"Let me tell you this." Danny turned serious. "I was a Boston cop for eight years. I rode or walked with all types. The safest I have ever felt is with Henry. Nobody will hurt him. And he thinks all of them, every last addict and thief, will turn out all right in the end. His hope will kill him faster than the liquor."

"Jesus," she said.

"I know." Danny added. "Tell me about it."

That night, at eleven, Danny picked up the Inspector and brought him for a ride.

"I met a friend of yours today."

"Who?"

"Pidge."

Coffin settled back. "The nurse. Runs the Opioid clinic."

"She didn't tell me that."

"She does."

"Seems nice."

"I think she is," he said. "I also think she killed J.T. Palmer with an overdose of morphine."

"The principal?"

"Yep."

Danny remembered the battering ram, and walking into the house to find the older woman gasping on the floor in her own stink.

"Was that a bad thing to do?"

Coffin looked at him and let his silence answer.

CHAPTER SIX

After a quiet night and a quieter morning, Danny went to pick up the Inspector at three in the afternoon. He parked the car halfway up on the sidewalk in front of the old man's house on Main Street. A plumber's van jerked around the cruiser, then accelerated down the street. Danny took note of the license plate, in case he needed to amuse himself with the rednecks later.

Inside, the old man sat in his kitchen, drinking coffee, and staring out at the birds in the backyard. The trash can was full of wrappers and boxes. His dishes were stacked in the sink. The kitchen table, on the other hand, was bare.

Pip lay at his feet with a stuffed gnome in his teeth.

"I am going to send cleaners."

"Don't bother."

Danny looked at the old man, then took out his phone and began taking pictures of the clutter, trash, and rotting food.

"Why are you doing that?"

"I need to check to see whether I am nuts. I will bring it to social services for Meals on Wheels. They might put you in a home."

The Inspector glared.

"Or I might show my wife."

"Don't do that."

"You are a danger to yourself," he said. "She still likes you. She will send you some dinner. And a nurse."

"I don't need a nurse."

"You need a fucking cleaner."

"I don't."

Danny felt a spike rising. The only man the Inspector would ever hurt is himself, and he would do that daily if he didn't get stopped.

"Get in the car, old man."

Coffin rose from the chair. He carried his coffee cup and saucer to the sink and set it next to four other ones. Then he put on a pair of socks and shoes and headed out the door.

At a last moment, he grabbed the leash. Pip came bolting to the door.

Zenas looked on without a word.

Outside, the traffic had slowed on both sides of the patrol car. Henry and Pip stepped outside.

"We can't take a dog."

"Why not?"

"Because we're cops. Because we might have to store someone in the back."

"If we arrest someone, Pip can ride up front with me."

Coffin opened the back door and Pip hopped in. Henry unsnapped the leash. The dog was excited at all of the smells buried into the cushions in the rear of a police car.

Danny got into the car and slammed the door.

Pip didn't understand the aggression. He sat up on the rear seat, looking straight ahead. He loved going for rides.

Danny turned to the Inspector.

Coffin folded his arms.

"In any other town…" Danny barked.

"We are on Nantucket. And he loves you."

"It doesn't matter."

"You're right."

Danny sighed and looked up Main Street. Both sides of the street were lined with multi-million dollar houses built by people living check to check, credit slip to credit slip..

"You know what pisses me off?"

"No."

"Privilege."

"Privilege?"

"Yep," Sergeant Abraham answered. "If a black officer shows up, in any other town, with dirt on his shoes, he gets written up. But out here, the old white man doesn't wear a uniform, doesn't carry a gun, or his shield, or an ID. He drinks on duty, he sleeps in the car, and, now, he brings his dog."

"You're right," Coffin allowed.

"I know."

Henry let him sit for a moment. Danny ran his fingers over the steering wheel.

"When you're ready, let's go to Lover's Lane."

This time, Danny approached the boat from Surfside Road. He drove through one subdivision, to another, and then only had to drive the big car over fifty yards of packed sand and pot holes.

By the time they had parked, Moira appeared on the deck of the boat. She picked up a paper bag, and then negotiated her way, backwards, down the ladder.

The pines and cabin cruiser were burnished in a September light; bright, blue, and dappled. Without the crush and noise of August, the green of the scrub oaks and pine glowed in Hobbit like familiarity. Life in a rotting, dry land "The Sea Breeze" seemed to be an adventure; it could be a tale told to grandchildren on a long car ride.

"Do we know whose house this is?" Danny asked.

"Doucette."

"Henri?"

"He's alive?" The Inspector raised an eyebrow.

"He died. It's his widow's," Danny said. "Do you want to look into it? Send the health inspector?"

The old man hung his head.

"No."

"In a month?"

Henry looked over. "You think they could be in this all winter?"

The black man shrugged.

"Yes, then," he said. "I'll come with him."

Coffin slipped out of the car. He'd opened the rear door, put Pip on a leash, and walked over with him. They had to pause at a blueberry bush.

Moira stood with a paper bag held in front her.

"Moira," Henry gestured with the leash, "This is Pip. He is very friendly."

She stood stock still.

"Bend down and let him sniff your hand."

The girl shifted the bag and half squatted with her hand out. Pip sniffed it, then licked it. He sniffed her legs, looked at her, then trotted back.

"He likes you."

"Good."

"Have you spent much time around dogs?"

"No."

"Well, he likes you."

She nodded. "I brought you her stuff."

"Okay. Usually I like to look at it in her space."

"Oh," she looked down.

"It's fine," he said. "Do you have her phone number?"

She paused and looked at him.

"Is her number on your phone?"

"Oh."

She looked at her phone for a moment.

He set the bag on the hood of the car and then began unpacking. Caroline had three sweaters, two pairs of tapered jeans, a white blouse, four t-shirts, and five sets of silken underwear in various permutations.

Moira picked up the bag and wrote a number on the side.

"Would you write your number on there as well. In case we have questions."

She paused as she looked at him.

At the very bottom of the bag was a copy of *The Prophet* by Kahil Gibran and *What I Know For Sure* by Oprah. Caroline had bought it for a dollar at the Hospital Thrift Shop. Inside the Gibran was a picture of a young boy in a basketball uniform and his mother. It was the first picture of Caroline he had seen.

Coffin put it aside.

"Her son," Moira answered. "Michael."

So it said on the back.

"Can I see where she slept?"

"I got you everything."

He smiled as best he could. "I know. I just want to see where her home was."

"It's not home."

"It was for the summer."

She didn't move.

"I won't disturb anyone. I'll just climb the ladder."

"I don't think…"

"It's just me, Moira. I'm not going to get anyone in trouble."

He began walking across the yard. She followed after him.

"Please," she said. "Please, don't. I gave you everything she had."

"I know."

She pulled on his hand. "Please."

And he stopped.

He knew what he would see. Two beds in the crawlspace in the bow, two under a tarp in the cockpit of the boat. A white mayonnaise bucket for waste. He knew it. It wasn't new. Poor people on island had lived like this for years. Perhaps they were hidden in tents on the Land Bank land. Perhaps they were in basements and crawlspaces. Perhaps they were living six to a room. They got a good job, they needed a place to sleep. Anywhere.

For Moira and Caroline, that was the "Sea Breeze," peeling and propped up, in Widow Doucette's driveway.

"Was she dating anyone?"

Moira looked stricken.

"Did she see anyone special?"

"I don't know."

The two stood in silence, with the truth darting overhead.

"Thanks for your help." He handed her one of Danny's cards. "If Pasquale or someone else gives you a hard time, let me know."

When he got back to the car, he repacked the paper bag, with the two books on top. Then he placed the bag in the trunk, next to Danny's riot gun. Pip popped into the back seat and sat in the center, waiting for the adventure to continue.

They drove off.

"What did you learn, Henry?"

"Caroline didn't leave on her own."

"No?"

"No."

CHAPTER SEVEN

Thursday night is the dawn of our weekend. The weekenders may have only started to cross the sound, but the wedding people had been arriving for days. The ceremony is on Saturday, but that meant that the only night that was without bridesmaid duties and Daddies was on Thursday. So it took a little longer for the bar to clear out. We had seen it before.

When Danny and Henry showed up at the Chicken Box, the band was slowly dismantling the sound equipment on the stage. In a quirk of musicianship, the gig at the Chicken Box wasn't about money, but housing. With a bed in the band room, they could play any number of other, better paying, gigs as long as they came back to play on Friday and Saturday night. Other than their 10 p.m. gigs at the Box, the bands played weddings twice on Friday, twice on Saturday, and once on Sunday. Tonight, they had already played before three audiences and moved their gear three times; Henry hoped everyone was going to be sleeping soundly.

When the two policemen arrived, the bartenders were still ringing out their drawers, the lights were up, and the brooms were sweeping. Pip came in on his leash. As always, he was on alert for snacks.

One man stood with a beer at the side of the bar. He wore a crisp Red Sox hat, a red windbreaker, and blue pants with a heavy crease. He eyed the dog with some surprise.

He was drinking a cup of coffee.

Danny looked at Jon-Jon.

Jon-Jon shrugged.

"Wait on your coffee, Henry," Danny said.

"I see him."

"Let me handle it."

"Nod when you need me."

The black officer snorted and walked directly at the man in the hat.

"Sir, you are aware that the bar has closed for the evening?"

"Sure. I am just finishing my coffee."

"On Nantucket, the closing hour is 1 A.M."

""I'll be done in a second."

"Great."

Danny, in full uniform, leaned against the bar five yards from the man. He watched the roadies take the monitors apart on stage over the man's shoulder.

In a short moment, the man with the hat put his cup of coffee down and started walking for the door. Danny stayed where he was, but when the man passed through the outer doors, Henry walked to a window. The man stepped into the passenger seat in Pink's cab.

When he returned to the bar, his mug of coffee and a cup of creamers waited for the Inspector. Jon-Jon drifted over.

"How long had he been here?" Henry asked.

"Two hours or so. Since midnight."

"Drink anything?"

"Diet Coke. A coffee. He adopted an empty beer bottle."

"On behalf of the entire law enforcement community, I apologize for him."

"I thought he was a pervert," Jon-Jon added. "He was hanging out near the ladies' bathroom."

Another cup of coffee, with the taste of Scotland, appeared next to the Inspector.

"Pink took him."

"Did he?"

"Not the ride I would expect."

"Maybe he is getting a check from the state."

"Maybe the state has him in its fist."

"Maybe."

Jon-Jon gestured to Pip.

"Have we had a change in the Health and Safety Code?"

"Not that I know of."

"Not sure if I can have a dog in here. Is he a service animal?"

"Not officially," Coffin replied.

Jon-Jon eyed the animal.

"Sit." He commanded.

Pip sat. And waited to be a "Good Boy."

Jon-Jon smiled. "He can stay. He is better behaved than either of you."

Coffin slipped the Good Boy a treat. Then he let him off the leash. The dog wandered off in search of all the good smells a dive bar would have.

"Henry," the bartender said. "He doesn't have any tags."

Coffin nodded. "Does he need them?"

"Have you been to the vet?"

"No."

"No?"

"Should I?"

The black bartender cast a glance at the black cop.

"Henry, you are a piece of work."

"We can take him to the vet."

"Do that."

Pip was sitting next to one of the young bartenders as she counted out her tips. He was looking up at her. In a moment, she stopped and scratched his head.

"This is good for you, Henry. When did you get him?"

Danny leaned in. "Six weeks. Someone abandoned him in a house this August."

"The Bradshaws of Weston," Coffin said. "I called."

Danny continued. "They left him alone in a house for a week. The cleaners showed up and got scared. They called us."

"And here we are."

Pip was sniffing along the front of the stage. He started licking at something.

"I hope that is spilled beer." Jon-Jon said.

The Inspector had brought the picture of Caroline Bird in. He removed it from his breast pocket and put it on the counter. "Can we talk business?"

"Sure."

"Have you seen her around here?"

The picture had a young woman, with blondish hair, sitting on a park bench with a darker little boy in a baseball jersey.

Henry pointed to it. "This is Caroline Bird, with her son Michael. She was working at the Atlantic Cafe up until after Labor Day. She appears to be missing."

"Appears?" Jon-Jon asked.

"Her friends and. co-workers are looking for her. Her phone is dead."

"Where was she staying?"

"Lover's Lane."

"Not the boat."

Coffin nodded.

"Let me hand it around," he said. "Atlantic Cafe workers don't come here much after hours."

In the next two cups of coffee, twelve of the regular crew slipped in. The Red Sox were on the west coast for the fans and college football was being played for the bettors.

The picture went around the groups.

Then it returned to the bar. Jon Jon tacked it to a post, then poured Henry another cup of coffee.

Pip had investigated the place. After he was clear on smells and treats, he returned to the Inspector and lay at his feet.

The Red Sox sent three up and three down.

An older woman, in a black skirt and a white blouse, came over to the Inspector while he was considering a third cup. Suzette had been married twice, bore four boys, two of which had been passengers in the Inspector's car before they became passengers in another squad car. The two boys who avoided the law were working in Boston. The two who knew Henry, carried the chip, met in the church every morning, swung hammers or shovels, and mostly kept out of the way. Mostly. One was due to get married to the mother of his son. If he could make enough to get out of his mother's house. We understand the struggle

"Henry, I have a story for you."

Coffin eyed her. "Does it have a happy ending?"

She cackled. "Not at all. Not tonight."

"Do you want a drink?" Coffin asked.

"If you're buying,"

He gestured to Jon-Jon. The owner filled a red cup with beer, then handed it to her. .

"Brian Swain was in to dinner tonight."

"He was?"

"Sure," she nodded. "That douchebag just sold a big place in Polpis and he was all in. He had the jacket, the tie, and one of those watches. And the new young wife."

Danny looked over, turned his ear to her, and listened without looking.

"So they get a bottle of wine, and then another and something after that. And she gets frisky. Takes her shoe off, starts on his leg under the table. Very discreet."

"Except for you."

"Of course," she said. "We know what's coming."

"Is he going to run out on his bill?"

"Well, not him," she said.

Coffin looked at her.

"Henry, do you remember being young and in love?"

"Vaguely."

"Well, the young lady is very much in love. She whispered in his ear, and then stepped to the Ladies Room before the Chocolate Pot Du Creme appeared on the table. We held up their service."

"Yes…"

"She stayed in there for a few minutes."

"Yes…"

"Henry, are you being dense?"

"I guess."

"Have you been in our bathrooms?"

Coffin looked dazed.

"Yes…"

"Would you say they are private and and are for one?"

"Yes…"

"Henry?"

The older man looked at his partner. His partner looked down at his shoes. Pip looked up at him sympathetically.

He shrugged.

She drank off her beer.

Jon-Jon had stayed close and was smothering a laugh with a bottle of beer. He looked at the Inspector.

He dropped the beer but kept the smile.

"Henry, the Langueduc bathrooms are great for blow jobs."

Danny nodded his head like a mad elephant, hiding his laughter.

"Henry, every night," Suzette said. "Somebody gets a smoothie in there. Young. Old. Man. Woman. We should put it on the menu. Or Cushions on the floor."

Coffin smiled. "I guess I learn something new every day."

"We need to find someone for the old man." Danny smiled.

"Yes," Jon-Jon agreed.

"Well, Henry," Suzette added. "This night was not like any other night. The lady left."

"Uh-oh." Jon-Jon added.

"She came out, knocked over her chair, took her bag and walked out. Left him there with his regrets, her dessert, and the bill."

"And blue balls," The bartender offered.

"Those too."

For his part, Danny realized, for the tenth time today, that this island is crazy.

After they left the Chicken Box, the two police officers went to the station. The Nantucket Police station had been a fire station in its first life. It had a magnificent front, with two big sliding doors for the fire trucks, marble and granite stonework, and a door around the side. But, in the ensuing years, when the town became busier and the fires became more likely away from the cobblestones, the fire department had moved and donated the building to the police.

As a result, every space inside had been modified and changed. Two jail cells now filled the space where the firemen had slept, the garages were filled with saw horses, motorcycles, jet-skis, and a boat on a trailer, and the offices and desks were jammed along a corridor.

Danny was sitting at his desk with the Inspector. Danny had the keyboard and the mouse in front of him; the old white man had his hands in his lap. Both men had more cups of coffee. And only coffee.

"So…" Danny asked.

"Okay." Coffin said. 'What do we know about Caroline?"

Danny swung over to the computer. Years of riding with the Inspector, eating the leftovers off his daughter's plate, and nibbling Goldfish at four in the morning had made him into a considerable man who overwhelmed his desk chair. He typed Caroline Bird and Massachusetts into his database.

"I have a Caroline Bird was convicted of receiving stolen goods, shop lifting, and burglary. Heroin possession, several times. There was a charge for assault and battery but it didn't go to court." Danny spun the computer to his partner, "Look familiar?"

The mug shot didn't flatter her. On the other hand, she didn't have her little boy in her lap.

"Who did she assault?"

"A man named Mark Shea. He didn't press charges."

"Any other family?"

"No."

"Father of Michael?"

"Doesn't say."

"Where's he?"

Danny typed in the name.

"No warrants, DUI, and…." He clicked one more screen., "He died two years ago. Found alone."

"Heroin."

"Or suicide."

"Is there a difference?" Coffin said. The sergeant didn't feel the need to press the argument.

"Any pictures?"

"He's dead."

Coffin shrugged.

"Do you want me to look?"

"I guess not." Henry cleared his throat. "I am sort of assuming that, if he didn't press charges, he might have been…close to her."

"How does that help us?"

Coffin didn't have an answer. His heart was more in line with the fact that Mark had died. Seeing his picture was somehow acknowledging that he had once been alive.

Sergeant Abraham saw how the old man was moping.

"Okay, let's search the Internet."

Danny took out his phone, opened up Facebook, and typed the man's name in. "Mark Shea" was a popular name, but he found a Mark in Marshfield with several posts filled with weeping angels.

Mark was black.

"So, he was a brother." Danny said.

"We're all brothers," Henry responded.

"Pardon me, Mr. Quaker. For a Black man, it doesn't often feel that way."

Coffin nodded, "Point taken."

Danny scrolled through the pictures on Facebook until he found one with a lighter skinned baby and mother. Caroline Bird was wearing sunglasses, a Smitty's Clam Bar work shirt ,and big smile.

"Print that."

Danny sighed. Now it was real for the old man. Now that he could see the kid and the Dad. Caroline had become a cause.

No noise penetrated the , other than the printing of the picture. The room glowed in the fluorescent daylight. Outside, the all night orange burned over the Steamship Wharf.

"Let's look up this boy. He's in the state system somewhere."

"Fair enough. Let's see if he has any warrants."

"He's six."

"We live in a crazy world. Let's see what the database has."

Danny peered at the screen, found the right window, and typed the name in.

"No warrants, but…"

Henry inched over.

"But, he has a couple of missing persons notes."

Both men were silent.

A picture of the little boy came up. He had curly hair, a big smile, and skin the color of light coffee.

After pausing to print the picture, Danny kept searching.

"He has a court appointment in a week."

"Why?"

"Mom wants custody."

Henry sighed.

"She has a lawyer. "

"Well, that sounds like a thread we can pull on."

When they left the station, the two officers returned to the Lifesaving Museum on Polpis Road. Pip had stretched out on the back seat and and fallen asleep with his head on his paws.

Surprisingly, Danny was able to pull over two speeders. One was a local pickup truck, with fishing poles stuck in PVC pipes on the bumper. He gave them a ticket on the basis that they should know better, since he and the Inspector hung out here every night. The fishermen were disrespecting the badge.

The second was a bartender from downtown, in a Honda hatchback, on his way out to his boyfriend's apartment, a boyfriend who was cheating. He was weeping. Even Danny, at his most official, didn't want to ticket him, but he did follow him all the way out to Wauwinet and a lighted house. Everybody has to live with their own messes. We learn this the hard way.

Then it started raining.

Like many storms that hit the island, this storm arrived with wind and a fine mist. After an hour, it increased to a solid tattoo on the roof. Danny had to flick the wipers to a higher speed.

Pip shook himself awake.

"Let's go to Lover's Lane," Coffin looked at the bushes shaking in the wind.

"We have other issues."

"Let's just go."

"Do we think there is going to be a crime there?"

"Just go."

So they went. Danny could see the hook working its way into the old man's soul. The little boy in foster care, the dead father, the recoveries from drugs, it all fit into a pattern. Real Police knew that people did this stuff to themselves everyday. Real Police didn't get sucked into the drama, they watched for weapons, and sudden moves, and opportunities to bring someone into a jail cell. Real Police believed that the social worker who took this lille boy from his mother, had seen enough of heroin and poverty and maybe even violence to act on it. Maybe somebody knew better than the old white man in the passenger seat.

But it wouldn't help. This is his privilege.

Danny parked the big cruiser in under the pines and waited for nothing to happen. The Inspector stepped outside and took Pip for a brief break in the **pines**. Both man and dog returned wet and smelly.

At four thirty in the morning, the Sea Breeze was just as exciting and positive as it was at four thirty in the afternoon. The girls had snapped a tarp onto the open top of the boat. Twenty years ago, Henri Doucette had taken this boat out past the jetties and watched the fireworks off of the beach. He, his wife, and their kids had crackers, cheese, Ernst and Julio Gallo in a box, and Bud Light. Everyone had a wonderful time.

That had been a long time ago. The boat hadn't seen saltwater for more than a decade. It hadn't been water-tight for even more time.

But now the rain was coming down so hard that it bounced off of the blue tarp and washed down the sides of the boat. And the hook got set further into his partner. He saw all of the rain falling, in the gray dawn, and the old man felt the damp chill inside the boat.

"Henry, we can find five boats just like this if we look around. And if we want to find people in the damp cold, we know they are camped out in the moors."

The old man nodded.

Danny sighed. "You have plenty of extra rooms if you really wanted to help."

Coffin sighed. He didn't see his house as a home, he saw it as a place for his personal penance. But it had four other empty bedrooms.

Nonetheless, it was a thought. As if Zenas had laid a finger on his forearm.

The rain picked up. Even under all of the pine trees, it started to drill the roof of the car. The water was building up from puddles to ponds. Drainage into the island sand never progressed as fast as we would hope. By six in the morning, Lover's Lane had returned to a series of small ponds. The driveway that the boat was propped up on was also developing a small stream.

Danny had his hand on the gear shift, when Pink's Cab came splashing down the road. He stopped on the wrong side of the road, so that his passengers, four women, had to put their feet into the sandy brown water. They held their shoes up and hurried over the street and wet driveway. They didn't have an umbrella or even a coat to hold over their heads. They were all wearing short party dresses, even Moira. They climbed the ladder, lifted the tarp, and disappeared into the boat.

When Danny saw his partner's face grow hard, he knew that they were going to spend more evenings by this boat. And for the incivility of making the women step into the puddle, Pink would pay.

Then they got a call to go to Madaquecham and everything went to hell.

CHAPTER EIGHT

We love Madequecham. Years ago, when hippies roamed the earth, a several day long party called the "Madaquecham Jam" broke out on the beach. The idea of an island without anyone but us and our buddies tickles our hearts. When the kegs came, it was even better

Madequecham rests in a gray area of the Land Bank land, between the airport and Tom Nevers. When the island had sheep, they chewed the bushes down to a bare rolling surface of sand and beach grass. But, the Conservation Foundation let the scrub oak and knotty pines grow, along with any number of bushes. In the glory days of August, the jeeps rode the sand roads and celebrated all of the preservation that Nantucket had enforced. In the off-season, the bushes and woods were left to the cold and the dark and the deer

And in that gray driving rain, we found Meaghan.

There was another woman standing on a dirt road, next to a black lab. She had a long down jacket, a pom pom hat, and gray face that neither officer knew. Danny waved his hand to the woman, as he drove past, and she waved back. Her black lab sat at her feet and didn't move as the big cruiser rolled by. Danny brought the big car to rest on a relatively rocky part of the dirt road. Henry stepped out.

Pip started barking from the back seat.

"My sister," Coffin asked. "Where is she?"

"Over there, in that thicket." The walker said. "My dog found her. She came right out."

Coffin looked through the murk and saw a blob of a bush, almost eight feet high. When he flashed his flashlight into it, even from a distance, he could see the shape of the tent.

"Did you look in?"

"Briefly," she said. "Mabel was pretty shook up."

"Is that her name? It's a good name."

"She's a good dog."

Coffin looked at the dog. Pip was still barking in the cruiser..

"How is she doing now?"

The dog was squirming.

"Not good."

He nodded. "I understand."

Both walker and Mabel continued on their way to some place drier and warmer. She had a story to tell to her friends in Greenwich.

Danny opened the rear of the car and removed a heavy Nantucket Police Poncho and draped it over the older man's shoulders. In the rain, with the drama, Henry accepted the warm covering. The rain began to bounce off of him.

Coffin walked up to the bush, found the tent, opened the flap and found a stiff and still Meaghan Ingersoll.

The two of them hoped that the girl was still alive and the two of them knew that the wish was foolish.

But for Coffin, Meaghan remained, motionless and cold and staring at the sky in a lightweight tent, miles from the nearest house.

There was a bike.

There was a laundry line.

There were two laundry baskets, with tarps, holding pots, pans, and a single burner.

There was a string of outdoor lights, hooked up to a series of D cell batteries.

There was a phone. The Inspector held it up to Meaghan's face and it unlocked. This was not the first time he had done this.

The last call, going out, was to Pink's Cab.

Meaghan Ingersoll was under her sleeping bag. Most of her clothes were balled up at her head. She had a shoe box for a bed side table, with a light, and a travel alarm clock, and, inside, twenty or so unused condoms and a vibrator.

And, in another box, were five clean needles, a book of matches, and a spoon. A sixth needle was next to her left arm.

In her senior year, at Nantucket High School, Meghan had come in third for Junior Miss. She had excited the crowd with a dance routine to Donna Summer's "Hot Stuff," but Andrea Miller's version of Adele's "Hello" really was the best. We all thought so.

Then, Meaghan had graduated and gone for a semester to UMass Amherst, but returned to help her mother clean rooms at the White Elephant, where you could make real money.

And then, carrying blankets, she slipped on a wet set of stairs, twisted her knee and did something to her lower back. Doctor Tupper prescribed some Vicodin for the pain and two hours a week at the physical therapist.

Her insurance didn't cover the therapy.

We lost track of her. She was around. Everyone has to clean up their own messes. We learn this the hard way.

And, five years later, she was found by Mabel and her person.

Inspector Coffin and Sergeant Abraham inventoried the site, took pictures of everything, and waited for the ambulance.

Then, after Meaghan was taken away, Danny drove the Inspector to Helen Ingersoll's house.

As they drove back to town, Danny didn't say anything to the old man.

Henry did his work. Those of us who complained about the old man, about his drinking, or his sleeping, or his uniform choices, had to acknowledge that he stood up. When bad things happened, he stood up and took charge. Of course, he would be the guy to knock on the door.

Danny couldn't do it.

When Coffin knocks on a door, we know what the bad news is. And still, he comes in. All of the prayers and all of the hopes and all of the sleepless nights came to nothing because what we all knew was going to happen, happened. Coffin's knock says that in all but words.

It happened in the parking lot at work when her husband found her.

It happened when the Jeep rolled over on Polpis Road.

It happened on a deserted beach.

We knew about Henry's son and the dock. We knew his pain. Nobody wanted it to be their pain. But it was and it would be and it had been. Again and again.

With grace, and calm words, and sympathy, he told them what they already knew. He showed them the tragedy and, a little, the redemption.

You could live with the pain.

He did.

He knew the sudden acid spray of grief, the long chemical burn of a life melting, and the scars that came afterward. He knew.

So he could sit. He could call family. He could call help. He had that privilege. He had license.

In an hour, after two minivans came to Helen Ingersoll's house and pried her away from her home and her searing memories, Coffin came out of the house grayer, older, heavier, and slumped into the car.

"Let's call it a night." Danny offered.

"No, let's find Pink."

Danny turned the car off.

"Henry, you need to listen."

"Okay."

"Pink is, what we in the police business call, a suspect. What we should do is head to the police station and start a file on him and get him, and the other drug dealers, for murder and drugs and everything else."

"Fine. Continue."

"What we shouldn't do is stop him on the road and let him know that he is a suspect. He will hide, the drug dealers will leave, and Meaghan and Caroline and the rest of the women on the boat will get no justice."

Sergeant Abraham stopped. "Are you listening to me, Henry?"

"Ye,." he said. "But the chances of everyone getting justice is pretty small. Nobody gets justice. I want to talk to Pink. We know him. I want to talk to him."

"Do you think you can stop him by talking to him?"

"I think I can get him to pause."

"We won't be able to prosecute him."

"We won't anyway. All we know is that Meaghan called him."

"Henry, can we, please, treat this as a police matter and not a counseling issue? You think you can get all of these people to look and find something good inside themselves. Pink isn't good. He's bad."

"If I talk to him, things could go better. It can't hurt."

"It could."

"Noted," the old man said. "Now, please, trust me. Let's find him."

He wasn't at his house.

He wasn't at the ferry.

At ten in the morning, the two exhausted policemen, and a hungry dog, were parked outside of Naushop development waiting for a heroin deal to happen.

The Naushop Development had been a realtor's dream. Fifteen acres of rusted trucks and overgrown farmland transformed into white picket fences, brick sidewalks and quarter acre lots. The one-way roads twisted about, the Home Owners Association was active and the buildings looked right, even if it was under the airport. And almost no-one lived there for more than a week. You rented the house on-line, arrived in a cab, then put your swim suit on. There weren't any little old ladies sitting on a porch wondering why all of those pick up trucks stopped at number 41. It was the perfect place for the Russians.

The Russians owned at least two houses in there. One of which Pink stopped by often.

The Russians were the current corporate drug dealers on island. They were the dirty truth you learned from the addicts and the overdosed and the family. They were responsible for the mis-spellings on the plastic bags. Their current brand was "Eternal Brutherhood."

Naushop was a drug dealer's dream. You drove in, stopped at a stop sign and had a word with a man on a bench, then you drove the path, until a kid in a bike pedaled by and dropped a package in a window. The cabs and the Ubers came in and out of that street all the time.

Within a half hour of waiting, Pink's Cab pulled out of the road. Instead of running the lights, Danny just followed him until he let his fare out at the Stop and Shop.

She disappeared into the store.

Danny pulled up and blocked the cab.

The sergeant didn't like it. But he kept his eyes open. Sometimes, he needed to remember that the Inspector wasn't real police and had never seen three children shot in a drug deal gone bad.

Coffin straightened himself and approached the driver's side of the cab.

"Morning, Pink."

"How can I help you, Inspector. Why have you pulled me over?"

"I wanted to have a conversation."

"You could call me. You could make an appointment. I could call a lawyer," he said. "We don't need to block the good people getting their groceries."

"They'll be fine. They know why I am here," Coffin said. "You're not being charged with anything today."

"So why should I stay? Why shouldn't I back up and drive away?"

"Because I would make your life awkward."

"No, you couldn't."

Currently, Ornette Coleman was playing on his speakers.

"Pink," Coffin sighed. "Let's suppose Danny and I set ourselves up on Old South Road every night and pull you over every time you leave Naushop. How would that look to you?"

"Like harassment."

"How would it look to the Russians?'

"What Russians?"

The Inspector rubbed his eyes. "Pink, I am trying to have a non-threatening conversation with you that doesn't involve you doing anything criminal, but I would like some information. Now, you know and I know that I can make your life unpleasant and you can merely annoy me. So, let's cut the bullshit and be friendly?"

"I don't know anything."

"Fine. What do you know about a girl named Meaghan Ingersoll?"

He looked at the Inspector with dull curiosity.

"Nothing. Never heard of her."

Coffin showed him a picture of her from her phone. "Anything now?"

"Nope."

Coffin sighed.

"You are the last person Meaghan called on her phone. Then she overdosed in a tent near Madequecham."

"If you say so."

"This call was around one in the morning today. She died hours later."

Pink made a show of looking at a clipboard. The Inspector was sure that this call was not on it.

"I don't have any record of that. I think you might have had the wrong cab."

"Pink…"

"Are we done here?"

"No."

"You're blocking me."

"You're right. Did the name Caroline Bird pop up in your memory"

"I know nothing about that," he stared straight ahead. "If you don't move, I will file harassment charges. I will take your badge."

"I don't have a badge."

Pink rolled his eyes.

"She had a son," Coffin said.

"She probably still has one."

"We'll meet again, my brother."

"Of course. I will have my lawyer with me."

"You do that."

CHAPTER NINE

Danny liked going to bed just after the shift ended in the morning. He and the old man would pick up his little girl, Hadley, drop her at school, drop the old man at his house, and then hit the hay seconds after he left the car. This morning, of course, the schedule was thrown off by two hours. Coffin needed to piss someone off. So Danny missed his little girl, his wife, and got to bed much later than he wanted. As he drifted off, he decided on calling in sick tonight.

The Swain Real Estate Office occupied an old house behind the whaling museum and within a short walk down Whaler's Lane to the Nantucket Yacht Club. Brian's father never joined the yacht club, because he didn't understand that those rich snobs bought and sold houses. But Brian did. He joined, he smiled, he helped with the races, he sent his daughters to have lessons, and he never set foot in a sailboat. Brian sold many, many houses to the sailors.

There were two other Swain offices, both with bigger conference rooms and more modern appointments, but Brian preferred to stay here in the old building. We knew what his presence said.

The Swain Real Estate office had swollen to fill almost every corner of the house; he didn't have it in his heart to set up any desks in the basement. But the computers and the staffers were upstairs in the old bedrooms, and the agents and their desks were lined up in the old living rooms and dining room, not that you could tell anymore. Brian's office sat at the back of the building in an expanded former kitchen, pantry, and closet. He had put in a conference table, chairs, Nantucket paintings and his father's big desk. He had taken out the oven, the sink, and everything else you needed to feed people. The big gas oven was now in his ex-wife's house.

The desk was as old as anything else in the building, and could probably place its age back to the end of the whaling business. But it was nicked, stained, split, and kicked into a peculiar shape. It had been his father's desk. We knew it.

His office had windows to the street and garden, but none to the inside desks and agents. So, Brian left the door open so he could see and hear what was going on in his office. When he closed the door, he was shut off. Which was a good thing. He didn't need to know too much about what the team was doing; he'd hired them and kept them because he trusted them. Occasionally, when he opened the door, he got surprised.

Inspector Henry Coffin sat in one of the winged customer chairs out in a waiting area. That was a surprise. None of the surprises that the Inspector brought were pleasant.

The rest of the office avoided looking at the old man. Many of them had met him on the Polpis Road after one too many. Others remembered him from the high school parties in the woods. And a few, including Big Jim, Brian's father, had met him at the front door to try and explain the crying that he could hear inside. Coffin knew something about almost everyone in the room.

And everyone remembered Henry's son.

Brian saw Coffin and understood what he had to do.. This was why he claimed the big check. When the man comes around, you get to stand up.

Brian was tall, big in the shoulders, with a haircut too short and a tan too brown; he gave the impression that he would rather be doing something that involved seawater and highly specialized toys, but he had to make a living. He wore Nantucket Reds that had faded to a fleshy pink, a short sleeve seer-sucker shirt, and a crisp and dark blue blazer with gold buttons (if you studied them) that resembled fishing lures.

The one accessory that made him the most money also cost him the most money. He wore a Rolex Oyster Imperial watch that stayed tactfully hidden under a cuff when the blazer was on, but when the blazer was off and business was being done, it glowed silver against his gold skin. Twenty thousand on the wrist put millions in the checkbook.

For his part, Coffin remembered the man when he was a lot younger and he had been summoned to drive his father home from the Admiralty Lodge. He also remembered a story he had heard a few nights ago about dessert at the Langueduc.

Brian walked out of his office in five great strides, extended his right hand, and pulled the old man into a grip.

"Inspector," he smiled. "How can I help?"

Coffin stood, still in the grip of the young man. "Well, let's go to your office."

The room dropped to silence.

Brian's office was as curated as the owner. Fishing rods across the ceiling, oriental rugs across the floor, and a bar cart against the wall. On his desk, Brian kept pictures of his two little girls, his parents (Big Jim and Mags), and his fiancee, Pidge.

Coffin sat in one of the client's chairs.

"How is Pidge?"

Brian looked at the Inspector a beat too long.

"She's great."

"I ran into her with Miss Palmer at the hospital?"

"Oh," he said. "Pidge doesn't talk about her work."

"I suppose she shouldn't."

"Yes, it's a bright line."

Coffin didn't believe this for a minute.

"Well, she was very generous to Miss Palmer. If her family knew what she did for her, they would thank her."

"Sure," Brian smiled at the old man.

"And you are very lucky."

"I'm glad you think so."

"You are."

"Thanks," Brian said. "How can I help you?"

"I am thinking of selling my house."

Everyone was still alive. There was no bad news. Brian relaxed.

The young man tented his hands in front of his face, and then folded the rest of the fingers together, but his pointer fingers.

"The brick one?"

"Yes."

"Do you own other property on island?"

"Why?"

Brian smiled. "I was wondering if you were moving off island."

"Oh, no," Coffin said. "I would find somewhere else to move to. Smaller."

Swain eased back into his chair. "Do you want to know the good news or the bad news?"

Coffin eyed him. "Go ahead."

Not getting an answer gave Brian a moment.

"The good news is that we could sell you house for eight to ten million dollars. The bad news is that you are going to have to do some work to it before it sells in order to get that price. And you may not be able to get that price. You might have to sell it for a lot less. It depends."

"What does it depend on?"

"You live in one of the most historic houses on the island. I don't know if you know what your parents, or forebears, did when they owned the house, but their might be a historic restriction on it. There probably is."

"What does that mean?"

"Well, whoever buys it can't do what they want. They might want to build a sun room, or a wine cellar or an entertainment room or put in a hot tub. All of that would require gutting the inside. A historical restriction would prevent that."

"Okay," Coffin said. He looked out the back windows onto Whaler's Lane. He spent a minute in his thoughts.

"What if I wanted to convert it into apartments?"

"Henry."

"Yes."

"You and I know what the boards and committees of this town are like. You want to change the zoning around your house so you could make it into condos. Can you imagine the meetings?"

Coffin could. He sighed.

"Henry," the realtor leaned forward. "Why do you want to sell your house?"

"A lot of people on this island need housing."

Brian stopped.

"You want to convert one of the the most historic houses on island into low income housing?"

"I suppose so."

"Have you talked to anyone in your family about this?"

Coffin looked at him.

Brian added. "I mean in the extended Coffin family. Cousins, aunts, nieces, nephews…lawyers."

"No, but I own the house. I have the title."

"Do you think that, in the entire Coffin family, there isn't someone who is going to challenge this sale? Someone isn't going to come up and say that you are insane?"

"It is my house."

"And lawyers will say…"

Coffin understood.

"Henry, I want to pour you a drink," Brian stood up and went to the bar cart. He showed the old man the label of Johnny Walker Blue. He pulled out two Angler's Club tumblers, dropped ice in each, opened the bottle, and poured two glasses. Brian placed both glasses in is left hand, as if they were robin's eggs, and brought them to the Inspector. He leaned against his desk.

Coffin sipped the moneyed whiskey.

"My brother, we drive around and find people working on this island and living five and six to a boat. I have a big and empty house. Don't I have to do something about this?"

The realtor smiled. "You may be the only person who have ever sat in this office and said this."

"Okay."

Brian swallowed more of the whiskey. He knew that the old man liked his brown drinks.

"All I know is real estate, Inspector. And I don't know astronomy, I don't know sailing, and, to listen to my father, I don't know fishing. Out here, the wisdom of real estate is that the poor sell their homes to the rich. If you were to put your home for sale, I could sell it in ten minutes. I would call your neighbor, the CEO of Black Rock, and he would wire the money by the end of the day. If I were to actually list it, we could get even more money, because you live at one of the premier addresses on island — they sell postcards of your house— but if you want to sell your house to poor people, none of those people will let me do it. They will sue, they will fill my office with lawyers and briefcases, and they will fill the newspapers with stories about heritage, history, and tradition. If you were to donate your house to a charitable organization, that group would almost immediately sell it for the money." He sipped the last of his drink. "And they would be right. They could sell your house for enough money to build two or three—maybe four houses somewhere else on island. And Henry, there would still be people living in boats and attics."

Coffin sipped his whiskey empty.

Brian continued.

"Since we are having this rare conversation, let me push it out for you. I know you feel compelled to help these people in basements and tents. I understand, but let me ask you this. Why do they need to be here? There are a lot of good cheap houses in Fall River, in Springfield, in Portland. People are leaving New England for Arizona and Florida. I am desperately trying to get Big Jim to go to Florida. These people don't need to be here."

Brian swirled the ice cubes in his glass.

"Henry, tell me I'm wrong."

"I would be helping."

"There still will be people living in holes, in basements, and in the moors. And when a better paying job shows up somewhere else, that's where they will go."

"So, this won't work."

"Not the way you want it to, but I want you to go home and think. I want you to consider it. If you really want to sell that house, let me know."

Coffin stood and shook hands. When he opened the door, the room glanced at him, including Brian's father, Big Jim, who stood with arms crossed in the waiting area.

"Inspector," Big Jim said to Coffin as he passed. "Have you found his fiancee? She may have slipped away when she went to the bathroom."

Coffin turned. Brian's face had closed and he waved the Inspector away.

CHAPTER TEN

Afternoon sleep is not the best; the doors open, noises happen, and, despite the best wishes of everyone involved, the sleep dissipates and leaves you lying in a room where the windows glow and life fritters itself outside.

When the lasts wisps of sleep had slipped away, Danny rolled out out of bed, wrapped himself in his bathrobe, and padded out to the living room. His wife, Sherrie, sat in the corner of the sofa, with three binders open around her and two legal pads on her legs.

"You got a call," she said.

Danny frowned.

"Your loving and adorable wife took your phone out of the bedroom so you could sleep."

"That is remarkably loving of you."

"Of course."

"Who was it?"

"Would I look?"

Danny had been married long enough not to answer that question. His phone was on the sofa next to her. Apparently, it was three o'clock. And the Chief of the Nantucket Police Department, and his lieutenant, had left a message asking him to come in when it was convenient.

Which, translating from White Cop in standard English, meant now.

"Would you like to watch your daughter play soccer this afternoon?" she asked.

"Yes," he said. "Alas, the old man has made a mess and I have to go to the station." He drank some of his coffee. "Do you know what he did last night?"

"No."

"He brought his dog along for the ride."

She looked up. "He has a dog?"

"A black lab," Danny answered. "Some rich prick abandoned it in Madaket. We rescued it."

"Coffin rescued it."

"I was there."

"We are not getting a dog."

"No."

"So he is the rescuer, not you."

"Touche"

Sherrie returned to her binders.

"Why can't he go?"

"Because they can't control him."

"Course not," she said. "But they have you."

"Yes."

"You don't need to take this."

Danny regarded his bride with something like affection. Old arguments never end. "Nice house we have here."

"Yup," she said. "They have nice houses in North Carolina as well."

"Yeah, but they are prejudiced there."

She harrumphed.

He patted her on the knee.

Beyond the bullet proof glass at the station, two supervisors waited for Sergeant Abraham.

Lieutenant Chris Macy had joined the force fifteen years previous, but through classes and tests and boyish humor, had been placed in a command position. He had a wonderful smile, a tight haircut, and a prosthetic leg below the knee. Somewhere in Afghanistan, he had stepped on something that had been waiting for him. Since then, he had come back, rehabilitated, joined the Nantucket Police and posed for a million pictures. Danny allowed that he wore clean clothes, smiled at the little old ladies, and was never late to the gym.

Chief Bramden was older, straight as a pencil, and had found a nice spot on a lake in Maine for his future summers. But for now, as the town fathers continued to pay him, he was behind this desk on Nantucket. He was also, perhaps, the only person Coffin would talk to, besides Danny.

But the old man wasn't here.

Just Sergeant Danny Abraham.

He had arrived in full uniform, armed and ready. He even saluted when he walked in the door. Macy, standing behind the Chief, snapped off a precise salute back, but the Chief did not. He merely looked up from the papers in front of him.

"Sergeant Abraham, sit down please."

"Yes sir."

"Danny," the chief relaxed in front of his subordinate. "I am told that you stopped Pink at the market this morning."

"Yes, sir."

"Did you give him a ticket or a warning? Was there a reason to stop him? Was he speeding?"

"No."

"Why did you stop him?"

"Henry wanted to talk to him."

"He did?"

"Yes."

"You're aware that you aren't supposed to use the car and the lights for that?" Macy underlined.

"This is the Inspector we are talking about."

The three men looked at each other and pondered the unsolvable mysteries of the earth.

"Go on," Bramden continued.

"Pink appears to be connected to two deaths. One of them was Meaghan Ingersoll, who we found this morning out in the brush in Madaquecham. Pink's number was the last one on her phone. We waited outside of Naushop, where the Inspector feels that there is a source of drugs, followed Pink to the grocery story where his fare bolted. So, Henry wanted to talk to him about that."

Lieutenant Macy glanced at the Chief. The Chief did not glance back.

Instead, he asked. "Who is the other death?"

"Caroline Bird."

"I don't believe we have a dead body that has that name."

Danny nodded, "Her coworkers say she is missing. She left all of her gear at the boat she was living in."

"Which boat?"

"One that is on the ground on Lover's Lane. She lives there with some other women who work at the Atlantic Cafe."

"Why does Henry think she connected to Pink?"

"Because we have seen Pink stopping at this house…or boat… for fares."

Macy looked down. "You said that she was dead."

"Henry thinks she is."

"Has he seen a body?"

Danny sighed, "No, the women at the boat gave him a bag of her clothes. It had a picture of her son in it."

The Chief continued. "And he thinks, because she left a picture of her son, she must be dead."

Danny saw, in the cold light of the afternoon, that the Chief wasn't wrong.

"Yes, sir."

"We don't have her body, we just have her absence."

"Yes, sir."

"We don't even have a missing persons report. She could be anywhere. Maybe even in a bed in a house?"

"Yes, sir."

The Chief settled back. The Lieutenant glowered. After glancing up at his inferior, he turned his attention back to his sergeant.

"Well, I understand the old man. Meaghan was unfortunate. And, knowing him, the detail about this woman's son is going to hit a sore spot."

"Yes."

"But, we can't go after ghosts. Either recent ones or older ones. So, let me ask you something?"

"Yes, sir."

"It is an ask, not an order, not anything else."

"Yes, sir."

"Let's leave Pink and the girls at that house…or boat, alone?"

"Yes, sir."

"Meaghan appears to have overdosed on her own? We have no evidence of murder? A solitary death of despair?"

"That's true."

"And Caroline Bird isn't even missing yet. Therefore, unless there is further evidence, there is no need to investigate."

Macy leaned in. "Danny, are you getting the message we are sending you?"

"Leave Pink alone," he answered.

"Yes."

The Chief looked at the sergeant with something between affection and pity. "Tell Henry that we, and others, are aware of Pink's role in all of this. Okay?"

"Yes, sir." Message received.

Danny for a moment considered who the "others" were?

CHAPTER ELEVEN

Sergeant Danny Abraham was pretty sure that his sick day or night would be accepted, endorsed, and even welcomed, as long as it was paired with his partner's. After he left the police station, he went out to the Delta fields to watch the second half of Hadley's game. Her team was up by six goals, but she remained in the middle of the field, patrolling from sideline to sideline. The Swain girls were also playing, with their mother in attendance. Pidge, however, was nowhere to be seen.

When Wendy saw Danny, she came over and gave him a birthday invitation, addressed to Hadley. "Jennifer would love to see her."

Of course.

With his daughter in the back seat, Danny drove back to town and to Henry Coffin. While he didn't know precisely what the old man was doing, he knew he could use a meal.

"Hadley, I am going to pick up my partner, Henry."

"Okay." She said. She was looking out the window. "He can smell bad."

"So can you. You aren't so sweet right now."

She sniffed her armpit. He loved her for that. "I'm fine."

"Well, hopefully he is fine as well."

The old man was puttering around his dining room table. He had stacked his bills and was organizing the envelopes.

Pip barked twice when Danny walked into the house. Then he walked between Danny's legs and waited for his butt to be scratched.

The sergeant was happy to see that the old man was wearing fresh clothes. As far as he could tell, Henry was presentable for dinner.

"You're not working tonight," he said.

"I'm not?"

"Unless you want to do it by yourself," Danny looked at him. "The two of us could use the night off."

Coffin moved into the kitchen. There were slightly fewer dishes in the sink. Danny didn't know if Coffin had washed some, hired someone, or had just stopped eating.

"You're not suspended, are you?"

"No, but..."

"But."

"We have been asked to leave Pink alone," Danny said. "They said that they were on it."

Henry snorted.

"Grab some of your beers," Danny continued. "Hadley is waiting for us in the car."

"Oh," then the old man paused, then put the papers on the table. "You didn't say she was here." His face cracked open, sprouted, and bloomed. "Well, let's go."

He pulled Pip's leash off a shelf.

"Maybe we should leave Pip here."

"Nonsense."

"Sherrie doesn't like dogs."

"Hadley does."

"I don't know about that."

"Let's see."

It turned out that Hadley loved dogs.

Pip was not going to come inside. In the face of his daughter and his partner, the dog remained in the back seat. He looked out the window and was sure that there had been some mistake. He was a Good Boy. Everyone said so.

Danny's moment of authority was brief.

"Mom!"

"Sweetheart," Sherrie stood in the hallway. She was tall, with an ankle length skirt, a tan blouse, and her hair was up.

"Can we let Pip in?"

"Whose Pip?"

"He's a nice dog."

"Maybe he likes it in the car?"

"He doesn't."

"How do you know?"

"He looks sad," she said. "His first people abandoned him. He hates being abandoned."

Henry said nothing. Danny was pretty sure a polite lie might solve this problem, but the Quaker wasn't one to tell a polite lie.

"Sweetie, are we sure he is housebroken?"

"Of course he is."

Sherrie hated when her husband conspired to make her the bad guy, so she cast a cold eye on the sergeant.

Her husband hated when his partner put him in yet another awkward situation, so he cast a cold eye on the Quaker.

The Quaker smiled, "Shall I get him?"

With that, his one brief moment of authority winked out and Pip came bouncing into the house.

There are things we don't talk about. For one, we don't talk about race. In its history, Nantucket has many wonderful stories about escaped slaves and African American whaling captains. We will tell those stories. We won't tell the ones about forcing everyone who wasn't white to live in one corner of town,"New Guinea" or of the assaults and murders, or of the separate burial ground out in Dead Horse Valley.

When Danny Abraham came out for his first job interview, we didn't know if he would be the right fit. He didn't know the island. He wasn't our kind. He had been in the inner city. He was urban. At this point, his competition was a rookie from Framingham and another gentleman who had been in three other departments before he came here. At this time, however, Pastor Anna Gardner was on the select board, saw Danny's resume, and 'liked the cut of his jib.' Chief Bromden, who was negotiating his own contract with the select board, agreed.

Before he signed a contract, Danny and his wife came out to find a place to live. The money was tremendous—half again as much as he was making—but...

No uniformed police were waiting at the dock. He had called realtors, but they weren't there either. Select-person Gardner was otherwise engaged.

On an April morning, Danny, Sherrie, and young Hadley had a map and the car they brought over.

Nobody turned around when he walked into the Steamship Authority Building.

When he walked into the police station, nobody came to the window. He rang the bell, sat on a bench and waited. After five minutes, he got up and left. Message received.

And Henry Coffin, just as rumpled, just as dirty, and five years younger met him as he walked out the door. Introduced himself, for the only time Danny had ever heard it, as a member of Nantucket Police Department. Could he ride along?

Together, they walked into a The Murray People Realty, and David Murray came up, shook Danny's hand, and agreed to show him some nice houses. David had been brought home from a drunken night six months ago and he remembered.

Then, when they found the house on Mizzenmast, The older woman remembered Henry very well. And Henry remembered removing her husband and a sledge hammer a year previous.

Finally, at the bank, Hank was so happy to help Henry and the town out with financing for this new policeman and his lovely family. Attorney Herman Lamb would be happy to take care of the details. Just sign here. And Here.

All told, the real estate transactions started at ten in the morning, and the signatures were finished by three.

They moved in a week later.

We were happy to see it happen. We weren't sure if he was in the right place, however.

Since that time, Danny and Sherrie knew what they owed and to whom. For her part, Sherrie was pretty sure that she could have lived without the gift. The idea of owing someone, even the Quaker, rubbed her wrong. Early on, Danny saw that the old man needed him more than the reverse. The Department, also, was happy that Danny was here to take on the care and feeding of the old man. They all loved the old man. They respected that he did the messy things they didn't want to. And the police union negotiations with the select board went by pretty easily with his presence. But they didn't want to work with him. If the new guy from the city wanted to spend the night with Henry, good for him.

After dinner, Hadley had to go to her room to complete her homework. Pip was NOT allowed upstairs. Homework, for a fourth grader, seemed excessive to the old man, but the world had taken many turns while he had walked it. And if she were just going upstairs to text her friends and play with the cat outside of adult eyes, that was fine with him. Pip returned to his place under the table and waited.

Sherrie disappeared into the kitchen to clean up the mess her husband had made in creating the baked salmon. She turned the radio on so as to give the impression she wasn't listening.

"What are the arrangements for Meaghan?" Danny, the father, asked.

Coffin shrugged. "Helen doesn't know. I don't think the family is very religious..

"So, no memorial service?"

"There will be some kids involved. She was young." Coffin said. "People will need to grieve. I'm sure there will be something."

"This weekend?"

Coffin shrugged. The moment paused.

Henry had settled into a faraway look. "I am thinking of the tent."

Abraham nodded.

Coffin continued. "There had been a fight with her Mom."

"Of course. Heroin."

"Mom believed in tough love. Not in my house. All of that."

The old man finished.

Danny nodded. "She never thought that she would just die out there.

"\You think they get cold and they come back."

"Sure."

Both men tapped their beer bottles. Sherrie sang along to Rihanna in the kitchen. Upstairs, they heard Hadley moving her chair. In that moment of comfortable noise, Danny thought of the echoing silence of the old house on Main Street. And of the noiseless footsteps of an eternal ghost.

"I'm going to Plymouth tomorrow," Coffin said.

"Okay."

"The sheriff is taking a bunch of men up for a hearing. I'm hitching a ride."

"Why?"

"I want to see if Caroline shows up," Danny remembered the court hearing for the boy.

"And if she doesn't?"

"Then I want to see that," he said. "She has a lawyer. She has money. She has a court date. She has a son."

Danny nodded, "Why are you doing this? You could just call the lawyer."

"I want to see it."

"Really."

"I want to be there."

"I don't know what you are going to find out that we can't find out on the phone."

"It's always good to shake hands. It's always good to be present."

"Present?"

"Sure."

"I hope she is there."

"Me, too."

He drove the old man and his dog back to his house and sent him back to his ghosts.

Danny knew many things. He didn't want to, but the fare you pay for living a long time are the unpleasant things you have to learn.

The old man was vain. He had been asked to look for Caroline and he was going to do it. Everyone likes to be needed.

He could tell Henry that she was a heroin addict. Bad things happened to addicts. She was someone's daughter, someone's mother. But at this point, she was only a missing person. And not really that.

Just like twenty other young women who had come to Nantucket this summer. Work appears in other places in September, and the workers move on. They might wear t-shirts, they might mow lawns, or they might work in one of those houses off Fairgrounds Road.

But there was something else.

The boat set him off. No question.

But, in the silence, Danny settled on the picture. The Inspector had lost a son. And this son, it appeared, had lost a mother.

Danny Abraham hoped that, for the cost of an evening, a salmon dinner, and his wife's annoyance, the old man realized that he was risking a lot more than the odd hours on his day off island.

CHAPTER TWELVE

The Inspector did not leave the island often. He hadn't driven on a highway in twenty years and had no desire to do so again.

So, as it happened, the sheriff's deputy was taking three Guatemalan men up to the Plymouth Court. If he didn't mind sitting in the shot gun seat, he could get a ride.

At seven in the morning, he squeezed into a seven seat Cessna with Jimmy Shaw, a young deputy and recent graduate from the high school. He was wearing the full brown uniform, complete with a Glock and nightstick. He sat next to the pilot, while the Inspector sat one seat behind, next to one of the handcuffed inmates. Coffin gave him a handshake before the plane took off.

We used to fly often. The airlines will sell ticket books and the contractors would buy dozens of them. Before high speed ferries serviced the islands, the sports teams would fly in DC-3s to the mainland. Then, when the decades caught up to that plane, we all jammed into nine seat Cessnas for a thirty minute flight. Five or six flights would go every hour. As the high speed ferries came and got more reliable, the magic of flying disappeared from our lives.

In Hyannis, a Plymouth District Court van had been brought up to the terminal. Jimmy took over the wheel, while the Inspector helped the shackled men get into the rear seats. After they were all seated and belted, he climbed into the passenger seat.

Deputy Jimmy Shaw pulled out and headed out Iyannough Road to Route 6. However, before he left Hyannis, he pulled into the Dunkin Donuts drive through.

"Coffee?"

"Sure. Small and black."

The van inched up to the speaker.

Coffin turned around. "Coffee?"

One of the inmates smiled. "Regular." He said. "Any chance for a donut?"

Coffin looked at his wallet. "We can do that."

Shaw looked aghast. Coffin smiled.

"I got it, son. A dozen donuts, three regulars, and a small black coffee for me," he said. "And whatever you want."

"We don't do that."

"Today, we do."

The young deputy glared at him. The speaker asked for an order.

Coffin recited it to the speaker. Then he gave the young man two twenties.

The donuts disappeared before the van left the Cape and crossed the Bourne Bridge, including a chocolate frosted for the deputy.

Powdered sugar and bits of glaze were stuck to the orange jumpsuits. Coffin smiled.

At the courthouse, the court officers, the lawyers, and the judge went about their business in a quick, courteous, and ruthless manner. People were remanded, people were paroled, people had court hearings scheduled. The Judge sat in his high seat, assisted by two clerks, and a series of officers who pushed people in an out of his view with brisk efficiency. The Guatemalans all stood, all nodded, and all were handed a new hearing date.

Shaw looked at Coffin and pointed at his watch.

He wasn't the only one with an eye on the old man. Everyone in the courtroom, had a purpose, a goal, and a pattern. Save one. One idle old man in a busy room attracted eyes.

Inspector Coffin was on a bit of a fishing exhibition. Caroline had a court appointment for this morning. She had hired a young lawyer, Jay Thomas, to represent her in an attempt to win back her son.

An hour after the Guatemalans were seen and dealt with, the matter of Caroline Bird came to the eyes of the court. A woman stood up for the Department of Social Services and a young man, in a gray suit, crisp haircut, and colorful tie stood next to her.

After the clerk called the case, the young man looked up.

"We beg the court's pardon, but we are unable to locate Ms. Bird. We ask, respectfully, to reschedule the hearing."

"Do you know where your client is?"

"She has been working on Nantucket, your honor, but she has not been responding to her phone."

The Judge looked at the Inspector. Henry did not recognize him. He paused, as if to offer Coffin a moment to speak. The Inspector did not.

Instead, Coffin was searching the room for a young man who also looked out of place.

Both lawyers saw who the judge was looking at, however.

"Is a new date amenable to the state?"

"If your honor would make an appropriate notation."

"So noted," he initialed something "Next."

Later, the court recessed for lunch.

Coffin made his way to the young attorneys. They both were looking at an open folder.

"Pardon me."

The folder closed, immediately.

"How can I help you, sir?"

The lawyer for the DSS caught the eye of a court officer.

"I am Henry Coffin from Nantucket. I work with the police department. I want to ask you some questions about Caroline Bird."

"Do you have a badge?"

"No."

"Do you have a Police I.D."

"No."

The DSS lawyer nodded at him with her head. The Court Officer approached.

"Sir, I cannot speak to you about this matter." The lawyer spoke and looked at the tall, white haired Court Officer. "Would you?"

"Please come with me, sir."

Coffin sighed.

Outside the court, but still inside the building, Inspector Coffin sat on one of the wooden benches. Sheriff Deputy Jimmy Shaw led the three Guatemalans out of the court and he stood near the door. The rest of the court was also moving, briefcases closed and phones at the ear.

Caroline's lawyer, Jay Thomas, opened a door and stepped out. He saw the Inspector and came over.

"Hey."

"Hello."

"Judge Farnsworth says you are a cop on Nantucket. An Inspector. I didn't know we still had Inspectors in Massachusetts."

"It's a title."

"Why aren't you in uniform?"

"I'm a Quaker."

The young man looked at the old one as if he just left an asparagus and chili fart in the courtroom.

"I wouldn't think there would be many Quakers in the police departments."

"Should be more."

A group of other younger men and women were waiting for him. Lunch plans were waiting. Thomas turned brusque. "Why are you here?"

"I am looking for your client. I thought she might be here."

"Why are you looking?"

"A bunch of her friends are missing her."

He stopped.

"That's it?"

"They asked me, I saw where she was living, I saw what she had, I saw that she left her…place without her stuff or her pictures of Michael. I think she might be dead. I hope she isn't."

"She isn't even missing yet."

"But we can't find her," Coffin said. "You can't either. You're her lawyer."

"You don't know much."

"No."

"How was she doing?"

"She was working."

"Working?"

"She was a waitress at a restaurant downtown. She lived in employee housing."

He nodded. "Was she doing any other work?"

"Maybe."

The word carried a world of meaning. The lawyer caught the wink in the word.

"Did you know that she paid me a five thousand dollar retainer? In hundreds?"

"No."

"Did you know that she has an apartment in Duxbury where she is going to live with her sister and her son?"

"No," he said. "And the sister hasn't seen her?"

"No," The lawyer continued. "Did you know that her son has been in three foster homes in the last year?"

"No," Coffin said. "And the boy hasn't talked to his Mom recently?"

Jay crossed his arms. "He is in isolation right now. Hospital. Has been there for a month."

Coffin peered at the lawyer, but read the sadness in the silence.

He nodded.

"Did you know that the state is going to allow her son to go back to her?"

"Really."

"Yes."

The young lawyer looked at the Inspector with both curiosity and annoyance. The Judge had pulled him over and asked him to speak to Coffin. He was known. He was respected. The attorney hadn't the foggiest idea why.

"Okay," Jay said. "Now, you know something."

"Would you do me a favor?" The old man asked.

"Depends."

"Would you report her missing? The court will record she missed a court date and with your letter, perhaps I can get some more resources on this."

"Twenty four days, Inspector. It takes twenty four days for a person to legally go missing."

"With a letter from you, a mention from the court, and my help, perhaps we can get things moving a little faster. Nantucket isn't like other places."

"Well, they do have an Inspector."

Coffin nodded.

"Inspector, the boy could really use his mother. He has been clinging to this rope. It means a lot to him." He said. "I will report her missing. I'll see what I can get from the clerk."

"Will you send me the contact information for the sister?"

"Sure."

"I'll do what I can."

"Good."

That night, Coffin slept soundly in the passenger seat of the patrol car.

Danny stepped outside to acknowledge both his age and the power of Volcanic Peruvian coffee.

September glowed overhead. The moon had set hours ago and, in the cool Canadian air, the constellations glistened and the Milky Way burned its ancient light. We are all small in the shadow of the galaxies.

Back inside the cruiser, he picked up his Kindle just in time for a 1976 Chevy Blazer to come weaving around the corner. One zig over the line and one zag back and a near brush with a scrub pine.

A touch of the lights and another on the accelerator brought the Inspector out of his sound sleep. A moment of pursuit brought the Blazer to a rest off the road and on the bike path.

Henry was blinking when Danny reached for the door handle.

"Wait," Coffin said.

"For what?"

"I got this."

"He better not be shitfaced."

"If he is, I'll signal you."

Danny sat back in the car and crossed his arms. Coffin opened the door.

Outside, in the blue light of the stars, Coffin noted that this old car might be the only regularly running car on island that was older than their police cruiser.

He walked up to the driver's side window and tapped it. The door opened.

"I'm sorry, but I don't think the window works."

The nurse, Pidge, sat behind the wheel. She wore tan pants, a blue blouse and a pair of subtle earrings that looked like rice.

"Hello, Pidge."

"Inspector?"

"Danny and I hang out at the life saving museum most nights. Do you have your license and registration."

"Sure."

But it was a process. Her license was in her clutch, but the registration was buried in the glove compartment. Beyond her, in the passenger seat, Paul Brody was asleep against the door.

"Is he okay?"

"He passed out."

"But we don't need an ambulance?"

"No," she said. Then, she reached up to his neck and measured his pulse. "Strong and steady."

"We carry Narcan."

"He's fine."

She resumed her dive through the glove compartment. Even though Pidge was banging on his legs and thighs through the search, Paul didn't move. Like her, he was dressed for dinner, but his shirt had slipped up in his slumber and some of his back tattoo showed.

Coffin wasn't surprised. He recognized the car when he woke up. Paul's father, Elliot, drove it when he was on island. Senior had been the second name on a law firm in Boston for thirty years. In the seventies, when you could still do this sort of thing, he built a fishing shack in Quaise on the eastern side. He loved his shack; it was a hundred yards from the ocean, had a bathroom, a hot plate, a deck, and a bar. It was about as feminine as a urinal. For ten years, while Junior was small, the old man stole time to fish for a week or so in the summer and fall. Then, when his boy got old enough, the lawyer paid a few locals to build a second floor, a kitchen, a real bathroom with a bathtub (and not just an outdoor shower) and put in the usual appliances that women like. Now, as the years had built up, and then washed away, the house and the son remained, albeit with the old man's fishing gear, his mother's water colors, and a gigantic, loud, Chevy Blazer.

In the deep dark past, the Inspector had found the Blazer parked in a series of driveways on Polpis Road, where the lawyer had parked to sleep the Canadian Club out of his system. More than once had he woken Senior with a tap on the window and an angry homeowner on a doorstep.

Pidge gave him both her license and the car's registration. He noticed that she was not wearing the big ring.

At the police car, Danny looked at the registration.

"He's a year out of date," the sergeant reached for the radio.

"Pidge is driving." Danny shuffled and found her license. Coffin looked at him. "She isn't wearing a ring."

"Ah, shit," he sat back. "So, that shit about the Langueduc…"

"Is probably true." Coffin added.

Both men stared at the back of the Blazer. The registration sticker, on the license plate, was covered with dirt.

"Do we want her to have this car impounded, have the two of them take taxi cab, and start a few more rumors?" Coffin asked.

"That's the law, Henry," he said. "And you have questions…"

"I'll drive the car to his house. We'll drop them off. Then I'll make sure it gets towed off tomorrow morning. Impound it then."

"This assumes that you are ready to drive."

"I am more than familiar with this car."

"Whatever."

Danny handed the paperwork back.

Coffin walked back to the Blazer. The nurse opened the door.

"Pidge, your license is fine, but this car's registration is a year out of date. Danny wants to impound it and call you a cab. He's right, but I have an idea that will keep you out of people's mouths for a while."

"What's your idea?"

"You get in the back and I will drive you home."

"Really?"

"Yeah, Paul will have to call for a tow tomorrow. We will be looking for this rig. Hard to miss it."

"No shit," she said.

"Subtlety was never a strength for the Brodys, both father and son." Coffin replied.

"Yeah," she said. "You knew his dad?"

"Professionally. He was the victim of bartenders." Coffin added. "His son may have a similar problem."

"He's a good sleeper."

"Father was too," Coffin said. "Okay, get in back."

The Brody fishing shack was five miles away. On the mainland, five miles is a short newspaper route, but on Nantucket, this involved several turns tom he dark, and a final push through a gravel and sand road along side the eastern shore. They drove in silence; Coffin knew the way.

In the years since Henry had come out here last, the building lots on all sides of the fishing shack had bloomed into cedar shingle fantasies. Porches came off the second floor bedrooms, gables lined the roofline and pools filled in the empty space between the ocean and the house. Coffin didn't think you would need a pool when the ocean was another twenty yards away, but the world kept spinning underneath him.

The Brody house remained dark, ramshackle, and quaint. He bounced the big car through the ruts and parked it next to Pidge's green Subaru.

Pidge thanked Henry, waved at Danny in the car, then opened to door to another man's house.

She let Paul sleep in the car.

When Coffin came back to the cruiser, he nodded to his partner.

"She thanked you."

"Good thing."

"I don't think she is going to be at that birthday party."

"Probably not."

At six-thirty, as they were about to go off shift, the officers returned to the shack in Quaise. Both cars were still there, although Paul had moved inside.

Danny called for Greg Moore at Nantucket Auto Body to impound the Blazer. In that way, peace was maintained and order was restored.

CHAPTER THIRTEEN

On Wednesday morning, Henry Coffin reported to Dickie Lewis' Funeral home. He left Pip at home. Too many people were coming to this service.

Meaghan Ingersoll had a closed coffin at her wake. The coffin lay in the front of the room at the funeral home with a spray of memories over it. Meaghan at prom, Meaghan at graduation, Meaghan dancing on stage at Junior Miss, Meaghan as a little girl playing in the grass with her dolls. Helen had put up a diploma, some toys when she was a little girl, and a small dancing outfit from her childhood. Two large sprays of white lilies framed the casket.

In the front row, Helen considered the impossible. Five women sat next to each other, all a similar age. Their men stood at the back of the room, praying for something to drink. A group of hispanic women walked in twenty minutes after the door opened, weighed down with food. Helen hugged them and cried.

Henry sat alone.

He remembered the tent in the moors, and the lights, and the shoe box.

He wouldn't have decorated the coffin with all of that stuff. He hadn't done that for Pete. He wasn't sure if he had been right; but he was sure that he couldn't live with that pain. Perhaps Helen could.

He did think of Pink. He wanted him to sit next to him in this metal folding chair, at the back of Dickie Lewis' Funeral Home.

We decided that Meaghan was going to have a funeral. All of Meaghan's people were Nantucketers. They had gone to Wee Whalers with her, cheered with her at the Boy's and Girl's Club, sat in Mrs. White's Social Studies Class, competed in Junior Miss, got drunk on Fireball and were fucked up at beach parties, graduated and worked here and there. Somewhere, at UMASS Amherst there might be a few boys who remembered her, or a roommate, or an adjunct who was there for her one semester. But everyone else, and everyone else who counted, was here. Some came back from college, some came back from off-island, but everyone else didn't have to come back to where they had always been.

The funeral was announced on the message board outside of the Hub on a piece of paper with a black border. Of course, we knew. But pictures were taken of the sheet and posted on Facebook and Instagram and shared. Words were said. Even the newspaper found out.

Wednesday, at eleven, was good time for a funeral. The midweek lunch rush, in September, was minimal. The White

Elephant hotel rooms had been cleaned already, the dinners could wait until four, and everyone else understood why the workers were late. Time would be taken for Meaghan. St. Mary's By the Sea, for its part, had not been booked weddings or anything else for the middle of the week. They had several wedding rehearsals for Thursday, but Wednesday was open.

So we had a funeral. The air glowed in the glory of the extended summer. If you had retired, or were rich enough, Wednesday was just right. The air was warm, the water warmer, and there was no waiting at the tennis courts and the cash registers.

Henry left the funeral home and walked down Union Street, then up to the church. He followed the hearse, but not formally. The presence of the big black car quieted the shoppers and the visitors for a moment. The street stared at it and asked. Let attention be paid.

St. Mary's had been built by poor people, filled by poor people, funded by poor people, and still attended by the same. The poor people, of course, had changed over time. The Irish, the Portuguese and the Cape Verdean, had been replaced by Central European, Honduran, and the Brazilian. Father Nunes offered his mass in English, Spanish, and Portuguese.

Henry sat in the last row on the left, just inside the door and deep in shadow. Above him, in the stained glass, Jesus carried his cross. The mourners followed in behind him. Her classmates, in Whaler jackets still, had left their jobsites and had come to pay respect. The women she had worked with at the White Elephant came, with their friends and family. Her mother's friends and co-workers filed in until the church was three quarters full.

Danny stepped in after the crowd. He wore his full dress uniform, unlike his partner.

"Y'know we can get paid for this."

Coffin looked at him.

"We have to lead the hearse to the burial."

"Great."

"I'll let you put the lights on, if you want."

Jon-Jon walked in and slipped up to the front of the church. He spoke to some people in the front row, then he walked back to the two policemen. They moved over for him.

The bartender reached over and touched Coffin's thigh. "You know this is where the black people sit, right?"

He grinned. Coffin tried to meet him with a smile.

"Hey," Jon-Jon added. "Chicken Box is hosting the after-party."

"It's not called an after-party. It's a collation." Coffin replied.

"Call it what you want. You're invited."

"Thanks."

"I have something for you," he said. "Someone saw Caroline at the Club Car."

The music began and Father Nunes bid everyone to rise.

By the time Meghan had been put to rest and the hearse had been put in its garage, the crowd had grown at the Chicken Box. Jon-Jon had covered the pool tables with plywood, then spread white table clothes over them. The mourners had brought macaroni and cheese, beans, and tamales. Others had brought barbecue: ribs, and pulled pork, and coleslaw. Finally, the White Elephant had sent over a fried chicken dinner for thirty, with mashed potatoes, green beans, and rolls.

The Chicken Box was not at its Friday night full, but the crowd was large and well fed. The bar, however, was only sparsely attended. Henry sat at his usual chair, with a plate of Jamaican and Honduran food. Jon-Jon brought him a Jim Beam on ice. Danny got a Coke.

Coffin nodded a thank you, then, with a mouthful of food, he put one hand on the bartender's hand.

"Jon-Jon, why isn't anyone drinking?"

"It's a cash bar."

"You're charging?"

"I have to pay people," he said. "Nobody works for free."

Coffin nodded. Then he put his plastic fork down.

"Free drinks. Tell your bartenders to keep a list and I'll pay it."

"Really?"

Danny looked at him. "Are you getting off your wallet?"

"Might as well."

Jon-Jon remained. "You will pay for everyone's drinks?"

"For the next hour," he said. "And it's anonymous."

"Okay."

Jon Jon then swept past all of the bartenders, had a word, and locked the registers. The mourners, almost all of whom had worked behind a bar at least once, knew what the locked registers meant. They drifted to the bar.

Henry had another bite of something spicy and brown.

"Is that oxtail?" His partner asked.

"I have no idea. Tastes like chicken."

"Let me taste it."

"Get your own."

"After I taste it."

Danny dipped a fork into Henry's lunch. For his part, he had a plate of scallops wrapped in bacon. Only on Nantucket, would you unfreeze these for a funeral. Someone here pulled the free food from the harbor last year; everyone else has to pay a hundred dollars a pound.

"Definitely chicken." he added. "I'll get some more. Have a scallop."

The bartenders were pouring a lot of wine. Not that it mattered what the mourners drank, but Coffin had thought that the crowd would start ordering mixed drinks. As the word passed, the lines at the bartenders lengthened. Even though the registers were closed, the tip jars remained open. Danny returned with a bowl full of whatever the Inspector had been eating. He brought two rolls with it, and dropped one on the old man's plate.

"For clean up."

Jon Jon was helping his staff. He was taking orders and pouring, working wherever the line was the longest. The crowd was thirsty, but orderly. They knew what it was like on the other side of the bar.

"How much is this going to set you back, old man."

"Nothing."

"Doesn't look like nothing. Looks like quite something."

"Looks like a lot of wine and beer. Nobody is ordering cocktails or champagne."

"I wouldn't think you would drink champagne at an afterparty."

"It's a collation. And you're right."

"I should drink something."

"You should." Coffin said. "But everyone would see you."

"They see you."

"They know I don't drive."

"True."

The big man ate three of his cooling scallops, then finished his coke. A bartender freshened it for him.

"Seriously," Danny asked.

"What?"

"Seriously, why are you paying for all of this?"

"I want to. I can."

"Beyond that."

Coffin stopped and he stared ahead. "This morning, I got up in bed and went to the bathroom. After I completed the necessities, I looked at the mirror. Do you know what I saw?"

"A silly, foolish, old white man."

Coffin cast a glance at his grinning partner. He answered. "I saw the frame. I saw the wall in front of me and behind me. I saw a house that I had been given that I have lived in for more than thirty years. I saw a house that was built and paid for by all of these people. These people worked on the whale ships and got paid nothing while my great grandfathers built their wealth. Now they mow lawns and paint walls and clean dirty sheets and serve drinks and still get paid nothing. I got handed a mansion on Main Street while Meaghan got a tent in Madaquecham and Caroline got a sleeping bag in a boat. So, sometimes, when the sun is right, I feel a little silly with the money that I have and the house that I live in. Free drinks is the utter least I can do. Frankly, it's an insult to their grandparents."

Danny patted the shoulder of the Quaker. The word had spread about his visit to Brian Swain. He would ask him later. "You're a good man, Henry."

"I should be better."

In a half hour, Helen Ingersoll left, along with her sisters and their husbands. After she left, a few came up for one more drink before they, too, began filtering out. They had to go home, or go to work, or to the beach or to another bar in another place.

The afternoon regulars began filing in. Without pausing a step, they grabbed a paper plate and began helping themselves. Jon-Jon looked at the Inspector from across the bar, and the old man gave him the nod. He walked around to each register and unlocked it. Grieving was over: the bar was open.

Jon-Jon repeated his walk, this time picking up the slips. He went to the rear of the bar and began to add up the tab, beneath a TV showing a college football game on Wednesday afternoon. When he finished, he walked over to Henry.

"Inspector, I think you owe about two thousand dollars."

"Does that include a tip?"

"They all got tipped well. You saw the pitchers fill up."

Coffin pulled a ragged leather wallet out of his pants. Inside, he extracted a paper check.

He looked at Jon-Jon. "Am I good?"

"I know where you work."

Coffin snorted. Then he wrote a check for three thousand dollars. "Take care of people, would you?"

"Of course."

Danny caught the bar owner's eye. While he kept the Jon-Jon in his sight, he eased to his left so Jon-Jon could see the guy behind him leaning against a wall, watching TV.

"You see a guy with a crisp Whaler's cap on?"

He looked over Danny's shoulder. "The undercover? Sure."

"How often is he here?"

"A lot. Not sure exactly."

"Does he talk to anyone?"

"Not that I notice," Jon Jon looked at him. "He pretty much shows up when you are here. If you aren't here, he leaves."

Coffin spoke. "Send him a beer on me."

"Sure."

Danny watched the beer get delivered. The undercover, to his credit, tipped it to the cops and drank. Jon-Jon returned.

"You see Pink much?"

"Nope. Not at all."

Coffin nodded.

"Is there a reason for that?" Jon Jon asked.

Danny cleared his throat. Coffin eyed him. Then continued.

"They did a nice job with that funeral, didn't they?"

Jon-Jon understood the communication. "People gotta help people."

"Yup," Coffin answered. "You said you have something?"

"You left that picture here."

"I did." Coffin replied.

"Well, this guy I know, Tobias, he recognized her."

Coffin grew a little. "Where did Tobias see her?"

"He is the maitre d at the Club Car. He said she was at dinner with a guy over Labor Day?"

"Did he say which day?"

"He thought Friday or Saturday. He wasn't sure. He remembered her because she brought the girls to the party?"

Coffin cocked his head in a question.

"She wore a very revealing dress to the Club Car."

"Some of his guests were upset?"

"And others were excited. There were complaints to him. They said she looked cheap."

"Did they have a reservation?"

"I don't know," he said. "Probably."

"We'll visit him," Coffin said. "Soon."

In the early evening, Danny dropped the old man off at his house then returned to his own. After six hours of interrupted and annoyed sleep later, for both men, Danny picked Henry up at eleven in the evening.

On his door, someone had left a green post-it. "Call me if you want to sell." Connecticut phone number at the bottom. On island, the only secrets we have are the ones we tell ourselves. The old man crumpled it and dropped it in a hall waste basket. He didn't comment.

Tonight, Pip returned to the back seat. The old man had brought out a ratty quilt (probably an antique) and tucked it into the rear seat. Pip hopped up and got settled.

The old man was back asleep in the passenger seat by eleven thirty. He had drunk too much. He had talked too much. And, probably, he needed company to sleep these days.

All of which did not make Danny feel any more comfortable when he thought about the undercover and the state police cruisers who drove by on the Polpis road.

The Inspector slept until four A.M.

Then, they got a call.

"Don't come in here, Henry."

"You know I have to."

"No, you don't."

"I have to come in."

Nancy filled the door. Her face had reddened, her hair was all over the place. She wore a Whaler's t-shirt and a blue pair of sweats. Behind her, on the stairs, two kids watched the front door. Beyond them, on the floor of the kitchen, Ronnie Folger lay on his back.

"We got called. We have to come in."

One of the kids pressed 911 and left the phone open.

They had done it before.

Coffin walked into her. She wanted to shove him, but didn't. Danny hurried right in behind him, with the Narcan hidden behind his back.

"Just let him die, Henry. He's miserable. We are going to lose the house because he can't stop. Just let him die."

"I can't, Nancy. I won't."

"He is miserable."

Danny knelt next to Ronnie. Ronnie was a mason; he carried bricks and cement across work sites, then he drank beers with his buddies before he came home. And he shot up.

Right now, he was still, he was white, and he had shit himself in his nylon shorts.

"Henry, Just…"

Danny shot the Narcan up the big man's nose. He popped up.

"What the fuck was that?"

"Narcan, again, Ronnie."

Nancy was wailing in the hallway.

"There's an ambulance coming, Ronnie. Get on it and go to the hospital."

"Shut the fuck up, you fat bitch!" He shouted at his wife.

Danny grabbed him by his shoulders and shook him. Ronnie looked at the black man.

"Get your hands off me, nigger."

Coffin got down to his level. "He just saved your life."

"The fuck he did. I was faking it."

Danny took his hands off, stood up, and stayed close.

"Ronnie, when the ambulance comes, get in and go to the hospital."

"Who is going to pay for that?"

"You have insurance, Ronnie."

"The fuck I do."

"We don't have insurance!" Nancy yelled.

"Not for a fucking joy ride in the ambulance!"

"Ronnie," Coffin lowered his voice.

The big man, in a white shirt and shit filled nylon athletic shorts, wouldn't look at him.

"Ronnie," Coffin continued. "Whatever you took might have been doctored. It might have fentanyl in it."

"I just drank beer."

"Ronnie, who sold it to you? We could have a whole bunch of dead people on island tonight?"

"Fuck you. It was just beer. I was faking it."

"You heard what happened to Meaghan? In a tent in Madaquecham?."

"I am not her."

"You can prevent some people from dying."

"I just drank beer."

Coffin stood.

Nancy screamed. "You should have let him die."

CHAPTER FOURTEEN

Hadley was ready for school at 7:15. The old man moved into the back seat, behind the grill, so that Hadley could ride up front with her Dad. But Hadley was having none of it.

"I want to sit with Pip."

So Coffin moved and Hadley sat on the seat for the criminals.

With the dog.

She was very happy, as was Pip. He licked her cheeks. Her hair was in tight rows.

"What day is it, sweetie?"

"Game Day."

"And what do we do on game day?"

"We win."

"That's right."

"Who do you play today?" Henry asked from the passenger seat.

"The Bluebirds."

"I hear their tough." Coffin said.

"We beat them six to nil two weeks ago."

"Well, you must be tougher."

"Course," she said. "Are you going to come to our game."

"Hopefully. You never know when police work will happen."

"Oh, puh-leeze."

They pulled into the fire lane. She kissed her Dad on the cheek. The door closed.

Pip watched her go all the way into the doors.

"There you go, Henry. We have done something good today."

Six hours later, Danny walked into Coffin's bedroom.

"Get up, old man."

Pip trotted behind him, barking.

Henry blinked in the sudden light from the hall. "What is it?"

"Do you have any clean clothes in here?"

"Sure."

"Put them on. A uniform would be good."

Danny was in uniform. Henry looked at his phone on the night stand. Eleven in the morning.

"Stop." Coffin asked.

Danny was opening the shades. He stopped.

"What is going on?" Henry asked.

"Did you call Susan Bird?"

Coffin thought for a moment. "No. Is that Caroline's sister?"

"Yup. She saw you at the court," Danny said. "You didn't call her?"

"No."

"You aren't lying to me?"

Coffin glared at him.

"No," he said. "I should have called her."

"I think the Chief would disagree with you there. As Caroline isn't a missing person yet. Did the Chief know you went to Plymouth?"

Coffin pulled on his pants.

"I don't know what he knows."

Danny nodded. His mortgage, his daughter's education, and his retirement is tied onto this idiot white boy.

"Well now, everyone wants to see you. The chief is angry, the one legged lieutenant is pissed, and Susan Bird has taken a ferry and is waiting with a full stomach to shit on your head. She's at the station. Chief wants you, and yours truly, there ten minutes ago. I have the lights going outside."

"Oh."

"Get dressed and wear your "Eating shit with a smile" clothes," he said. "We both will be getting full plates."

Pip was ready for an adventure, but the Quaker decided the good boy should stay for the moment.

Ten minutes later, blinking and unshaven, Henry appeared at the police station downtown.

Just off of police property, a thin woman in jeans and a sweater smoked fast and hard. She looked hard at the police car as Danny emerged. Coffin saw her, then opened the door.

He walked straight for her.

"Susan Bird, I am Henry Coffin."

"Where is my sister?"

"I don't know."

She sucked on the cigarette, then blew a long plume.

"What do you know?"

"Not much."

"Who the fuck are you then?" She flashed at the Inspector. "And who's he?"

"Sergeant Danny Abraham," Danny stood just behind Coffin.

"So, who the fuck are you?" She returned to Coffin.

"I am Henry Coffin, I work with the Nantucket Police department."

"But you aren't a cop?"

"I work here."

"But you aren't a cop?" She pressed.

Danny stepped in, on cue. "This is Inspector Henry Coffin. He is a Quaker which makes him a bit of a problem on introductions."

"Why the fuck is that?" She returned her attention to the old man in a flannel and gray chinos.

"Quakers don't like titles, uniforms, guns, badges or anything else that makes someone seem more important than anyone else." Coffin answered.

"That seems fucked up for someone who is a cop." She looked at Danny, "He is a cop?"

"He is."

"Susan, let's sit on this bench," The Inspector suggested. "Let's talk about your sister."

"Hold on," Susan said. She held her hand up in a stop gesture. "Why aren't you guys working right now?"

"Well…" Coffin started.

Danny glanced at him, "We work the night shift."

"Hold the fucking phone. Shut the fuck up." She swung her cigarette in a circle. "My sister is missing and the two people in charge of this don't even work on the day shift? One guy who looks like he's going to die and…you." She gestured at Danny. "You are not even the J.V. for cops are you?"

"Let's talk about your sister," Coffin said, moving towards the bench.

"Do they even let you in the station?"

"Ma'am?" Danny retreated into his uniform. "The station called us in. He is 100% police, even if he looks weird. We can go inside, you can put your cigarette out, and we can all talk to the Chief."

"I talked to that clown."

"Or, we can talk out here, where you can smoke."

She looked at Danny. Then she walked over and sat at the bench. Henry sat next to her, but Danny, feeling the racist vibe, decided to stand in front her. Let her see the nightstick, the Glock, and the badge.

Coffin opened a legal pad. Danny knew that he never used the legal pad, except to make some people feel better about talking to him. If he had that out, he must be listening.

She lit a new cigarette.

"When was the last time you talked to Caroline?"

"Just before Labor Day, Friday, at four."

"What did she say?"

"Nothing. Hi. How are you? We talked about the court date and Michael. Work. Shit like that."

"How often did you talk?"

"Enough."

"Once a week?"

"Like that."

Coffin wrote that down.

"You were going to move in together?"

"Well, we are going to move in together."

Coffin looked up. "Sorry."

"You should be."

"I am."

She blew out a long plume.

"I found a good apartment in Duxbury. They have good schools in Duxbury. For Michael."

Coffin wrote that down.

"In that phone call, what did she say about work?"

"Usual shit. It was hard. Lot of dick sucking. Paid well." She said. "She must. The lawyer costs a frigging fortune. And she gave me money on a downpayment."

"So you have a rental agreement?"

"Yeah."

"Where?"

"Colonial Corners, Duxbury. But she ain't fucking there, now is she?"

"I assume not."

"No. she is not."

"Did she talk about anybody on island?"

"Like who? Customers? Clients?"

Danny glanced at Coffin, but the old man kept focussing on Susan.

"No." She continued.

"A guy? Did she have a date?"

"She always had dates. She said there was a guy who was her partner. A while ago."

"What did she say?"

"She said he was a spoiled little boy."

"Okay."

"She said that he liked things a little weird."

"Weird?"

"I don't care. Guys are guys. They are all freaks." She sucked in the smoke, then blew it out in a blue-gray column. "He liked to choke her."

The Quaker looked up. Danny shuffled.

"Was this consensual?"

"What the fuck do you think?" Susan said. "Do you think she was making a bag of money as a waitress?"

Danny appreciated the ashy color of his partner. The things he didn't think of.

"Would it be fair to say that Caroline had…an arrangement with this guy?" Coffin asked.

"Is that what you call it out here with the billionaires?"

"Yeah."

"Well, she had an arrangement."

Coffin wrote it down.

"What is his name?"

"Why?"

"Maybe he could tell us something."

"I know guys like this. He won't say shit."

Danny stepped in. "I know the Inspector looks a little gray, but he's good at this."

She looked at the little old man in the flannel shirt. "You're an Inspector?"

"Everyone gets a title."

"Like Inspector Gadget?"

"Yes," Coffin smiled. "But we really want to find Caroline. Anything will help."

"How about this?"

Susan fiddled with her broken screen on her phone, swiped up several times, and showed a picture of her sister with blue and purple and even green bruises around her neck.

Now, Danny turned away.

Coffin looked at it. "Would you send that to me?"

Susan eyed him. "Don't get him in trouble. He paid her a lot of cash."

"She said it was consensual?"

"She did."

"So it's no crime. But it will help us."

"Fine. What's your number?"

Coffin gave it to her. The horrible picture came to his phone.

"Do you have any more pictures of her?"

"Sure."

"We only have the one with her son."

"I'll send you a bunch."

And she did. Susan shared pictures of cigarette burns, noose marks, scars across her sister's bottom and across her back.

She also sent one from a year back, at Christmas with Michael.

Coffin assumed a serene expression.

"Did she ever tell you who her partner was?"

"He was very good to her."

Danny walked away. Coffin continued to listen.

"He's not in trouble. But he may have seen her before she disappeared, so we would like to ask."

"She said his name was Cam Christmas."

Coffin wrote the name down. Danny plugged the name into his phone and came up with an address in New York, Greenwich, Jupiter Island, Park City, and 61 Baxter Road, Nantucket.

"She said he had a lacrosse stick tattooed on his ass."

Coffin nodded. "Did she know how old he was?"

"Young guy. Twenties."

Coffin nodded.

"You don't know where they met?"

"No," she said. "But he was fucking loaded."

"How loaded?"

"He paid her a thousand per...visit."

"Okay," Coffin nodded. Susan watched Henry write the information on a notepad. Then he capped his pen and put it in his pocket.

Danny returned.

"One last question," he looked at her and smiled. "Do you know why she sent you these pictures?"

Susan looked at the old man. "I don't know."

But she did. It was a chain of evidence. It was a trail of breadcrumbs leading into the dark woods.

The silence breathed in cigarette smoke.

Coffin folded up his notepad. "Would you do us a favor and file a missing person report? It will help us look for her."

"The Chief said she couldn't be missing for 24 days."

"Well, that's true," he said. "But If I can get the D.A. to sign off on a search warrant, I could trace her phone."

"It's out of power. I called her."

"We can use the phone company to trace it. I would love to find her in Florida."

"I would be pissed."

"Would you fill out the form, anyway?"

"Sure."

CHAPTER FIFTEEN

After Susan left, the two officers filed into the Chief's office.

As he watched, Danny Abraham could appreciate the predicament that the Chief was in. Coffin folded his hands over his stomach and leaned back, Danny sat at attention, and the Chief had his hands tented on his desk, leaning forward.

He had no options, other than an appeal to good sense and prudence. Or he could threaten Coffin's long suffering partner. His partner, a handsome, dark-skinned, and considerable sergeant from Boston, had a wife, a daughter who needed cleats, a college fund, and a mortgage. If the Chief wanted Danny's attention, he could do it with a gesture. Just hold a certain paycheck on his desk and Danny would sit, stay, beg, or shake hands. But the Chief was too much of a gentleman to threaten Danny directly, or he knew what the Inspector could let loose.

But the Inspector did not need the money for a wife, a child, or a mortgage. His wife had left, his child had died, and he lived in a house that was on calendars. There wasn't a room on island that he wouldn't be recognized in, wasn't a person who didn't owe him for something, and there wasn't anything he wanted. If the Chief fired him, Coffin would just get worse.

So the two old men played out their cribbage game. If you listened, you could hear how they pegged out and the Inspector won again. He walked away, with some promises and some understanding, but no change.

When Sgt. Danny Abraham picked up the Inspector that evening, the old man was in the same clothes, perhaps a bit more rumpled, a little bit drunk, and tired.

Pip was not. Pip was ready for more adventure. He waited at the door to the cruiser. When Henry opened it, the dog leapt in, then sat in the center of the seat.

Two more post-it's were stuck to the Henry's door. One was yellow, the other green.

Coffin closed the car door, locked it, and put on his seatbelt.

"Where to?'

"61 Baxter."

Danny sighed.

"I want to see the house."

"No, you don't."

"Of course, I do."

"No, you want to go, knock on their door, show them the nasty pictures, and make sure that I lose my job."

"You won't lose your job."

"Why do you think I was in the office with you?" he said. "If they wanted to yell at you, they would just sit you down. They made sure my big black ass was in there as well. I'm the hostage. You're the mutineer."

"Kidnapper."

"Mutineer." He said. "They always have shiny ideals."

Coffin sighed, "Let's go. I just want to see the house."

"Not tonight."

"Why not?"

"It's Thursday, I have had no sleep today, I missed a soccer game, and Cam Christmas is back in New York. Tomorrow, we can go out there and you can threaten my job."

"Your job is fine."

"Are you going to help me move out?"

"Don't be dramatic."

"Henry, it's Thursday night. They aren't here."

Henry crossed his arms. "We can check."

"First, tell me something." Danny barked.

"What?"

"Are you selling your house?" He put the two post-its on his fingers.

Coffin pinched the bridge of his nose. "I don't think so."

"Henry, what does that mean?"

The old man sighed.

"I should."

"Why?"

"What do I need five bedrooms for? I wanted to divide it up into apartments or condos."

"Why?"

"Housing."

Sergeant Danny Abraham knew it. "Henry, you saw the boat and you thought you could give them your house."

"Well, not quite like that…". He said.

"How is it, old man?"

"We have to do something," he said. "I need to do something."

"This is why you bought everyone drinks."

"No."

"Yes." Danny crowed. "You felt guilty."

"Of course I feel guilty. I have money. I have a house. I have five bedrooms." .

He was a man. You had to always give him that. He was a man in full. He was full of contradictions and cowardice and bad habits and good thoughts. He drank too much and he expected too much and he was sorry for himself. But he didn't lie to himself. He knew his privilege, he knew what it had cost and he knew that he owed.

"Henry, do you think you are more than what your parents gave you?"

He paused and looked out the window.

"Old man, answer me."

"Of course."

"Five people asked me, today, why you were selling your house. Because there are no secrets on this fucking island."

"Sorry."

"They are afraid you are going to leave."

"I am not going to leave."

"Good," Danny said. "Because I am the only black man in the department and, without you I would be sent on my way before you could say 'Zippity-Doo-dah.'"

Coffin sighed.

"I am going to give you some advice. If you want to fill your house, rent the bedrooms to some people. Fill that old mansion with young people who drink, who laugh, and who fuck. Talk to your lawyer and make the leases fucking bullet proof, then bring in a carpenter to make sure you can handle eight or so guests. It's an old house."

Coffin looked out the window and nodded.

Danny felt his sermon coming to an end.

"There have always been and will always be poor people living in tents and in boats. It's a shitty world. Every day, you help without writing a check."

At three in the morning, Main Street was empty. No cars were parked, no movies were letting out, no bars were open. Where there had once been apartments above the stores, now was only dark windows. The gaslights remained bright and the cobblestones glistened.

The big car rocked over them. Danny turned up Orange Street into the light of the town clock tower. The times was neither wrong nor right; they have been acquainted with the night. For an impish reason, Coffin asked his partner to turn right, and then headed up Fair Street.

"Stop."

"I'd have to park in front of a hydrant."

"Okay. Do that." Coffin nodded. "Look around."

Danny was aware of the tongue-lashing he has given the old man and relented. Blocking a fire hydrant with a police car might be the easiest gift to the old man's vanity.

All of the houses were dark, but one. Coffin got out of the car. He opened the door and Pip stretched, then exited. He trotted to the fire hydrant and made use of it.

"What are we doing?" Danny asked.

"Wellness check."

"On who?"

"Helen Ingersoll."

"She should be well medicated and asleep."

"But it's three in the morning and her light is on."

And it was. Danny realized that a few more drunk drivers would either get home, or not, this evening; he was going to be babysitting two old people.

Coffin stepped up the worn and paint-less wooden steps. He knocked on the door while Danny called their location in to the dispatcher.

The door opened with a tired old woman in a cat sweatshirt and blue sweatpants standing in her slippers.

"Henry."

"Good evening, Helen. How are you doing?"

"Oh, you know."

"I do," he stepped inside. "Can Danny come in?"

"Of course."

"Can I introduce you to Pip?"

"Hello, Pip." She bent over and scratched his chest. Pip allowed her this. He even lifted a paw to make it easier.

Then they all came inside.

Her house was close to the center of town. It had been an oldish house when they bought it, in a place that few had really wanted to live in. And then the years turned, and the boats came, and now her neighbors were millionaires who wanted to put hot tubs in the back yards where people used to keep pigs more than a century ago.

Her sitting room was in the very front of the house. The windows looked out onto the street, the neighbors, and, a hundred to so feet above, the glowing clock tower.

Helen returned to her wing chair.

Coffin and his partner sat on an overstuffed and ancient sofa that hadn't not felt that weight in years.

Pip, of course, was overwhelmed with smells and began patrolling the room. He found some treats.

The room had newspaper on the floor, empty cardboard boxes, empty bottles of seltzer, and a T.V. that was silently watching Guy Fieri make marinade for a pork shoulder. On every flat surface, Helen had put a picture of her daughter, Meaghan.

"Have people been by, Helen?"

"Oh, of course. Nobody wants to leave an old woman alone. Even you."

"Do they get you out of the house?"

"Oh, of course. They take me to the Salt Marsh Center, or to get my hair done, or to get lunch."

"Well, that's nice."

"They want me to go to a home."

"I doubt that."

"My sisters want to sell this house."

Coffin nodded.

"They do. That pig of a husband, Butchie, wants a new boat."

Butchie was seventy and was a deacon in the church. Fish and chips on a paper plate wore him out, never mind bluefish on a line.

"Well, I'm glad they come by," Henry said.

"I wish they would leave me alone."

He stood up. "I'm gonna get something to drink. Do you want something?"

"No."

Coffin moved into the kitchen. The trash had been taken, the dishes were clean, and there were leftovers in the fridge.

"Danny, do you want a Pepsi?"

"Sure."

Henry began fussing with ice cubes. Helen turned to Danny and whispered.

"Is he selling his house??"

"No. He is just being dramatic."

She looked arch, but smiled. "He has always been a pain in the ass."

Coffin returned with two glasses of Bushmill's with ice and one can of warm Pepsi.

"Henry, you couldn't have poured my Pepsi, could you?" Danny asked.

"Oh, I didn't think of it."

Danny got up. Sure enough, there was a pint glass with ice cubes in it sitting on the counter.

Coffin grinned when his partner returned.

"You white people have a strange sense of humor."

Coffin handed the other whiskey to Helen.

"Henry, this whiskey hasn't been opened in ten years."

"So it has aged, has it?"

"It's gone bad."

"Helen, I have been drinking whiskey for more than fifty years. I have never found a bottle that has gone bad."

"I don't know what you think you are doing trying to get me drunk."

"Not that I can do much about it."

Helen laughed.

"Henry, don't do that," she said. "It hurts when I laugh."

"What else are we going to do?"

She paused. She sipped the whiskey. Henry followed along.

Helen sat back in her wing chair and sighed. Pip found a comfortable spot on the rug and lay down.

"She was lovely."

"Yes, she was."

She sipped her drink.

"I think I hear her all the time."

"Me, too."

"Petey?"

"Yup."

"Doesn't it kill you?"

"It makes me live. While I live, he lives."

She had nothing to say. Then she said.

"Father Nunes says it gets easier."

"It doesn't."

She sipped again. There wasn't much left in the glass.

"My sister thinks I should get rid of the pictures. She wants to do it one afternoon when I am away."

"Just makes it worse."

"Do you have his pictures up?"

"No."

She took another sip. Helen was starting to slip.

"I don't know why I am still here. I should have gone first," she said.

"I didn't," Coffin responded.

"No. But I wonder what to do."

Coffin nodded, "Help."

"Help who?"

"I don't know. Help."

"You're a weird man, Henry." Helen said, "Help me upstairs and don't take advantage of a drunken woman."

A half hour later, Detective Abraham was back at the Lifesaving Museum while his partner snored in Irish. The night remained dark, and very few drove past.

When Coffin woke up at five, Danny got him some water and some Tylenol. This wasn't his first morning with a hung over Quaker in the car.

Henry Coffin, Inspector and father of a boy who had drowned, looked to his partner and asked if he could help take Hadley to school today.

Danny Abraham, husband of a loving wife and father of a very much alive little girl, nodded.

CHAPTER SIXTEEN

Herman Lamb Esquire appeared two minutes early, which Henry had anticipated.

Pip had not been informed of a guest. When Herman rang the bell, Pip went into full alarm mode, with barking and running. When the lawyer entered the house, Pip barked at him, and then got a warm sniff of dachshund. The lawyer had had a dachshund in his life since he was ten years old. His current dog, Frederic, had lovingly decorated Herman's pants with hair and dander. Pip was curious. Herman stroked the side of the dog. Pip enjoyed this, lay down, and rolled over for a tummy rub. The old lawyer, with a briefcase and a hat, squatted down and helped a doggo out.

After a few years on island, you became a caricature of yourself; under the influence of money, clients, and isolation, the restraints of polite society came off, and the quirks and peculiarities of your character come out. Henry Coffin, the most public Quaker on island, knew this more than most. Eccentricity wasn't hidden on island, it was a brand. Herman Lamb was that brand.

Herman did not belong on a sunny Nantucket; he was pale enough to burn in the sun, heavy enough to dislike the beach or the boat, and sober enough to be in bed by nine . Instead, he worked. He had been the go to lawyer for an entire generation of men who were now retiring, selling the family house, divorcing, writing wills, or just needing some representation.

He drove a twenty year old Ford Explorer, complete with some rust and some spots. We keep cars that could be kept going for decades longer than the manufacturers intended. When the average commute is less than five miles, you worry more about your exhaust system rotting than the tires wearing out.

While Pip luxuriated in the afterglow of his belly rub, Herman took his hat off, and stepped onto the sailcloth flooring. The entering hallway to Coffin's house hadn't changed in a hundred years, The stairs wound up to the second floor, the mirrors on the walls glistened, and the mortgage button, (an ivory knob) sat up ostentatiously on the post at the end of the railing. It signified that the mortgage had been paid; even though the last dollar crossed the bank's counter a hundred and twenty five years ago. .

Coffin led the lawyer past Zenas Coffin and his stare. Henry had stacked all of the statements from Bank of America (formerly Pacific National), Rockland Savings (formerly Nantucket Bank) and Fidelity. He had made a rectangular space for the lawyer to put his case.

Herman was looking around at the kitchen, and he looked into the dining room. He also noted the dirty dishes and the kitchen trash.

Silence is the lawyer's best friend.

"Herman, I think I need your help."

The lawyer nodded, remembering something a little bird had told him.

"Yes."

"Herman, I would like to rent out some rooms."

The lawyer looked up.

"I had heard you wanted to sell?" He answered.

Coffin smiled.

"I thought about it. I don't know how much good it would do."

The lawyer nodded.

"So, do you want to make this an apartment building? Do you want to break it into condos?"

"What would happen?"

"Well, you couldn't."

"Why not?"

"Well, three reasons that come to mind, immediately. I am 99% sure that your grandfather, back in the fifties, got a historic restriction on the house. Saved him, and you, a bunch in taxes. But it means that you can't really change the house."

"We changed the kitchen."

"Yes, but it wasn't visible from the street. When we did that, we also had to bring it up to code. We had a loophole."

"I see."

"Second, you are on Main Street, in an area that is not only historic, but zoned single family. Your neighbors, and their representatives, certainly don't want to change the zoning and change their tax assessments. You would be paying me to fight in court for ten years. Third, we have very stringent rules about apartment buildings, condos, and the like. If you wanted to make this into apartments or condos, you would need separate doors, parking, sewerage, probably some sort of structural work. It would cost a fortune. I would be happy to help you get permits, but…"

Coffin sighed.

"Can I get you a glass of water, or something?" The Inspector asked.

"I'm fine, Henry."

Coffin nodded.

"Henry, you live in one of the most famous buildings on island. If we got it cleaned, and updated, it will certainly suit your purposes. And if you want to sell…"

"I don't really want to sell."

"Why not?"

Coffin had thought about this. He had reflected. He had labored. And he knew he was wrong. But he felt that, as a native and an islander, he should hold onto a piece of the island. The bankers could own everything else. He thought this one spot should still be Nantucket's. Or as he thought Nantucket should be.

But as soon as he put it into words, it sounded silly.

"I would rather keep it right now."

"Do you need the money?"

"No." He gestured at all of the envelopes.

"So…"

Coffin shrugged. "I need to do something. I need to help."

"Have you thought about an AirBnB? You would have to hire a housekeeper and a cook?"

"No."

"Henry, I don't understand the problem."

"I know" Coffin said. "What if I had guests here?"

"Guests? Like a guest house?"

"Not formal."

"You're zoning doesn't allow it."

"How long could guests stay?"

"Henry, let's talk hypothetically, because I wouldn't want to give you advice on running an illegal guest house."

"Of course not."

"If it was, say, a cousin, nobody would have trouble up to about three months. Hypothetically." Herman eased back in his chair and put his hands behind his head. "But you would have no protection. Your insurance would just see them as guests. No tax advantages."

Coffin nodded.

Lamb knew the Inspector. They had worked together years ago when there was a wife and a son. He had the will, the estate, and the trusts. Which still existed, while the boy didn't.

"Henry, I don't know what you want to do. I don't know who you want to help. Or how. The best thing, legally, for you to do might just be to sell it. I am sure it will fetch many millions. And then you can use that."

"I don't really want to sell."

"Well, I'm not sure how I can help," he said. "But, we do need to get together, you and I, and update your instructions."

"Instructions?"

"Your will and the estate."

"Sure," Coffin nodded. "Not today."

Then he led the lawyer out, past Zenas, past Pip, and into the warm afternoon.

Eleven o'clock came early that evening. Henry hadn't been able to sleep after the lawyer left. Instead he wandered around the house, picking up things and putting them down. Pip led him on a long walk out to the cemetery and back.

On the other hand, Danny had had a full day's sleep, picked up his daughter from school, went to the library, and then, for dinner, picked up a half mushroom, half sausage pizza. Hadley wanted a Caesar salad. Good luck with that.

When the sergeant pulled up to the house on Main Street, Pip was ready at the door. Henry put his collar on and led him to his seat.

"I got a text," Danny told his partner.

"From?"

"Jon-Jon. He said Tobias is at the bar."

"We are still going out to 61 Baxter."

"We can stop. When did you ever turn down a stop at the Chicken Box?"

Coffin crossed his arms.

Tobias wasn't at the bar. The undercover, in his sporty hat, was.

Jon-Jon shrugged.

"He was just here," he said. "There is his glass."

On the bar was a larger looking shot glass that smelled of Grand Marnier.

"Did Tobias see our friend over there?" Coffin asked, without turning around.

"Maybe," Jon-Jon replied

"Did he see you texting?"

"Not unless he can look through doors."

Coffin smiled. He wasn't surprised at all of this.

"Tobias saw her. At dinner?" He asked.

"That's what he said. She made a disturbance."

"My brother," Coffin said. "We will drop by the restaurant some time. We'll get him there. And send my undercover colleague another beer."

"He's been drinking ginger ale."

"Let's see what he does."

The beer sat in front of him.

Jon-Jon plucked at Coffin's sleeve. "Hey, you're not selling, are you?"

Henry rolled to him. "No. I don't think so."

"Danny says you feel bad about five bedrooms."

The old man looked at his partner. The sergeant flashed a wave.

"Well, people shouldn't have to live like dogs."

"Amen to that."

"Well, perhaps like your dog."

"Perhaps."

The Club of Nantucket draws up its velvet curtain in September. If the membership committee had any say over it, the overture would start in mid-August, or perhaps even in the last weeks of July. The house lights would flash, the members would take their seats, and everyone else would be shoved out on the sidewalk.

By September, the water around the island is still warm enough for jellyfish, sharks, and bankers. The air remains warm, although not hot enough for air conditioning. The staff at the Club open the windows, set the tables outside, and put the Mojitos on the front page of the menu.

For the Members, the pleasure of September isn't who is on island, but who isn't. The families have gone home, along with the weekenders, the partiers, and the ice cream scoopers. The General Managers, the Junior Partners, and the C-Suite professionals have gone back to work, but the Members have the golf courses to themselves, the club, the restaurants, and the beaches. The Board of Directors has settled their feet in the sand. Perhaps, if they are up to it, the kids can bring the grandchildren out for a week at the beginning of school. The island grows quiet, interrupted by the well-tutored swing of a golf club and the thump of a tennis ball.

While the entire island returns to the Members, they prefer to live in Sconset; the town was built at the end of a train line, with hotels and guest houses. But as is the way with guest houses, they got bought by rich men with large families and larger parties. Now, the entire village is in the hands of trust fund lawyers and accountants, with keys handed out to the new generation of Club Members.

As the two policeman rolled into their midnight shift on Friday, most of Sconset had dropped to sleep. Dinner service had finished at the Sankaty Club, the bar was getting wiped down at the Chanticleer, and the piano was silent at the Summer House.

Baxter Road had been one of the addresses on an island that was itself an address. But time, tide, and Exxon had worked their considerable magic and several addresses had slid down the bank and into the Atlantic. Owning a house on Baxter Road no longer counted as an investment in generational wealth. Instead, it was the scent of a burning cigar; rich, decadent, and temporary. Owning one of these houses was the equivalent of burning money or sponsoring fireworks. For a few summers, it would be spectacular, then it would be gone. So the Members, and their lawyers, sold the houses off to Hedgefunders during Christmas bonus season and everyone was happy with the arrangement.

61 Baxter was perhaps a third of the way down the road, on the ocean side. At midnight, the house was well-lit but silent. The two policemen watched shadows move back and forth across the windows. Beyond the well cared house and the trimmed and approved lawn, the Atlantic rolled and a rising moon lit a path across the waters to the seething shore.

Coffin unrolled his window so that he could hear the waves better. They came and left in slow tidal breaths. Danny had parked two houses up, slightly behind a Japanese Maple. While they weren't obvious to the people inside the house, they weren't hiding. And no other house nearby was lit or had cars in the driveway.

"Well, this is fun," Danny said. "We should come out here more often."

"It's one in the morning on a Friday." Coffin said.

"People have parties on Fridays."

"Not on this street."

Danny sighed.

Coffin unlocked his door.

"If you get out of the car, I will drive away and leave you here."

"I am going to take Pip for a walk, on a public way, and I may take pictures of the license plates."

"Because…"

"You never know who may have a warrant."

"Don't YOU need a warrant?"

"Nope," He said. "F.B.I. used to run the tags outside the Malcolm X rallies."

"Then what?"

"Then we go back to looking for drunks and speeders, my brother."

Danny sighed. Henry left the car. Pip surveyed the hedges and cars. The dog smells were unfamiliar, but he needed to leave a signature.

Henry walked down the center of the moon illuminated street. Then, as he approached 61, he started snapping pictures of the cars on the street. He paused outside of the driveway and got the cars that were parked close to the house. For his part, he wasn't bringing the phone up to his face.

Pip sat on the yellow line and scratched.

One figure inside stopped in the window and pulled the curtain aside. Henry took a picture of him as well. Then he walked back to the car.

Inside the squad car, he started transferring the plate numbers to his legal pad.

"We can go now," Coffin said without looking up.

"No, we can't."

Pink's cab pulled up. Three women, in evening wear and high heels, walked the path and opened the door. Apparently, they were welcomed.

As far as Coffin could tell, they had not paid Pink.

"We're not going to pull him over." Danny warned.

"I know."

CHAPTER SIXTEEN

Herman Lamb Esquire appeared two minutes early, which Henry had anticipated.

Pip had not been informed of a guest. When Herman rang the bell, Pip went into full alarm mode, with barking and running. When the lawyer entered the house, Pip barked at him, and then got a warm sniff of dachshund. The lawyer had had a dachshund in his life since he was ten years old. His current dog, Frederic, had lovingly decorated Herman's pants with hair and dander. Pip was curious. Herman stroked the side of the dog. Pip enjoyed this, lay down, and rolled over for a tummy rub. The old lawyer, with a briefcase and a hat, squatted down and helped a doggo out.

After a few years on island, you became a caricature of yourself; under the influence of money, clients, and isolation, the restraints of polite society came off, and the quirks and peculiarities of your character come out. Henry Coffin, the most public Quaker on island, knew this more than most. Eccentricity wasn't hidden on island, it was a brand. Herman Lamb was that brand.

Herman did not belong on a sunny Nantucket; he was pale enough to burn in the sun, heavy enough to dislike the beach or the boat, and sober enough to be in bed by nine . Instead, he worked. He had been the go to lawyer for an entire generation of men who were now retiring, selling the family house, divorcing, writing wills, or just needing some representation.

He drove a twenty year old Ford Explorer, complete with some rust and some spots. We keep cars that could be kept going for decades longer than the manufacturers intended. When the average commute is less than five miles, you worry more about your exhaust system rotting than the tires wearing out.

While Pip luxuriated in the afterglow of his belly rub, Herman took his hat off, and stepped onto the sailcloth flooring. The entering hallway to Coffin's house hadn't changed in a hundred years, The stairs wound up to the second floor, the mirrors on the walls glistened, and the mortgage button, (an ivory knob) sat up ostentatiously on the post at the end of the railing. It signified that the mortgage had been paid; even though the last dollar crossed the bank's counter a hundred and twenty five years ago. .

Coffin led the lawyer past Zenas Coffin and his stare. Henry had stacked all of the statements from Bank of America (formerly Pacific National), Rockland Savings (formerly Nantucket Bank) and Fidelity. He had made a rectangular space for the lawyer to put his case.

Herman was looking around at the kitchen, and he looked into the dining room. He also noted the dirty dishes and the kitchen trash.

Silence is the lawyer's best friend.

"Herman, I think I need your help."

The lawyer nodded, remembering something a little bird had told him.

"Yes."

"Herman, I would like to rent out some rooms."

The lawyer looked up.

"I had heard you wanted to sell?" He answered.

Coffin smiled.

"I thought about it. I don't know how much good it would do."

The lawyer nodded.

"So, do you want to make this an apartment building? Do you want to break it into condos?"

"What would happen?"

"Well, you couldn't."

"Why not?"

"Well, three reasons that come to mind, immediately. I am 99% sure that your grandfather, back in the fifties, got a historic restriction on the house. Saved him, and you, a bunch in taxes. But it means that you can't really change the house."

"We changed the kitchen."

"Yes, but it wasn't visible from the street. When we did that, we also had to bring it up to code. We had a loophole."

"I see."

"Second, you are on Main Street, in an area that is not only historic, but zoned single family. Your neighbors, and their representatives, certainly don't want to change the zoning and change their tax assessments. You would be paying me to fight in court for ten years. Third, we have very stringent rules about apartment buildings, condos, and the like. If you wanted to make this into apartments or condos, you would need separate doors, parking, sewerage, probably some sort of structural work. It would cost a fortune. I would be happy to help you get permits, but…"

Coffin sighed.

"Can I get you a glass of water, or something?" The Inspector asked.

"I'm fine, Henry."

Coffin nodded.

"Henry, you live in one of the most famous buildings on island. If we got it cleaned, and updated, it will certainly suit your purposes. And if you want to sell…"

"I don't really want to sell."

"Why not?"

Coffin had thought about this. He had reflected. He had labored. And he knew he was wrong. But he felt that, as a native and an islander, he should hold onto a piece of the island. The bankers could own everything else. He thought this one spot should still be Nantucket's. Or as he thought Nantucket should be.

But as soon as he put it into words, it sounded silly.

"I would rather keep it right now."

"Do you need the money?"

"No." He gestured at all of the envelopes.

"So…"

Coffin shrugged. "I need to do something. I need to help."

"Have you thought about an AirBnB? You would have to hire a housekeeper and a cook?"

"No."

"Henry, I don't understand the problem."

"I know" Coffin said. "What if I had guests here?"

"Guests? Like a guest house?"

"Not formal."

"You're zoning doesn't allow it."

"How long could guests stay?"

"Henry, let's talk hypothetically, because I wouldn't want to give you advice on running an illegal guest house."

"Of course not."

"If it was, say, a cousin, nobody would have trouble up to about three months. Hypothetically." Herman eased back in his chair and put his hands behind his head. "But you would have no protection. Your insurance would just see them as guests. No tax advantages."

Coffin nodded.

Lamb knew the Inspector. They had worked together years ago when there was a wife and a son. He had the will, the estate, and the trusts. Which still existed, while the boy didn't.

"Henry, I don't know what you want to do. I don't know who you want to help. Or how. The best thing, legally, for you to do might just be to sell it. I am sure it will fetch many millions. And then you can use that."

"I don't really want to sell."

"Well, I'm not sure how I can help," he said. "But, we do need to get together, you and I, and update your instructions."

"Instructions?"

"Your will and the estate."

"Sure," Coffin nodded. "Not today."

Then he led the lawyer out, past Zenas, past Pip, and into the warm afternoon.

Eleven o'clock came early that evening. Henry hadn't been able to sleep after the lawyer left. Instead he wandered around the house, picking up things and putting them down. Pip led him on a long walk out to the cemetery and back.

On the other hand, Danny had had a full day's sleep, picked up his daughter from school, went to the library, and then, for dinner, picked up a half mushroom, half sausage pizza. Hadley wanted a Caesar salad. Good luck with that.

When the sergeant pulled up to the house on Main Street, Pip was ready at the door. Henry put his collar on and led him to his seat.

"I got a text," Danny told his partner.

"From?"

"Jon-Jon. He said Tobias is at the bar."

"We are still going out to 61 Baxter."

"We can stop. When did you ever turn down a stop at the Chicken Box?"

Coffin crossed his arms.

Tobias wasn't at the bar. The undercover, in his sporty hat, was.

Jon-Jon shrugged.

"He was just here," he said. "There is his glass."

On the bar was a larger looking shot glass that smelled of Grand Marnier.

"Did Tobias see our friend over there?" Coffin asked, without turning around.

"Maybe," Jon-Jon replied

"Did he see you texting?"

"Not unless he can look through doors."

Coffin smiled. He wasn't surprised at all of this.

"Tobias saw her. At dinner?" He asked.

"That's what he said. She made a disturbance."

"My brother," Coffin said. "We will drop by the restaurant some time. We'll get him there. And send my undercover colleague another beer."

"He's been drinking ginger ale."

"Let's see what he does."

The beer sat in front of him.

Jon-Jon plucked at Coffin's sleeve. "Hey, you're not selling, are you?"

Henry rolled to him. "No. I don't think so."

"Danny says you feel bad about five bedrooms."

The old man looked at his partner. The sergeant flashed a wave.

"Well, people shouldn't have to live like dogs."

"Amen to that."

"Well, perhaps like your dog."

"Perhaps."

The Club of Nantucket draws up its velvet curtain in September. If the membership committee had any say over it, the overture would start in mid-August, or perhaps even in the last weeks of July. The house lights would flash, the members would take their seats, and everyone else would be shoved out on the sidewalk.

By September, the water around the island is still warm enough for jellyfish, sharks, and bankers. The air remains warm, although not hot enough for air conditioning. The staff at the Club open the windows, set the tables outside, and put the Mojitos on the front page of the menu.

For the Members, the pleasure of September isn't who is on island, but who isn't. The families have gone home, along with the weekenders, the partiers, and the ice cream scoopers. The General Managers, the Junior Partners, and the C-Suite professionals have gone back to work, but the Members have the golf courses to themselves, the club, the restaurants, and the beaches. The Board of Directors has settled their feet in the sand. Perhaps, if they are up to it, the kids can bring the grandchildren out for a week at the beginning of school. The island grows quiet, interrupted by the well-tutored swing of a golf club and the thump of a tennis ball.

While the entire island returns to the Members, they prefer to live in Sconset; the town was built at the end of a train line, with hotels and guest houses. But as is the way with guest houses, they got bought by rich men with large families and larger parties. Now, the entire village is in the hands of trust fund lawyers and accountants, with keys handed out to the new generation of Club Members.

As the two policeman rolled into their midnight shift on Friday, most of Sconset had dropped to sleep. Dinner service had finished at the Sankaty Club, the bar was getting wiped down at the Chanticleer, and the piano was silent at the Summer House.

Baxter Road had been one of the addresses on an island that was itself an address. But time, tide, and Exxon had worked their considerable magic and several addresses had slid down the bank and into the Atlantic. Owning a house on Baxter Road no longer counted as an investment in generational wealth. Instead, it was the scent of a burning cigar; rich, decadent, and temporary. Owning one of these houses was the equivalent of burning money or sponsoring fireworks. For a few summers, it would be spectacular, then it would be gone. So the Members, and their lawyers, sold the houses off to Hedgefunders during Christmas bonus season and everyone was happy with the arrangement.

61 Baxter was perhaps a third of the way down the road, on the ocean side. At midnight, the house was well-lit but silent. The two policemen watched shadows move back and forth across the windows. Beyond the well cared house and the trimmed and approved lawn, the Atlantic rolled and a rising moon lit a path across the waters to the seething shore.

Coffin unrolled his window so that he could hear the waves better. They came and left in slow tidal breaths. Danny had parked two houses up, slightly behind a Japanese Maple. While they weren't obvious to the people inside the house, they weren't hiding. And no other house nearby was lit or had cars in the driveway.

"Well, this is fun," Danny said. "We should come out here more often."

"It's one in the morning on a Friday." Coffin said.

"People have parties on Fridays."

"Not on this street."

Danny sighed.

Coffin unlocked his door.

"If you get out of the car, I will drive away and leave you here."

"I am going to take Pip for a walk, on a public way, and I may take pictures of the license plates."

"Because…"

"You never know who may have a warrant."

"Don't YOU need a warrant?"

"Nope," He said. "F.B.I. used to run the tags outside the Malcolm X rallies."

"Then what?"

"Then we go back to looking for drunks and speeders, my brother."

Danny sighed. Henry left the car. Pip surveyed the hedges and cars. The dog smells were unfamiliar, but he needed to leave a signature.

Henry walked down the center of the moon illuminated street. Then, as he approached 61, he started snapping pictures of the cars on the street. He paused outside of the driveway and got the cars that were parked close to the house. For his part, he wasn't bringing the phone up to his face.

Pip sat on the yellow line and scratched.

One figure inside stopped in the window and pulled the curtain aside. Henry took a picture of him as well. Then he walked back to the car.

Inside the squad car, he started transferring the plate numbers to his legal pad.

"We can go now," Coffin said without looking up.

"No, we can't."

Pink's cab pulled up. Three women, in evening wear and high heels, walked the path and opened the door. Apparently, they were welcomed.

As far as Coffin could tell, they had not paid Pink.

"We're not going to pull him over." Danny warned.

"I know."

CHAPTER SEVENTEEN

For a change, the two policeman waited by the side of Milestone Road, instead of the Polpis Road. Sconset was attached to the rest of Nantucket by one long loop. You drove out on the straight and flat Milestone Road, between the moors on either side, slowed to an old mans sedate walk in Sconset, made the turn, and then came back the twisty and curvy Polpis Road. Most over-served visitors to the clubs and restaurants of Sconset chose the Polpis Road to return to town. It's turns and curves suggest a back way to the drunken safety of bed. Islanders knew, of course, that on most nights Henry waited at the LifeSaving Museum. So, the local drunks took their chances on the straight road.

Inspector Coffin had searched all of the license plates he had photographed and found warrants outstanding on two of the owners. One man had walked out on child support, court ordered anger management, and damages from breaking the windows on his ex-wife's Land Rover Discovery. The other had let his E-Z Pass go out of date. He owed thirteen dollars.

So they waited.

At twelve minutes past four, a bright red BMW X3 passed them doing sixty in a forty five.

"Tally Ho," Coffin said.

Danny looked at him, "Really?"

"Absolutely, lights and siren."

Danny put the big car in gear and began accelerating. He flipped on the lights and the siren, screaming through the night.

Pip barked. Things had gotten confusing in a hurry.

Two hundred yards ahead of them, the car accelerated, and then, twenty seconds later, flashed its hazards and pulled over.

Danny parked twenty yards behind him.

"This one has an anger management issue. I would be careful," Coffin noted.

"Why don't you take care of it?"

"You're so much better at this, my brother."

Danny opened his door.

"Always send out the black man first."

"You make everything about race."

Danny grunted and got out of the squad car. He strolled slowly up to the red BMW. In the dark and quiet of the island, the strobe lights on top of the squad car were visible for miles.

He tapped the window.

"License and registration."

The driver had turned on the inside lights, had both of his hands on the steering wheel, and had unrolled the window an inch. With exaggerated slowness, he picked up the papers and slid them through the window. When he saw Danny's complexion, he grunted and smiled.

"Where you coming from tonight?" Danny asked.

"I don't need to answer any questions without representation."

Danny nodded.

"It's late at night."

The driver remained silent.

The driver had seen forty years, and raised it a few chips. He was well tanned, athletic, tall, and trying desperately to hang onto his hair. His left hand had a shimmery watch that, had Danny known more about watches, he would have recognized.

The driver knew that this one couldn't recognize that, nor could he recognize his bespoke Indian cotton shirt.

Inspector Coffin ran the numbers and found, again, what he had been looking for.

He opened his door.

"Be ready for this guy to shoot me," Coffin warned.

"He's rich. He just called his lawyer. Rich guys don't shoot cops."

"Sure they do. They have lawyers."

"Then he would have shot the black guy."

Coffin nodded, "Good point."

He patted the door and walked out with his iPad, his legal pad, and the driver, Bruno St. Vincent's, paperwork.

Coffin walked up the side of the car. Not real police.

"My brother," he said.

Bruno turned to see. The Inspector stood by the door. Unlike his well trained and professional partner, Coffin stood by the rear view mirror. If Bruno wanted to shoot him, the Inspector was obliging.

"Who are you?"

"Henry Coffin. I work with my partner, Danny."

"Are you a cop?"

"I work for the police."

"Where's you badge?"

"Left it at home."

"Give me my papers."

"In a moment."

"I am going to bring my lawyer in."

"Go ahead."

Bruno jabbed a finger onto his glowing console. The name 'Herman Lamb, esq.' popped up. Coffin smiled. He hadn't spoken to Herman so much in years.

"Good morning, Bruno." Lamb was groggy, but professional. To him, the use of a first name had a critical edge. The driver may have missed that.

"Attorney Lamb, I have been pulled over on a bullshit speeding ticket on Milestone Road."

"Okay. On Milestone Road?"

"Yes." Bruno stared at the console for a moment.

"Okay."

"There's a guy who doesn't have a badge with my papers. He says his name is Coffin."

Herman Lamb sighed. "Yes."

"What should I do?"

"Henry, are you there?"

"Sure."

"What law did my client break?"

"Well, we pulled him over for speeding."

"Henry, I know you well enough to know that there is more to that sentence."

Coffin smiled.

Bruno looked at his console and at the Inspector.

"My brother, your client has several outstanding warrants, including avoiding child support and breaking his ex-wive's windows. I am considering arresting him and putting him in the station."

Herman was silent for a moment.

"Henry, would you walk away for a moment so that I may consult with my client?"

"Of course."

The headlights, the spotlights, and the rotating lights were still going. Coffin walked five steps to the rear of the car. Three cars passed at thirty five miles an hour. Coffin flashed a thumb's up to his partner.

After another car passed, Bruno rolled his window down.

"My lawyer wants to talk to you."

"Sure," Coffin stepped back to the car. "Herman?"

"My client acknowledges that he has made some organizational and calendar mistakes that I will rectify as soon as the courts open on Monday. I would hope that my assurance to you would obviate the need to impound my client's car and arrest him."

"Well, that's great, my brother. I actually want to ask him about something else."

"Are you charging him with another crime?"

"No."

"Is he a target in another investigation?"

"Not to my knowledge."

"Is that a no?"

"Other investigators don't like to include me, my brother. I don't know what else Bruno might have done, but I want some information for another case."

"Are you looking for an understanding, Henry?"

"Cooperation."

"Nothing that requires a statement?"

"I doubt it."

"Can you promise that?"

"Herman…I can't make promises. I am looking for some help understanding something."

Bruno blazed red at his console.

Herman Lamb cleared his throat.

"Mr. St. Vincent, you are in the presence of Inspector Henry Coffin, the only Inspector in the state of Massachusetts. He is a Quaker, which makes him both a pacifist and a bad liar. I would counsel you to answer his questions so that the three of us can come to an understanding that will let you drive home."

"Or?"

"Or," Coffin spoke. "I take you to jail, lock you up for having outstanding warrants and you go before a Magistrate in two days." Coffin intoned.

"That is precisely correct." Herman said.

"What do you want to know?" Bruno sighed at Coffin.

Coffin signaled to his partner and the lights on the squad car went out.

"Do you know Cam Christmas?"

"I have met him."

"Weren't you just at his house this evening?"

"Yes, but I was playing poker. Not with him."

"You've met him, though?"

"Yes."

"Okay," Coffin said. "I need your help identifying a woman in the picture."

"Do I know this person?"

"I don't know. That is why I am asking you."

Coffin opened his iPad and presented a picture of Caroline Bird with a minor bruise.

"Do you know her?"

Bruno shook his head. "No."

Henry showed him a picture with purple and green bruises.

"How about her?" He said. "Have you ever seen her?"

"It's the same woman."

"Is it?" Coffin said. "Ever seen her?"

"No."

"No?" Henry questioned.

"Did she say she knew me?"

"I couldn't say that." Coffin said. "One more."

The last picture was of her back, laced with thin red welts and drips of blood.

"No."

Coffin closed his iPad.

"Is that it?" Bruno asked.

"For now."

"Henry?" Herman spoke from the car.

"That will do it. Mr. St. Vincent, you are free to go. If I have any more questions, I will address Herman."

"Thank you, Henry." The lawyer spoke through the car.

Coffin slid the paper work to Bruno. Mr. St. Vincent waved them off, started his car, and drove away.

Coffin stood on the grass beside the road and watched them go. The sky was lightening to the east. Danny drove the squad car up next to the old man.

"So?"

"So, now we see."

"Bruno didn't beat her?"

"I don't know about that. I don't think he killed her."

"So what were you doing?"

"Just tugging on a string."

CHAPTER EIGHTEEN

On Saturday afternoon, Attorney Charles Hampden, of the firm Fitzgerald, Cromwell, and Hampden, visited the island and the police station. Charles was the same height of an NBA point guard, but he had chosen squash instead. The veins bulged in his hand, roped up his neck, and even, in the hour that he waited, on his temple. Attorney Hampden came fully armed, with a bespoke gray Italian suit from Milan, wingtips, a watch that cost more than his Mercedes, a diamond stud earring, and a briefcase that was constructed with either buttery Italian leather or fresh Florida manatee. Were he in New York, attention would be paid. Unfortunately, he was sitting amid the dust, chewing gum, and Marlboro Lights of the Nantucket Police Station.

His hours generally stopped on Friday afternoon, often just at noon. However, Cam was a special client and his guest room was available.

At four o'clock, Sergeant Danny Abraham and Inspector Coffin followed this legal vision into a conference room.

Danny, of course, was in uniform. Coffin wore a flannel shirt he found at Hospital Thrift Shop ten years ago.

"My brother," the Inspector said. "How can we help?"

Charles took a moment to consider Coffin. He had been informed. One doesn't become a partner young enough to keep a full head of hair without doing your own due diligence. They had said that he was sharp. They had said he made you underestimate him. They had not mentioned that he looked like Grampa on his second Seven and Seven right after Candlepins for Cash finished for the afternoon.

"I represent a Mr. Cam Christmas." Charles said.

"I see."

"I understand that you have been asking questions about my client. I thought I could make my self available to answer questions as to Mr. Christmas and his businesses."

"Is Mr. Christmas on island?" Danny asked.

"He is, but we both felt that I could answer any questions you might have."

Danny looked at Henry. The old man had an indeterminate look on his face.

Coffin spoke. "We are looking for a women named Caroline Bird. Her sister told us that she … had been seeing Mr. Christmas."

"Indeed." The lawyer looked unsurprised. He waited for the Inspector to continue.

"Her sister shared with us some disturbing pictures. I wonder if you give us some help understanding these pictures."

The lawyer made a gesture that both encouraged the Inspector to show him the pictures and that suggested that all of this bored him. Danny was impressed with the performance. He hoped he could vote for him on Yelp.

Coffin opened his iPad, selected a picture, and showed it to the lawyer.

Charles nodded.

Coffin proceeded to show him all nine of the pictures.

Charles nodded at each one.

At the end of the show, Coffin shut the book.

"Permit me to ask you some questions, Inspector."

"Go ahead, my brother." The lawyer considered whether the old man was pulling his leg.

"How do you have these pictures? They are Mr. Christmas' property."

"Caroline Bird's sister had them. She sent them to us. She told us that her sister sent them to her."

"I presume that you have a statement to that effect."

"Not right now."

"Have you, or anyone in the department, tampered with the metadata?"

"No."

"Have you or anyone in the department, made other copies? Have you circulated this data to other people? Other than Mr. St. Vincent. "

"No. I have made a back-up."

"Is that here at the station?"

"It is in the cloud."

"But within your control?"

"Yes."

"I'm going to ask you to destroy all copies of this, then to have an affidavit from you, your partner, the Chief, and the IT specialist that you have destroyed these pictures and possess no copies."

Charles smiled.

Henry also smiled.

"Right now, Caroline Bird may be the subject of a criminal case. We may be investigating her murder. These pictures may be evidence of a crime."

"I can assure you they aren't."

Danny let his hand fall to the table.

"Nevertheless, my brother, we will be keeping these pictures until the case is resolved," Coffin continued.

"Again, I can assure you that Mr. Christmas has committed no crime and these pictures are his exclusive property. Miss Bird has committed theft from my client and I will be looking for redress."

Danny raised his hand. "So, what you are saying is that these pictures with all the bruises, the blood, and the lashings, aren't evidence of a crime?"

"Surely not."

"You are saying you are going to sue Caroline, should we find her?"

"I am."

"And that your client is not a deviant who likes to hurt women."

Charles considered the Sergeant. "I would hope that this is the last time that you refer to my client as a deviant. I will be sending a "Cease and Desist' order tomorrow morning, along with a remand for the pictures and the affidavits."

Danny rolled his eyes.

Coffin remained intrigued.

"So, my brother, can you prove that these pictures are not evidence of battery?"

"Of course."

He put his briefcase on the table and opened it, and produced a thin manilla folder. It was labeled "Nantucket Police Department."

"I have ten contracts in this folder, dated, signed, and witnessed between Caroline Bird and my client. Each contract details what will happen to Miss Bird as a part of a performance, and what her consideration was to be. At no point was she in mortal danger and, as you will see, the contracts specified that a nurse with appropriate equipment and training would be on site."

The lawyer slid the folder to Coffin.

"Now, I do not have these photos, but I believe each one of the photos was taken a short period of time after the contracts were signed. I am sure that, if necessary in your investigation you may need to match up all of the contracts, we can do that."

"So, Counselor," Danny drew the words out and let his Dorchester background squash the vowels. "You are telling us that each of these beatings was a performance that these contracts excuse?"

"Officer, they don't excuse, they detail. Everything is expressly laid out in paper."

"They detail…"

"Mr. Christmas is an artist, like a movie director or a painter. He helped to create these images."

"By choking, whipping, and beating Caroline Bird."

"If that is what the contract required, yes."

"For fuck sake…". Danny looked at the Quaker, but Henry wasn't alarmed.

"She signed the contracts freely, received appropriate medical attention, and received due consideration."

Danny got up and walked out of the interview room.

Charles Hampden, Esquire turned his expensive and considered attention to the old man in a dirty flannel shirt.

Coffin looked at the contracts with a maddening slowness. Charles was familiar with such performances.

"My brother," Coffin intoned. "The contract for August 24 is for twice as much money as the previous nine." Coffin pushed the document across the table. Charles did not look down.

"Yes."

"What was the additional money for?"

"I do not know."

"We have nine pictures, but ten contracts. August 24 is near her disappearance."

"It details a performance on a Catherine Wheel."

"I haven't used a Catherine wheel, but I am not an artist. Could you find out for us, or would you bring him in for some explanation?"

"I will ask."

Coffin continued to mess with the documents. "All of these…contracts…are for Sundays."

"Yes."

"My brother, where was your client on September first, the Sunday of Labor Day weekend."

The attorney cocked his head. "I am not sure. But he generally takes his family and friends for a three day sail."

"You did not accompany him on this trip."

"No."

"Is there a contract with Caroline Bird for services on that date?"

"I don't believe so."

Coffin nodded. "Would you ask your client for a schedule of his activities on Labor Day weekend and if there is a contract for that weekend? I would like to know what his boat is, where it is berthed, and if there were any security cameras on it. I would ask you to preserve any recordings. And I would like that tenth picture."

"Is Cam a suspect in this case?"

"We'll see, my brother. We'll see."

CHAPTER NINETEEN

The old police car was parked behind the Club Car in a slot often hidden, and almost always used by the head chef. The head chef, of course, had gone home by nine.

Tobias loomed over the hosting station. He wore a white dinner jacket, a red bow tie, and a smile for service. His hair was immaculate, his fingers were golden, and his skin glowed with a deeper tan.

Danny knew immediately why he ran from the cop at the Chicken Box.

Both officers stood around the corner from the door, out of his eyesight.

"Henry, let me approach him."

"He's working. Where is he going to go?"

"You're too white."

"You're in a uniform."

Danny had to concede the point.

"I'll just walk in. You can go stand by the back door. Make sure he doesn't run." Henry said.

"Send the black man to the servants' entrance?"

"What will these lovely customers do when you walk in in uniform with a gun?"

Danny also had to concede that point as well.

After he left, Coffin entered. The Club Car had two distinctive rooms. One was the old Club Car from the train line that had served the island. It had been a diner, but it now served French champagne, Negronis, and single malts from unpronounceable Scottish towns. The other room, connected to it, was a dining room that looked out on the passing tourists. Coffin stood in front of the dais at the opening to the dining room.

Tobias was confused for a moment. The Inspector wore his flannel shirt, while the Club Car remained jacket and tie. Further, he was a half hour after the kitchen closed. Tobias assumed his best refusal-of-service face.

Then he recognized that something was wrong.

"My brother," Coffin smiled.

"Um. Who are you?"

"I am Henry Coffin. Jon-Jon said you wanted to talk to me."

Tobias took a step back.

"My brother," the old man continued, "I assume Jon-Jon told you who I was?"

"You're the Inspector."

"Sure," Coffin said. "I have one question, then I will fade away."

"I don't know if I can answer it."

Unfortunately, many of the people in the dining room recognized the Inspector. He had stopped them, perhaps, or he had knocked on their door. To them, his presence, at this hour of night, was something to be noted. They looked at the exchange with the frank and rude curiosity that only the rich and untouchable can bring.

Tobias noted.

Coffin kept smiling "Tobias, can I ask you a question?"

He nodded.

"You recognized the picture of Caroline Bird that Jon-Jon had at the Chicken Box."

Tobias nodded.

"She came to dinner on Friday of Labor Day weekend?" The old man asked.

"Saturday."

"Good," Coffin nodded. "What was the reservation under?"

"I don't think…"

"You're not in trouble. And you won't be in trouble."

Tobias turned the pages of the red leather book in front of him. He drew his hand down the line of handwritten names.

"Brody."

"You're certain."

"Yes. Mr. Brody."

"Big guy?"

He nodded.

"He probably thought all of the commotion was funny?"

He nodded.

"Thank you, my brother."

Coffin smiled into the dining room and gave half remembered faces a half hearted wave, then he opened the door and stepped out.

Out back, Danny stood with Anthony Cabral, the current owner of the restaurant. He wore jeans and a sweatshirt.

Pip looked out the back window of the car. He wasn't sure why he wasn't invited to the party.

"Henry," Anthony said. "If you want to come by, I'll set you up with the best meal you ever had."

"I'm sure," Coffin nodded. "This was a business call."

"Is there trouble?"

"No. Not with Tobias."

"I don't like him. Ever since that incident with the actor…"

"He was fine. Be nice to him. He helped."

"He did?"

"We are looking for a missing girl. She came to dinner here two weeks ago Friday."

Cabral frowned.

"She …caused some excitement."

Coffin looked up.

"I heard. She was with a big guy."

"Yup. Former soldier. Ranger." Coffin explained. "Paul Brody."

"Ow," Danny said.

"He didn't do anything to her?" Cabral asked.

Coffin shook his head. "Probably not."

"Good."

At ten on a Sunday morning, Cam Christmas and his lawyer appeared at the station. Arrangements had been made for a conference room.

Lieutenant Macy let the two men in, got them coffee, and watched as a tired Sergeant Abraham and Inspector Coffin filed in. Macy had informed the Chief of the previous afternoon's shenanigans, so that he could witness this as well. And Danny resigned himself to another meeting this afternoon.

Coffin and Danny made their own cups of coffee, then filed into the conference room. The Chief and his lieutenant retreated to the office.

Cam Christmas was dressed as carefully, and as expensively, as his lawyer. He also wore a suit, a watch, and loafers. However, as a sign of who held the pen in their relationship, Cam did not wear a tie and his lawyer did.

"My brother, thank you for bringing in your client." Coffin smiled.

"Inspector? Sergeant?" The well rested lawyer looked at the two of them. "I have brought my client in so that he can answer some questions directly. Before he does, he has a statement he would like to make."

Danny looked at the beautiful man.

Cam held a piece of paper before him and read. "I am deeply saddened that Caroline Bird, my partner and my muse, is missing. Miss Bird and I collaborated on a series of tableaux over the course of the summer and we drew quite close. I am willing to offer any aid I can that will help her safe return."

Danny scoffed.

Both client and lawyer ignored him.

Coffin cleared his throat. "Thank you, Mr. Christmas. We will be happy to keep you informed of our investigations."

The man nodded.

"Mr. Christmas, can you tell us about the …piece you created on August 25. We have a contract, but no picture."

"We have that picture. Caroline did not want to share it with her sister, but we have a picture." The lawyer produced a silver iPad Pro and, after a swipe or two, produced a picture.

"Inspector, are you familiar with a Catherine wheel?"

"That's what that is?" he said. "It's medieval?"

"Yes. Well, not completely. No bones are broken. But the model is placed in the…"

"I can see." Danny said.

"And then, she was whipped?" Coffin noted.

"She chose a rattan cane."

Henry looked closely. He saw the tattoo of her son's name clearly on her ankle.

He straightened.

"Inspector, Caroline enjoyed the work, but, clearly, felt uncomfortable sharing this with her sister."

Coffin supped full of horrors. He sat back and regarded the expensively dressed man in front of him. He noticed that Cam's hair was arranged and placed in such a way that it did not move much when his head moved. Its seeming carelessness had been professionally created.

The man smiled at him. His teeth were perfect.

Coffin glanced up. "There was a nurse present?"

"Of course."

"Did she witness this?"

"She was not in the audience, but she was in another room"

Danny muttered "Audience."

Charles leaned forward. "Officers, we are cooperating here. Caroline Bird has a signed contract, she accepted payment, she performed as her contract required…"

"Better."

Charles nodded to his client.

Coffin looked at the two of them.

"There was another matter, On Labor Day weekend. Is there any video of the sailing?"

"On Labor Day?" The lawyer asked.

"Yes. The three day trip."

"We have a photo of the group leaving the harbor and we are willing to share that with you. Frankly, we don't feel the need to share the rest of the video you requested. Of course, if you have a warrant…"

Cam waved his hands. "I am sure the Inspector will realize that the video will show them nothing."

Charles, spun the iPad around, swiped twice and produced a picture with Cam, his parents, his wife, their children, and three other youngish couples. Behind them, the Steamship approached the dock. Charles had brought out the metadata of the picture, where it was and when it was taken.

Coffin put a hand to his chin.

Both men seemed excited to watch him. Danny noticed this.

They were enjoying this, as much as they must have enjoyed flogging the girl and anything they did after that. The excitement of walking these pictures into a police department, waving under the nose of the law, and walking out, fulfilled these two rich men. Danny wanted to offer them a warm towel.

What good is privilege if you couldn't use it?

Five minutes after lawyer and client left the police department, Chief Bramden and Lieutenant Macy slipped into the conference room.

"Do you mind if we join you in here?" The Chief offered.

"Suit yourself."

He sat while Macy stood at the door, with his hands joined in front of his belt.

"So, what happened here today?"

Coffin sat up. "The man without a tie, Cam Christmas, has an artistic side. He likes to beat up women and photograph them."

Coffin opened his iPad, selected the pictures, and pushed it over to the Bramden.

Bramden's expression stiffened. Macy did not look at the pictures.

"His lawyer, the one with the tie, brought a series of signed contracts that showed that the woman in the pictures, Caroline Bird, agreed to the beatings and got paid for them. The pictures, we are told, are the property of Mr. Christmas and we need to get rid of them."

"Mr. Christmas…" the Chief said.

"The Holly, Jolly one himself." Danny added.

Bramden closed the iPad and pushed it aside. He looked at Danny. "I thought we talked about Caroline Bird."

"I thought we talked about Pink." Coffin said.

Bramden was not angry or annoyed. The pictures had unsettled him and he found himself on familiar ground with the Inspector. Coffin wasn't wrong, but…

"Henry, tell me about this case."

"Caroline Bird appears to have gone missing on Labor Day weekend. Her co-workers come to us with concerns. We go to the landed boat she was living in, with four or five other women. We go digging and find that she had a court date in Plymouth, where she was going to get her son back. She and her sister were going to move to an apartment in Duxbury and raise the boy. Caroline has paid first, last, and a deposit of several thousand dollars. Caroline doesn't show at court, but her lawyer does. Caroline also had enough money to pay his retainer Further, the state had guaranteed that her boy would go back to her. She didn't show. Her sister comes down here afterward and shows me these pictures and sends me to Mr. Christmas. And Christmas has come to us."

Danny noted that the truth telling Quaker had left out one little bit: Tobias.

Lieutenant Macy had folded his arms across his chest.

"Do we have Caroline Bird's body?"

"No."

"Do we know that she isn't living right now?"

"No."

"Has it been 24 days since Labor Day? Is it October?"

"No."

The Chief raised his hand. "You're right, Lieutenant."

Macy fell silent.

"Henry, you see the problem here."

"Yes."

"Danny?"

"Absolutely."

"Henry, what would you like?"

"I would like you to support my application for a warrant for her cell phone. I want to find out where it was over Labor Day weekend."

"You won't get it, Henry." Macy spoke.

"Maybe."

Bramden turned and looked at Macy. The tall lieutenant made no gesture.

"You won't get it, you know that." The Chief repeated.

"Maybe with these pictures?"

"Henry, I'll sign it, but you won't get it."

"Okay."

That night, at one in the morning, the two officers were tucked into the brush off of Lover's Lane. The moon had not risen, nor had the overcast broken; the night still held all of its secrets.

Pip chased rabbits in his dreams. They were in the back yard of the house on Main Street. He knew he could catch one. The officers saw his legs twitch.

At two, four women walked up the street in their "Atlantic Cafe" shirts and skirts. Using their cellphones to light the way, they picked their path down the sandy road, avoiding the puddled pot holes and rocks. Both men saw them walking.

"Apparently Pink doesn't drop them off down here anymore." Danny noted.

"Do you think we did that?"

"A little bit."

"Pink makes his choices, we don't."

"They're still walking, aren't they?"

Coffin folded his arms.

Then he unfolded them.

"How many of them have contracts with Mr. Christmas?" Danny asked.

"None."

"None?"

"If they were making thousands on the side, would they be sleeping on the boat?"

"Maybe."

"Unlikely. And what are we going to do? Ask them?"

They fell to silence. The women climbed the ladder up to the gunwales of the docked cruiser. The light flicked on under the cabin. Then, in a moment, it flicked out.

As their eyes readjusted to the dark, the boat disappeared into the night.

"Let's go make trouble. Let's find Brody."

"You drove his car home the other night."

"I did."

Danny put the car in gear.

CHAPTER TWENTY

Brody's neighbors had gone home.

Sergeant Abraham poked the car along the dark road. Out here, in Squam, the Members drove gigantic SUV's that lit up fifty yards in front of them. They kept the roads in rough condition to keep out anyone with a car that cost less than eighty thousand dollars.

Paul Brody's house was as dark as all of the others. However, Pidge's Subaru was pulled up near the door and the Blazer, probably with a fresh registration, was next to it. Danny carefully picked his way among the ruts, then parked the big sedan. They eased the doors open and shut. Pip only shifted in his sleep.

With the engine off and the lights dark, both men let their eyes adjust.

Above them, the Milky Way stretched from horizon to horizon. In the slow walk of Autumn, the summer houses had grown darker and the stars had gone brighter. In the crisp clarity of night, they could watch the stars creep over the eastern horizon. The eyes of the Ancient Ones flickered and blazed. Beyond the dunes, the ocean rolled in its sleep.

Brody spoke from the porch. His voice was clear, but soft and detached. The words would have drowned in a wave.

"Around here, Henry."

Coffin came around the house. He remained in his flannel shirt and gray chinos. Danny followed at a distance. He stood on the grass, out of the light. Let the Inspector do his work.

"Inspector?"

"Paul," Henry replied. "Nice to see you."

"Nice to be here," He breathed. "Thanks for your help the other night."

"I'm glad it all worked out."

The Inspector looked around a familiar deck. He put his hand on one of the rod holders. "I wouldn't think you could catch one from here."

"In the last year with Dad, he wasn't always sure where he was if I didn't put a rod or two in a holder. Then he was sure that he was on a boat. It gave him some pleasure."

"It's a shame."

"He loved it. It put him in a good place. He always felt that there was going to be a fish on a line. Gave him something to look forward to."

The Inspector sat in a twenty year old cast iron chair beside a twenty five year old glass table.

"How can I help you, Inspector?"

"Tell me about Caroline Bird."

"Is she in trouble?" He didn't stutter or stumble; he knew precisely of what he was speaking. Even lying down, he seemed calm. His voice was almost conversational.

"I don't know. Nobody knows where she is. She left all her stuff at her rental."

"The boat."

"Just so."

"Well, she left."

"She did?"

"Labor Day. I took her out to dinner at the Club Car, then we spent the night here. In the morning, she said that she had to go to Florida for a job. And she left."

"Just like that."

"I believe there may have been a free and candid discussion about housing opportunities on island."

"You didn't want to house her?"

"No," he said. "And when she would think about it, she didn't really want to be here."

"Better than the Sea Breeze."

"I am not sure how many nights she spent there."

Coffin looked at him.

Brody slowly sat up and focussed on the Inspector. "Henry, I think Caroline is wonderful and I want the best for her. I know that the best for her is not on this island or in this house. This can be a very hard island if you have to work to stay here."

"And you can be a hard man to live with."

"That is the general tenor of the customer reviews I have collected." Brody smiled.

"So, you took her to the steamship?"

"No, she called Pink. He took her away."

"Pink?"

"Pink's Cab. He was playing the Modern Jazz Quartet at the time." Brody closed his eyes. "Love the vibrophone."

"You're sure?"

"Positive." Brody sat back in the chair.

"Pink swears he never met her."

"Well, he might say that to you," Brody asked. "Why are you involved, Inspector?"

"She missed a court date."

"She wouldn't be the first waitress to skip a court date."

"She was trying to regain custody of her son."

Brody rested his hands behind his head. He took his time. "I did not know that."

"His name is Michael."

Brody looked at him. "Okay."

"He's in Plymouth. Foster home."

"No shit."

"Yup."

Brody brought his arms down.

"She had a son. Wow."

Coffin noted the change in tense.

Inside the house, a light went on. Pidge, in sweatpants and a t-shirt, stepped outside.

"Inspector. How is the night?"

"Getting longer," she said. "Sorry to wake you."

"Not at all. Glad you did."

She looked at Paul. "We talked about this."

"What?"

She picked up the pitcher of lemonade. "This."

Pidge stepped to the oceanside of the porch and poured it over the wooden railing and onto a rosa rugosa bush. .

Paul sighed and regarded the Inspector.

Pidge smiled. "Henry, I will see you around."

Then she opened the sliding door, stepped into the kitchen, rinsed out the pitcher, then picked up a plastic laundry basket and walked out the door.

The Subaru lights lit up the front of the house, then receded out the driveway.

"There goes a pearl of very great price." Coffin said.

"She'll be back," Paul said from his chair. "Where is she going to go?"

CHAPTER TWENTY-ONE

The Assistant District Attorney for the Cape and Islands is based in Hyannis. Once a week, usually on a Friday, she comes over for the various perfunctory court hearings and pleadings. Generally, the A.D.A. rides the high speed ferry with many of the lawyers she will meet in the court in an hour. They gossip, trade newspapers, and, occasionally, cut a quick deal on the defendants. Then, they all go through the dance moves of the court room, break for lunch, dance again until the four o'clock boat, then return to hearth and home.

Court was not in session on a Wednesday, yet an A.D.A. was on island, in an office in the town building.

In the last year, Attorney Erika Albertson had come over to do all of the legal scut work on island. The police liked her because she didn't cut many deals with the multiple losers. She was also six foot two, brunette, powerful, beautiful, and as of September, seven months pregnant with her first child.

Not many knew that she was on island. Coffin knew.

Sergeant Danny Abraham got the Inspector to put on a cleaner shirt, and drove him down to the town building and courthouse. Erika had an empty desk in front of her.

"Erika. Always a pleasure." Coffin stood and waited for her to acknowledge them. .

"Inspector. Sergeant." She gestured at the two chairs.

"Thank you for coming over. I didn't think I would have the pleasure of meeting you in person."

She rolled her eyes.

"Inspector, thanks to you, I have the opportunity to sleep alone in a hotel bed and get room service on the taxpayer's bill. I get a free three days on Nantucket. I might visit the windmill." She shifted in her chair. "Are we done with the horseshit?"

"Sure."

"Inspector, Caroline Bird has been missing for less than 24 days. If we use your count, we have another ten days. If we use the report from Plymouth County Court, we have fourteen days to go. No judge is going to permit any sort of warrant until the alarm rings on those twenty four days."

Henry cleared his throat.

"It doesn't matter what you have produced or who has written a statement, nothing happens until twenty four days are up."

Danny smiled. "Okay," he said. "What happens at day twenty five?"

"You declare her missing and we enjoin all sorts of agencies to help us find her. You can put out a BOLO and we can put her picture on a milk carton."

"What if she is dead by then?" Coffin said.

"Inspector," she settled back. "She might be dead right now, she might have been dead for ten days. Or she might be on the run, hiding from an abusive man. We don't know."

Coffin felt the current of the conversation. Erika smiled, not without warmth and understanding.

"We won't ask for an electronic warrant for her phone." She raised her hand, although neither man was going to interrupt her. "We don't have any hint of a crime here. So, even if I found the most fascist judge in the Commonwealth, he isn't going to give me a warrant to search the electronic history of an innocent woman. Even if she is missing."

Attorney Albertson was speaking without notes or a legal pad.

"In every other courtroom, the judge would remind me about all of the women that are beaten, maimed, and killed by intimate partners. He would suggest that this particular party might want to hide, even if she had to miss a court date for her son. If that judge saw some pictures that I believe you have on that iPad of yours, he really would want her to stay hidden. And he would be right. So that warrant is out."

"Okay," the word escaped Coffin's lips.

"So," she said. "I remain eager to work with you on any other matters, but we are going to have to wait to see what develops here. Let's see what happens in ten to fourteen days. And then, if we find her after that, we can proceed. Okay?"

"Sure." The Inspector, in his clean shirt, stood.

Danny shook the attorney's hand. "Enjoy the week, Erika. It's a good time to be out here."

"Thanks Danny."

In the car, The Inspector was smiling.

Danny put the engine into gear then crept into the line of cars leaving the ferry.

"What are you so happy about?"

"I'm not really happy."

"You seem pretty happy."

"Well, I get to work tonight." The Inspector looked out the window.

"Henry, whenever you get like this, I feel like I am about to get another letter in my file." Danny turned onto the cobblestones of Main Street. "Give me fair warning."

"There is something afoot."

"There is?"

"Yes," he looked back at his partner. "There is no way that the state authorizes Erika to come over for three days just to shoot us down."

"No?"

"No."

"What if they are aware of what a pain in the ass you are and they know that no-one on island can stop you from doing something dumb, but a pregnant Erika Albertson might prevail upon you to hesitate."

"They might, but they wouldn't do it on a Wednesday. They might on a Monday."

They passed by the Pacific National Bank and rocked up a reddening and yellowing Main Street.

"Henry, when you reach, you really reach."

"We'll see."

"Tomorrow, not tonight."

"Tomorrow," he agreed.

CHAPTER TWENTY-TWO

Tomorrow bloomed in big purple weight of hydrangea, bunched and hanging heavy at the end of a sturdy green stem. The warm air pedaled past, sun-drenched and tank-topped, the clouds drifted high above, and cast down five seconds of brief shade onto the golf courses and lawns, before returning to a healthy warmth in the midst of an American Express Blue sky.

Danny had anticipated his two-thirty alarm, and was dressed when it went off. The Nantucket Police Sergeant got to stay on the hanger in the closet, while Dad got to come out of the drawers. Dad got a late Meatball and Provolone Sub for lunch, spilled some marinara sauce on his jeans, and rolled forward, in the minivan, to the big soccer battle out at the Delta Fields. This afternoon, for the first battle in a series of ten years, the Nantucket Pixies were taking on the Martha's Vineyard Pixies.

This morning, while her father had collapsed into the bed, Hadley had painted her face blue and white, then wore her clean uniform to school. She would have wore her cleats, if her mother hadn't intervened and saved the school floors. Throughout the day, from Gym to Science Lab to Lunch, she had been a quivering battery of lightning, ready for the big game.

And it was a big game. She had never played soccer against strangers before. All of her games had come against the same cast of characters that wandered the halls of Nantucket Elementary School, save for the few girls who went to the two private elementary schools on island. Sometimes Brianna and Brooklyn put the cheer skirt aside and picked up the soccer shorts, but mostly Hadley played in a Round Robin against the same three teams; interrupted by a few games against older girls and the clucking of the Popsicle mothers who were afraid their daughters would get broken.

The Vineyard was a bigger island, with a wider residential profile. It had more poor kids, for now, and more kids of color. But because it was bigger and had Brazilians and Hondurans on the team, with futbol fanatic Dads to match, the Vineyard girls usually beat the Nantucketers.

Hadley had left a note, in Blue and White Whaler colors, informing her father that he was responsible for orange slices and for filling the Gatorade water bucket with water. It had to come from the hose, nowhere else. Water from the hose was good luck.

So, of course, he filled it from the hose.

Having the cooler and the oranges gave him pride of place. Danny got to drive his minivan close to the field. One of the assistant coaches came over to help him with the bucket (which he could take care of himself, thank you).

Hadley was in the middle of the pitch, with her blue and white, freshly laundered team uniform, stretching while the purple team did passing drills.

The parents watched the Vineyarders. They seemed big, fast, and none of their passes went strolling over the lines and into the bushes. Ten or so parents had come over with their girls.

We like playing the Vineyard. We get to pretend that they are a rival island, even though they are bigger and closer to the mainland. While Martha's Vineyard was only twenty or so miles away, the arrangements and the trip was convoluted and long. The Vineyarders had to take a ferry to the mainland, then a bus for forty five minutes from Falmouth to Hyannis, and then an hour long high speed ferry ride to this island; they needed three hours to come over and another three hours to go back.

Hadley saw her Dad and waved at him. With the sudden burst of happiness, her father staggered a wave back.

"Do you think they stand a chance?" Brian Swain asked him. He had left his realtor clothes in his closet and was also wearing Dad gear. He had shorts that fell beyond his knee and a polo shirt that advertised a fishing tournament from five years ago. Danny, still enjoying the sunshine of his daughter's love, was too surprised to back away from the white man. He knew too much about the man's private life to talk to him. But, here he was.

"Not a chance."

"No?"

"I think the Vineyard team has Brazilian twins on it. And they look bigger."

"Hadley will knock them back." Brian answered.

"Well, you don't know until the clock starts."

The two men watched the players warm up.

"Are you keeping next Friday available? Stephanie will be turning nine." Swain noted.

"Absolutely. After school?"

"Pizza. Bouncy House. Cupcakes. Starts at five, Over by seven."

"We'll be there. Sherrie too."

"Great."

Danny hesitated.

"Is Wendy coming today?"

"No," Swain said. "She had a closing. She tried to move it, but the client wouldn't budge."

"That's a shame."

"She tried to get me to do it."

"You don't work together…?"

"Oh, no. Not after divorce. She is a competitor."

"And she wanted you to close?"

"She knew I wouldn't. I bet she'll shake hands, watch them sign, and then ditch them on Herman."

The Nantucket Pixies lined up to take shots on goal.

"You guys get along?"

"We have to," he said. "What's more important than what's out there, right?"

"Sure."

"Is Sherrie coming?"

"Maybe. Same thing. She has a teleconference with Mass General at three. They wouldn't move it."

"I hope she makes it."

"Me, too."

Neither man was going to mention the third woman, Pidge.

In that silence, Danny noticed the other parents. We weren't staring, but they noticed. We were keeping score. Brian was here, Wendy and Pidge were not. We had heard the story about the Langueduc. We knew.

This was how it was. Your shame was known to all. Every horrible story, true or untrue, was public knowledge. And you went on. That is what Brian did. That is what the Inspector did. That is what we did.

Brian turned to him. "Let me ask you a question about your partner?"

"Sure. I don't think there is much about him that you don't know already."

"Do you think he really wants to sell his house?"

"Have you been putting the post-its on his door?"

"I will if it will help," The realtor laughed.

"For what it's worth, I don't think so."

"I didn't think so either. I told him he shouldn't."

Danny snorted.

"I told him he should. Sell, and move to Hawaii. Getting a tan, lose some weight, and drink Boat Drinks."

"We would miss him."

Danny looked at the other Dad.

"Yeah, but…" Danny said. "The shit we see. The shit we see."

CHAPTER TWENTY-THREE

If they had to arrest anyone, Danny was not sure where that person would go. Pip had a blanket to lie on. Of course, the blanket wasn't always comfortable so it had to be bunched and moved about until it fit the canine's needs. Pip also had a bag that he travelled with, carrying water, treats, a towel, and some spare chew toys. In the middle of the night, while Danny was mid-novel, Pip might wake up and growl at his plastic squirrel. He was very ferocious.

Danny did insist that, when Pip needed a walk, the Inspector would perform that office. Then, if there was an emergency during said walk, Danny could save a life while Henry could sit on a bench.

On Thursday night, Sergeant Abraham and the Inspector Coffin were back on their stationary patrol. This night, however, they were at the Milestone rotary and not tucked away at the lifesaving museum. Visibility did not stop the Inspector's sleeping habits, nor did it change Danny's reading. It did, however, cause several cars and trucks to tap on the brakes more firmly than they planned as the drove away from town and dinner.

Before he fell asleep, the Inspector asked Danny to wake him if he saw Pink's cab. They weren't going to pursue, but he wanted to be aware. And then he passed out.

However, Pink's Cab had not appeared by one in the morning when the bars "closed." On a Thursday, in late September, very few of the bars would have after hours. As a matter of fact, since the plutocrats had claimed dominion over the island, the drunk college students had retreated off-island to Newport and Weirs Beach. After one in the morning, the drunkest drivers were the Masters of Industry leaving the yacht clubs and headed back to Sconset. Danny waited to see how well they could negotiate the rotary before he ran the lights.

By two in the morning, the traffic ceased. The dishwashers, bartenders, and chefs made their way home.

At two thirty, a red Chevy Tahoe took the rotary too quickly, drove onto the grass and the bike path, and then swerved back onto the road. Danny turned on the lights and accelerated after the drunk. The Tahoe pulled over after two hundred yards and set his hazards.

Coffin and Pip had woken up. Nothing like sudden acceleration to end his dreams. As they came to a gentle stop, Coffin blinked.

"I got it," he said.

Danny, with his door open, glanced at his partner. "You just woke up."

"I'm fine," Coffin said. "Call Norm and get a flatbed here."

Danny shut his door.

Coffin rubbed his eyes, put the dog on a leash, and walked up the driver's side of the car. He gestured at the dog, and Pip sat.

"My brother, I need to see your license and registration."

The driver was not sure who he was seeing. While he had been pulled over before, usually there was a man in a uniform, tapping on the window with a flashlight. Not an old man in a flannel shirt with a dog.

The driver was drunk, he knew he was drunk, and he knew he had just swung out over the bike path. This was obvious. But the road was straight back to his house and he could get there just fine.

"Who are you?"

"I am Henry Coffin. I work with the police."

"Are you police?"

"Not really."

This sort of distinction wasn't registering with a man who had been drinking Patron Platinum for three hours.

"License and registration, please." Coffin asked.

"I want to call my lawyer."

"My brother, you can call your lawyer and bring him out here and we can make a big old issue of this or you can just give me your license and registration and we can be reasonable."

The driver rolled his window up.

Coffin walked back to the squad car. He opened the door. "He wants to call his lawyer."

"Let me talk to him."

"Go ahead."

Pip and his old man walked across the bike path to a the edge of some trees. The dog made sure that everyone would know he had been there. The pair of them returned to the patrol car. Pip sat up in the back seat, prepared and eager.

Danny walked up and stood next to the driver's window, rapping with his flashlight. The driver unrolled his window an inch and dropped his lawyer's card. Danny picked it up off the pavement and walked back.

"Fuck him."

"Who is his lawyer?"

"Herman Lamb."

"Oh, that's ridiculous. Herman isn't going to come out of bed for this."

"It's a nice car."

"Herman doesn't need the money."

"Well, I know what we would do off-island."

"And how long would you be in court?" Coffin said. "As you said, he has a nice car."

"We could call for back-up. I believe that is what technically happens when someone gets stuck like this."

Coffin smiled.

"Let's make a call."

"To Herman."

"No," he said. "To Pink."

Danny leaned back in his chair and closed his eyes. "Is that a smart thing? Really?"

"Call and say you have a drunk who needs a ride home. Send it through the switchboard so we have a nice record."

"He can't refuse."

"He can't. And if it turns out that he is busy, we can pin something down. Perhaps we can show him a way out of his troubles"

"You like trouble."

"I do," Coffin admitted. "But I think this will be a lot easier. Pink comes here, talks the guy out of the car and into his van, drives him off and everybody goes home."

So Danny radioed the station, they called Pink, and he came after making up three different excuses as to why he couldn't.

Pink arrived a few minutes after the call, along with Norman Moore and his wrecker. Norman knew enough to keep clear until the driver was long gone.

Pink pulled up in front of the Tahoe.

The cabbie stopped Chet Baker with a slam of the door and stomped past the red car. He looked in at the driver. He saw an older man with a green jacket and a fifty thousand dollar watch.

Coffin was leaning against the side of the patrol car. Danny had the window open. "Pink, let's talk."

"What the fuck are you playing at, Henry?"

"Absolutely nothing. You and I can do each other a favor."

"You could have called Triple A, You could have called Clyde's."

"Pink, you can do this and those guys can't."

The cabbie stopped.

"Pink, I don't want to arrest this guy, and I don't want to argue with Herman Lamb at three in the morning, and I don't want to spend the next three years in court with a rich drunk driver. 'He's too cocked to drive. You can see the trough he dug in the grass back there. He can't drive home."

Pink looked back. Moore's headlights lit up the marks in the dirt.

"He will talk to you. He won't talk to me. So, we play a little game to get him in the cab, charge him what you want, and young Norman will tow the car away for the night."

"What if he won't get out of the car?"

"Well, he thinks Herman Lamb is getting out of bed right now and coming to save him."

"That's not Herman."

"No," Coffin said. "So, if he doesn't get out of his car, I will call for back up and the Staties will come and take over, since this is a state road." Pink's eyes fell. The only state road on Nantucket was this one, and they would show up. "Then I hand it off to them and you don't get the thousand dollars you can bullshit out of him."

"At least," Danny added.

"We're all on the same team here." Coffin added.

Pink shot a look. "I don't trust you."

"Do you want me to call for back up or do you want to fleece this guy?"

Pink stepped back, shook his head, then stared up at the stars. "Jumping Jesus in short pants."

"Okay. Go to it."

Pink shook his head and tossed his hands in the air.

Then he turned and walked back to the window of the red Tahoe.

Coffin, for his part, stood by the driver's side door. Danny rolled down the rear window so Pip could stick his nose out.

Within five minutes, the cabbie returned.

"He wants to know if you will write him up."

"Only if he doesn't get in your cab."

Pink threw his hands out.

Coffin understood he was acting for an audience of one.

So Coffin looked at Danny. Then Coffin also threw his hands up.

Pink put his hand on the Inspector's shoulder.

The Inspector pumped his hand then winked.

Pink walked back to the Tahoe. The driver opened the door, stood and stumbled. Pink braced him up and walked him to the side of his taxi. In the glare of the headlights, the driver took off his watch and handed it to the cabbie.

Pink waved back and Coffin returned the favor.

As the cab drove away, the old man turned to his partner. "He's good at this shit, I'll give him that."

Having made contact with Pink, the two officers drove to the Lifesaving Museum and settled in.

At four in the morning, a blue Ford Explorer rushed by the Life Saving Museum at eighty miles an hour. Coffin was snoring, but Danny couldn't let this one slide. So, he pulled out, accelerated and started the lights. No siren, though. None of the good plutocrats who live along the road wanted to wake up to a siren. This wasn't New York, sir.

As soon as the headlights hit the Explorer, the car slowed, put on its flashers, and eased over onto the sand shoulder.

Danny brought the squad car to rest twenty yards behind. Coffin was blinking himself awake.

Danny keyed the license plate into the computer.

No alerts.

"Stay here and keep awake."

"Sure."

Sergeant Abraham stepped from the car, adjusted his belt, clicked on the flashlight, and walked up to the Explorer. The car had been sitting somewhere for a while. The wheel walls were rusted, as was the body work around them. The back seat of car was whistle clean.

Which threw a red flag.

The driver had not unrolled his window.

Another red flag.

Danny put his hand on his gun.

When he turned the flashlight into the driver's seat, it caught, brightly, a state police badge.

Danny put the light down.

The window unrolled. "Sergeant, would you bring the Inspector up here. We can have a conversation. Quickly."

Naturally, it was the white guy. Whalers hat, polo shirt with an undershirt beneath it. Chicken Box Cop. Figures.

"One minute."

Back at the car, Danny looked at the Inspector. "It's another white person you have pissed off. State cop from the Chicken Box. He wants to talk to us."

Coffin nodded, opened the door, and made his way to the passenger side of the Explorer. He opened the door and sat inside.

He surprised the state cop. Danny smiled. The old man had a way with other policemen.

"You're the Inspector?" In the state cop's mouth, it was either a question or an accusation.

"Henry Coffin."

"Yeah," he looked at Danny on the other side of him. He didn't need to ask the Sergeant. For one thing, he had a nameplate and a badge. For another, he was the only black man in the department.

"The two of you like to be assholes, don't you?"

Danny shifted his feet.

"Pink solved a problem for us tonight," Coffin said.

"What problem was that? The drunk you didn't call in?"

"That one," Coffin replied.

"Stop fucking with Pink."

"Okay," Coffin agreed.

The cop relaxed a bit.

"I can help you guys out," he admitted.

"Okay."

"We are in the middle of rolling up a major drug operation out here. Caroline was in the middle of it. She was my C.I."

Coffin kept smiling. "She was your informant?"

"I just said that."

"So you have interviews, records, history and all of that?"

"Its a part of this investigation."

Coffin heard the official footprint on the word "this."

"You know, of course, that she missed her hearing for regaining her son." Henry said.

"We do."

Coffin stroked his chin.

"Look," the statie said. "We are going to roll up this operation soon. All you need to do is wait."

"Wait?"

"Wait," he said. "We can help you with your…missing person…then, okay?"

"I understand."

"I am sure you understand. Will you avoid fucking with Pink?"

Danny crossed his arms.

Coffin smiled even more broadly. Danny was glad that the old man had had his teeth fixed. "What would you like us to avoid doing? We spend almost every night sleeping in that parking slot you passed us."

"I know. Just don't fuck with us and nobody has any trouble."

"What would you like us to avoid?"

The old man loved this Brer Rabbit shit, Danny thought. He loved sitting there and playing stupid in front of bureaucrats. In the past, Danny had tried to explain it to him that this was part of his privilege. Coffin couldn't be fired and he couldn't lose his paycheck or his pension, so he was immune. Henry shot the same shit eating grin back at him: "To whom much is given, much is expected." Danny pointed out that, as a black husband and father on this white island, he didn't quite have the same privilege.

The undercover statie looked at Danny, then back at Coffin.

"Just don't fuck it up for the sake of one dead junkie, all right?"

"Thank you, all clear," Coffin said. "Danny, do you understand?"

"Sho' Nuff."

The statie didn't even look at him.

"Have a good night officer." Coffin said as he left the car. "Drive safe and take care of yourself."

That morning, Henry and Danny parked their cruiser within distant sight of the "Sea Breeze." At five in the morning, no light seeped from the boat, nor did any in any nearby house.

"We shouldn't be here," Danny said.

"No, we shouldn't," Coffin said. "You're right."

"But," the sergeant said. "Here. We. Are."

"In a minute."

"Is something going to happen?"

"I doubt it."

"Maybe somebody will throw their shit over the side."

"I'm sure that they carry it down and throw it somewhere."

"Woods?"

"Probably a toilet," he said. "It would cause a problem in the woods. After a week or so."

Danny drummed his fingers on the wheel.

"The staties probably have a camera in the woods or a drone or something."

"They probably don't," Coffin said. "The women don't make the case. And they have Pink. Pink gives them all they need from this crew. There are no cameras here."

Danny looked at him. Then he put the car in reverse.

"Henry, you know I love you, but you also know that if we go to any job site on island and follow someone brown home, we are going to find families in crawl spaces, in boats, and in tents. And if we follow some young rich boys around, or even just some fishermen, we will probably find some working women in a rented house on dirty sheets."

"Maybe."

"Whoring is an old time Nantucket business. When those whale ships came in, paid off their sailors and let them loose in town, what do you suppose happened?"

"Danny."

"Yup."

"Danny, we can't fix everything. I can't fix the past."

"Nope."

"We can fix this. We can mend this rip, right here. I can't help where people choose to live and choose to work, but we have a problem right in front of us. We can fix that."

"Can we let the fellas with the flat hats and funny pants do it? Or does it have to be you?"

Henry sighed.

"Let's go mend the world, one drunk driver at a time, shall we?"

Danny put the car into drive and heading back up Boulevard.

CHAPTER TWENTY-FOUR

On Friday night ,the Chicken Box was jumping. The line stretched down Dave Street, the music pulsed out the doors and windows, and you could hear the chatter as you drove by.

"Henry, we can't go there."

"Not yet."

"Not for a while. What do you want to do that won't get me fired?"

The Inspector bit his thumb nail. This was a new tic for the old man, but not a bad one.

He was silent for a long minute. Pip let out a growl and twitched a leg. Even in dreams, the rabbits were too fast.

"I don't know," he muttered.

"Let's stop drunk drivers," Danny suggested.

Coffin nodded.

And so they did. The wedding season peaked in October, but late September was a great time for Chad and Stacy to come to the island and celebrate at their Frat brothers wedding with something Classic.

Coffin has earned many descriptors over his life, but the term "classic" is one of the favorites. So they sat at the Rotary in the center of the island and waited for the unsteady and over-served to come to them. Classic.

And they did.

Hours later, after closing time, the two officers drove the squad car to the parking lot of the Chicken Box, parked in the center, and ran the lights. Both officers leaned against the front bumper and waited for the drivers to get the message.

Many started walking to town.

Others called cabs and other rides.

A few more sat in their cars, waiting for the cops to leave. When they didn't, at least two nodded off to sleep.

At two in the morning, when the cars were dark and the drunks were in mid-walk, the two men turned off the lights, locked the car, and walked inside for their coffee. Pip jogged along without a leash.

Jon-Jon had two cups ready.

Pip had his own bowl in the center of the floor.

"Is this a new service?" Jon-Jon asked.

"I have been told not to start any trouble," Coffin responded.

"By me," his partner added.

"Well, I appreciate it. If you could make this a policy, my insurance rates will dip."

"We may have real work to do soon," Henry added.

"Maybe."

The after hours crowds filled the well lit bar. The bartenders, the waitresses, the cooks, and the dishwashers filed in, looking for some company at the end of a long night of celebrating newlyweds and their families.

He didn't see the undercover with the Whaler hat.

Among the crowd, Coffin saw many familiar faces. In one crowd of excited young women, he recognized Gabby from the hospital. She worked with Pidge on the night shift.

The six women drew the eyes of the crowd. They were not in the service industry, not the way the island understood it. As a result, they stood at the door and waited. When Coffin slipped over to them, attention was paid. The bartenders, the bouncers, even Jon-Jon waited for the old man to give a sign.

"My sister?" Henry tapped Gabby on the elbow

"Can we come in?"

"Sure."

"I thought we might…"

"You're all nurses, aren't you?"

"Mostly."

"Well, don't make a mess. Everyone here is tired."

Coffin caught Jon-Jon's eye and flashed a thumb. He nodded. Henry stopped one of the women coming in.

"I am sorry, but isn't your name Gabby?"

"Sure. You're the Inspector."

He walked away from the crowd and she followed.

She continued. "You broke up my graduation party."

"Well, I'm sorry."

"No, it's okay. Bad things were going to happen. I just didn't want to be responsible for someone else being an asshole. How can I help?"

"How well do you know Pidge?"

"Pretty well."

Coffin watched the woman's guard go up.

"Is she okay?"

"I think so. She isn't here."

"I saw that."

"I mean she isn't on island. She is covering for a friend at Brigham and Women's. She left on a Med-Evac helicopter two days ago."

"Does she do that often?"

"No," The word trailed away. "Why do you ask?"

Coffin sighed. He felt the conversation going sideways. "I don't think she has done anything illegal. I am just worried about her."

"Worried?"

Coffin shrugged. "It's difficult to say…She…"

Gabby understood the intricacies of snitching and just talking.

"She asked about you." Gabby offered.

"She did? Back when Miss Palmer was on the floor?"

"No, the other day. You came up to her… boyfriend's house."

"What did you say?"

"I said you were a good guy. I said you didn't arrest people."

"True," he smiled. "Not often."

"I said that if you were sniffing around her boyfriend, she might want to take a moment to think things over."

Coffin nodded.

"I guess I am sniffing around."

"Well, that might be why she is up in Boston for the week," she said. "He left a note for her at the clinic today. Taped it to her door."

Coffin looked at the young woman and took apart the information she had told him and the message that she hadn't. She smiled back.

Paul Brody was making it obvious and undeniable.

"You have fun with your friends, okay?" he said. "Don't drive home."

"Sure."

An hour and two cups of coffee later, the two officers drove out the Polpis Road. Danny was happy to see that no drunks had wrapped themselves around a tree or a sign while they were in the Chicken Box.

They made the turn into the moonless darkness of Wauwinet Road. Along the way, they scared some deer back into the woods. The road to Squam was even darker. The stars were so bright that they reflected off of the ocean.

The darkness enveloped Brody's house.

Coffin left the car and walked up the driveway. The Blazer was gone. He circled around to the porch and found a pint glass on the old table. Through the sliding doors, he poked through the electric twilight of clocks and red power lights. The door slid open but, sensing that he knew the answer, Coffin did not step in.

When he returned to the car, he asked Danny to run the lights.

After a minute of stillness, he snapped them off.

"Well, he must be gone," Coffin said.

"Imagine that. People leaving Nantucket."

"Well, you remember Pidge?"

"And her poor choice in men?"

"She is in Boston."

"So?"

"Paul Brody took Caroline Bird out to dinner over Labor Day weekend, then she disappeared. Pidge left her fiancé…"

"At the Langueduc."

"Then she was with Paul and now…"

"Do you think she is dead?"

"Well, no."

"Do you want to call Brigham and Women?"

Coffin understood how odd it seemed.

In his indecisive silence, the two men heard the faint buzz of a helicopter.

Danny turned the car around and headed back to town. While he still could not put the siren or the lights on, he pushed the engine.

Pip sat up and was ready for an adventure.

CHAPTER TWENTY-FIVE

When they arrived at the rotary, the morning sky was lit with the flashing blue and white lights of eight state police cars. The helicopter was over the center of the island, near the airport and shining a spotlight on the action below.

"Danny, let's go to Lover's Lane. Let's get to the boat. Go around on Surfside."

Danny nodded.

Lover's Lane was a sand road that disappeared into the woods. The Staties, in their vast and superior knowledge of pavement would block all the hard surfaces around the Russians in Naushop. They love that precision driving and high speed pursuit, but Nantucket is more sand than asphalt. The Russians knew that and would take another route.

In the gray dark, the policemen accelerated up Sparks Avenue and turned left on Surfside. At four in the morning, the road and the bike path was still, save for one pair of lights approaching.

Pink's Cab passed them at high speed.

Danny flipped the lights on and braked.

"No." Coffin barked. "They can't go anywhere. I"ll call it in. Go to the boat."

Danny resumed his speed. He had often been second guessed by the Inspector but the old man had seldom been wrong. The road remained empty. When they turned on the Boulevard, they saw the flashing lights against the clouds and fog off in the distance. Danny took the left hard, and bounced up the dirt on Lover's Lane. Then braked.

The boat was dark.

But, in front of them, a van was parked in the middle of the road. Lights were off and the engine was silent.

Coffin opened the door and he saw them. Three men were jogging across the backyard to the "Sea Breeze." Two carried shot guns, and one carried a can of gasoline.

"They're going to burn the boat!" Henry barked.

The unarmed old man went shuffling across the driveway, waving his hands. "Wait. Stop."

Pip sat back on the seat, and lay down. The world was too much.

Danny flicked the lights and siren on, then followed the old man with full lights flashing. The man with the gas can started emptying the gas can on the bottom of the boat. A man with a shot gun kicked the ladder over and the other shotgun aimed at the car, then fired overhead.

Henry kept shuffling and waving his arms. "Stop this. Don't do this. Don't kill anyone."

The first thought in Danny's head was that he was going to watch the old man explode in front of him.

Danny parked and jumped out of the car. He unholstered the Glock, aimed, and fired at the shot gun.

He missed high.

"Don't shoot." Coffin yelled.

The women inside were up and looking over the edge. The other man with a shot gun fired into the hull.

Henry kept jogging to the boat. The shot gun turned and began tracking him.

Danny fired at that gun.

He missed again, but gun turned for the police car and its lights.

Danny didn't miss with his third shot.

The sound of a bullet hitting a body is an unmistakeable thud. His spinning death caught all eyes.

Save Danny's

He followed the old man.

In his old man hobble, he came up to the other Russian. He had dropped the gas can and was trying to start his lighter.

Coffin reached out and put his hands around the lighter.

The second shot gun stood on the other side of the boat. As he came around the front, the gun swung towards the old man.

For the fourth time in his life, Danny fired his Glock at a person. The shot went into the boat, but it distracted the shot gun. The gun wavered between both men, then retreated.

Danny had never felt his heart pound like this. He knelt with his gun. He peered around the boat, but he saw nothing. The man had disappeared in the woods.

Henry had both his hands locked on the lighter. The younger Russian was hammering the old man with his left hand. He connected with his head, his shoulders, his arms. Coffin continued to hold the lighter.

Then he tried to kick Henry, but it went wild.

The man continued to try to punch the side of Coffin's head, but the old man wouldn't let loose.

Finally, the Russian tried to pull his other hand away,.

Danny put his gun in the man's face.

"Your buddy ran. Kneel."

The eyes went wild. Danny laid the hot barrel against his cheek.

"Kneel."

His attention wavered. Coffin peeled the lighter from his hand and tossed it towards the squad car.

Then he fell in the gasoline soaked grass.

Danny kept the hot gun on the man's cheek.

He knelt.

"Hands over your head."

Danny handcuffed him to one of the metal struts holding up the boat.

He jerked at the cuff, but it didn't move.

"You all right, old man?" Danny whispered.

Coffin flashed a thumbs up, though he remained lying on the ground.

"Call it in, please."

So Danny did.

By the time the staties came down Lover's Lane, Danny had replaced the ladder and brought the five women over to the back of the squad car. Henry had stood up and limped back with them. His face was cut and swelling, his arm and shoulder hurt, and something was grinding in his right hand.

Four gray state trooper cars came pounding down the dirt road. They drove on the yard and lit up the boat in their headlights.

The dead body and the gas can man glowed.

One of the cars circled across the yard cut behind the old Nantucket cruiser, and headed off in search of the last gunman.

"We have got to go," Henry said.

"You aren't going anywhere but a hospital and a retirement home." Danny muttered.

"No, we have to go."

"We can't."

"We have to."

Danny looked at him. Two of the troopers, including the one who had warned them off, were walking up the road.

Danny looked at the five women. They all were in shorts and t-shirts.

"Go and talk to those cops, would you?"

And as they moved, Danny got into the driver's seat, eased the car backwards.

The trooper who had warned him, the one with the baseball cap, hammered on the trunk.

Danny waved, then slipped the gears into drive and pulled away.

And there was no barking. Pip whimpered on the floor of the back seat. Coffin draped his hand over the seat back and scratched the dog's neck.

As the drove back up the Boulevard, the lights from the state trooper's cars and trucks lit up the whole street. Somewhere overhead, a helicopter was circling and its searchlight was picking along the beach.

"Where the fuck are we going?" Danny said.

"Town pier. That is where Pink is."

"Henry, I'm not in shape to do any more of this shit."

"It will be fine."

"You look like death." Coffin was pale and swelling.

"One stop. Then we can go to the hospital."

On Surfside Road, the parade had started. Other police cars, fire trucks, and ambulances raced their lights to the Boulevard.

On the radio, various voices demanded that the two of them return to "process the scene." Danny switched it off.

Once in town, the lights from the action faded to a glow against the sky. They slowed to a reasonable rate, turned at five corners and rolled down to the harbor.

"He wasn't driving." Henry said.

"You saw them."

"I did."

"So, do I have to reload?"

"The bad guys are on a boat."

"How do you know that?"

"How else are they going to leave?"

Pink's cab was parked in the handicap slot, next to the Harbormaster's office at the end of the town wharf.

A large cabin cruiser was motoring away from the dock. Its running lights were on, but the rest of the boat was dark.

Danny parked the patrol car behind the cab. Henry stepped out.

"Danny, call it in. The Coasties can pull that one boat in quickly."

Coffin was outside the car and limping to the cab.

It was empty.

In the driver's seat, three CD's were ground into the floor on the driver's side. Inside the console, under a stack of brochures, Henry found the drunk's gold watch.

On the rear seats, a spray of blood traced a line from the seat, up the window to a drop or two caught in the ceiling.

Coffin opened the rear hatch, but found nothing and no one.

He looked out to the harbor and hoped for the best.

From the wharf, the two officers watched what the State Police spokesman would call "a successful Joint Operation." The Statie's helicopter came spinning from the south shore and put a spot light on the escaping cabin cruiser. Two men on the flying bridge tried to shoot the spotlight out, but the copter was too high.

Under the illumination of that spotlight, however, the Coast Guard's 21 foot cutter, Endeavor, with a .50 calibre mounted to the deck, took up pursuit. The Coast Guard base was poised at the opening of the harbor, the boat ready at the dock, and the crew got the boat going shortly. The cabin cruiser under full power in the channel tried to out run both the helicopter and the cutter, but a burst of bullets in front of the bow took away their last desperate choice. The cabin cruiser cut the engine and passengers knelt on the rear deck, with hands on their heads and guns rattling across the deck..

The Coasties found two Russians on board. No one else.

Coffin saw the chopper fly over, but he returned to the taxi. He opened one of the rear doors and got on his hands and knees.

"Henry, it's a crime scene," The sergeant warned him.

"I am looking for something."

"You're looking to fuck up a crime scene."

"Not yet."

The old man got up off the ground, closed the door, and then walked over to the driver's side of the car. Once more he dropped on his knees. He swept underneath the driver's seat.

He found what he wanted, pulled it out and sat on the ground with a cell phone in a pink case.

He spit into the ground.

CHAPTER TWENTY-SIX

They kept Henry at the hospital.

When Nurse Stein was going off from her familiar third shift in the Emergency Room, he was the only patient on the floor, and he was still sleeping. His face had puffed up and turned shades of purple and green.

Dr. Tupper's notes said to keep him sedated.

For a shadow of a second, she wanted to question him. But that shadow slipped away into a life that she had not chosen and she let him sleep. We don't need to know, do we? Let the old man keep his secrets.

She read the numbers, marked the chart, and hung it on the door.

By noon on Wednesday two days later, Coffin was annoyed and poking around the room. He had gone to the bathroom, then returned to the bed and his phone. He did not turn the TV on.

Dressed in his uniform, Danny came to him around two in the afternoon. Coffin's clothes had been soaked in gasoline;

they had been bagged and disposed of as if they were hazardous material. The only clothing he had was a hospital johnny.

Danny knocked on the door and stepped in.

He didn't bring him any clothes.

"Well, look what the cat dragged in." Coffin said from his bed.

"Always a pleasure, Henry," he said. "How do you feel?"

"Sore. Sour. Bored."

"I have good news."

"Pip?"

"He's with Hadley.." Danny said. "I have a picture."

The weight of sorrow lifted from the old man's chest.

Danny pressed his phone onto him. "See?"

Pip was sitting at the ASPCA steps, with a new collar and new tags.

"Is he legal?"

"They said you adopted him."

Coffin weighed it in his mind. "Okay."

"Hadley may not let you take him back."

"Her mother?"

"The puppo is growing on her as well."

The old man sighed. "I better get out of here soon."

"Maybe."

"Tupper won't sign me out."

"Can't imagine why."

"I don't need a hospital."

"Have you looked in the mirror?"

"Do I need to?"

Danny smiled, "Maybe you should take advantage of the medicine and get some rest. You aren't going on patrol tonight. Or soon."

"Soon?"

"Officer involved shooting. You're a witness. We need a review," he said. "We are on paid leave while the department investigates."

"That should be good," he said. "Why are you in uniform, then?"

"Debriefing and incident report," he said. "I'm sure you will get your turn."

"I was hoping the troopers were going to take the credit."

"'Fraid not. Everything went haywire. They want to blame us."

"Of course."

Coffin sat. Outside his window, a flock of starlings darted over the African American burial ground in Dead Horse Valley.

"You shot a man." Coffin said.

"I killed a man," Danny corrected him. "Took three shots."

"What do we know about him?"

"He's dead."

"What was he when he was alive?"

"Henry," Danny fumed. "Henry, he was a pimp and a drug dealer, and a would-be murderer who was going to cut you in half with his shot gun as you did your old man shuffle in front of him."

Coffin made a face. Danny continued.

"You would have died, they would have lit the boat on fire, and I would be taking fire from three guys." He said. "So I killed him."

"You're going to live with it."

"That's fine. I have my share of ghosts. He can join the line."

"You have killed others?"

"Not directly. Not with a gun. They crashed or they exploded or they got shot by someone else. But they died. And I was there helping it happen."

Coffin sighed.

"Henry, I know what you believe." Danny said. "And I love you. And I have seen you do some remarkable things with dangerous men. If it weren't for you, a lot of people on this island would have been dead. But you are just going to have to accept the fact that the reason you are walking around right now is because I killed a man who was going to kill you."

The old man wasn't looking at him.

"And the five women in that boat now have a chance to do something else with their lives because I shot that man and he didn't shoot you and you had the chance to continue to be a complete fucking idiot and wrestle with someone thirty years younger over a lighter."

"Would you have shot him too?"

"In a heartbeat. But I was dealing with a third guy who also wanted to kill you. So I tried to shoot him first. Lucky for him, he ran. But, if I had run out of bullets, I would have choked that guy to death."

The old man put his hand over his mouth.

"I love you, Henry. And I trust you even when you do stupid things that no-one else understands. But you and I have a fundamental disagreement. I believe that there are bad people in the world that need to be stopped, either with a jail, a nightstick, or a gun. You don't believe in those bad people."

"There's no such thing."

"So you are going to have to make your peace with the fact that you are still alive because I killed a person who wanted to kill you. "

Coffin turned and looked at him. Danny saw the idea rise and cross his beaten face; there was an argument, there was a statement of faith, there was an urge to come out with some thoughtful query.

"Henry, a bad man died last night. Five women did not perish, screaming, in a fire. My wife still has her husband, my daughter has her father, and I will sleep, snore, and rise with Norwegian wood for the foreseeable future." He patted him. "And you will continue to be a silly old man."

Henry Coffin had been alone with these truths for the morning. They didn't surprise him. But he didn't like them.

Pidge came in when the Inspector appeared to be sleeping. The lights were off in the room, a sliver of a moon glowed in the window, and all of the machines were beeping happily.

One of the skills she had learned very early, back in Maine when the bed and breakfast was a going concern and two parents drank early morning coffee, was silent walking. When she got up to start the coffee and bake the muffins, she learned how to Indian walk down the old stairs. In the twists and turns, bedrooms and stair cases after that, she could walk as quiet as a goldfish.

The Inspector, on the other hand, didn't sleep and listened to the ghosts in the darkness.

"Welcome back." He croaked.

"You're supposed to be asleep," she said.

"I am not very good at things I am supposed to do."

Pidge was writing down the numbers on the machines. Since he was awake, she took his temperature and pulse as well.

He noticed her ring finger.

"So, you're back?"

"I'm back."

"Happy about that?"

Pidge looked at him, "You're supposed to be polite and sedated."

"Again, I am not very good at things I am supposed to be good at."

"I can increase your sedation."

"Please don't."

The silence swung like a pendulum.

"How was Boston?" Coffin asked.

She sighed. "So we are going to have this conversation?"

"I would like to."

"Okay."

In the blue monitor light, she sat in the green plastic chair and crossed her legs.

"When I worked up there, regularly, I was certified and hired for the NICU. You know what that is?"

"Sick babies."

"Precisely," she added. "And there is nothing that can put your life in very clear perspective than to watch a tiny baby struggle to breath. If God is anywhere, he had better be on the floor of the NICU. The parents wear the scrubs and the booties and the headgear and all of it, just to stare and wait and hope 32 becomes 33 and then become 40. They want the next five minutes, then the next ten." She paused and looked out at the setting moon. "Stupid shit gets left behind fast outside the doors of the NICU."

Henry Coffin could imagine what those parents felt. It didn't take much.

"I have never been inside one."

"That was a blessing," she said. "You get perspective. Here are these women who have carried this tiny little thing, hoping against hope. Every doctor, every nurse, everyone looks, and asks with "care.". And then the birth. And then the disappointment. And then the blame. No big, fat baby to bring to the grandparents, no happy christening, no blissful normal. The Mom fucked up. If she hadn't had that glass of wine, if she hadn't eaten that donut, drank that coffee. And all of that has to get dropped at the door. There is no room for bullshit in the NICU."

They sat in silence.

"Did Brody visit?"

She turn her face from the window to the patient.

"How do you know that?"

"Just a guess. He wasn't here. I heard he left a message."
She sighed.
"He did."
"That didn't go well."
"No."
Both were quiet.
"They don't change, Henry."
"Some do."
"Very few," she continued.
"Well, I'm sorry."
"Don't be," he said. "When I saw the two of you out there, and that pitcher, the lights came up in the room and I saw everything a lot more clearly."

She looked back outside.

"All junkies die soon. They don't pick the hour, but they pick the method. I saw you out there, with him, and his drink, and I thought he was dead. And then I realized that is exactly what it was going to look like. You. Him. Doctored Lemonade. And when I drove away, I realized I was going to spend the next few weeks or months or even years dumping out pitchers of Oramorph."

"Morphine?"

"Medical. You can drink it. It's for bad cancer. He gets it from the V.A. Totally legal."

"And Brian?"

"He's a good man. He's not an addict," she said. "What about you?"

"I got clubbed by a bad guy."

"He's in jail now?"

"Yes."

"And one of them is dead?"

"Yes," he said. "And Pink. Pink is dead. And Caroline Bird. They are all dead."

"Well, I'm glad you are still here."

"Me, too."

CHAPTER TWENTY-SEVEN

"Get up old man." Danny walked in on Thursday morning with a paper bag full of clothes. He dropped them on the bed. "You're getting out."

The bag had two sets of laundered jeans, two flannel shirts, a package of fresh underwear, some socks, and a set of sneakers.

"Brought you something to wear."

"Does that mean I can leave?"

"I'm not a doctor."

"They said I could sign out, but I would need someone to pick me up. Someone wasn't answering his phone."

"Really?" Danny made a show of looking at his phone.

Much of the bruising on the old man's head had faded to orange and brown. He looked rested, filled out, and even clean.

"Did you get a sponge bath?"

"No. They threatened," he said. "They sat outside of the shower."

"Get dressed," Danny snorted. "We have an incident to inspect, and you are the Inspector."

"Give me some privacy, for once."

Danny didn't argue, but he spun about and left the room to Coffin and his clothes.

Minutes later, as Coffin was threading his belt through his pants, the two men walked out the door.

"What is it?"

"Brian Swain overdosed this morning."

Both men were inside the car and moving. Coffin looked in the back seat and found it empty.

They met the ambulance on its way to the hos[ital. It thundered up Cliff Road; lights, siren, and everything else sounding to rouse the idle rich on a Thursday morning. Sergeant Abraham, with his own lights going, let them pass, and roared.

Brian had built a home for his family at the far end of Cliff Road, on Capaum Pond Road, in the shadow of the water tower, in vision of the Atlantic and Nantucket Sound. The pond itself was hidden by brush and another house, but Coffin imagined, when Brian went up to the master bedroom, he would have a pretty good view of the first harbor white people had landed in.

The house stretched out across the lawn, with a second story rising up in the center, a porch on one side, and an another room on the other. In front of the house, two other police cars parked on the lawn. Danny zipped into the space recently emptied by the ambulance.

Coffin popped out of the car as soon as it stopped. Danny put it into park and followed the old man.

Inside, one patrolman stood in the entry way, another was in the kitchen, and Lieutenant Macy had the bathroom door open and was taking pictures on his phone. In the dining room, near two bowls of cereal, two crying girls stood in the firm grasp of Pidge. Furious, angry, and hurt; her eyes blazed at Henry.

"My brothers!" Coffin shouted at the cops..

The officers stopped moving.The voice resounded in the stairway,

Somewhat softer, he followed with. "Let's meet outside."

The officers looked at the Lieutenant. Macy nodded and strode to the front door. The other two officers walked outside and stood on the marble steps.

"My brothers, this is now a crime scene."

Macy took a step back. "Henry…"

"We have a man who collapsed in his house and we don't know why?"

"Henry, we know why. He overdosed."

Coffin glared and stumbled. They do come across heroin addicts passed out in front of their families regularly. Coffin felt himself slide into a dead end where he claimed Brian was special because…

Coffin sighed.

"His daughters are in there. Pidge is in there. Maybe we should think about them?"

"They could be hiding evidence right now," Macy noted.

"Is that what you saw when you saw the three of them in the living room?"

All three men stared at Coffin.

"Danny, bring our sample bags. It's a crime scene."

Macy shrugged. One of the ironies of the his life was that, when you looked at the organization chart, Coffin out-ranked him.

The three officers returned to their cars, but did not leave. Coffin wasn't sure what to make of that.

Inside the girls and Pidge hadn't moved. The cereal bowls remained on the table. Coffin walked to the girls.

"Girls, we aren't going to let anything happen to you. Your Dad is going to get the best care possible."

They didn't look reassured.

He looked at Pidge. "Have you called Wendy?"

Pidge shook her head.

"Would you?"

"Of course."

Danny stood in the kitchen in blue booties, a hair net and wearing blue gloves. He handed a set of each for the Inspector. He turned and looked at the girls.

"Right now, we need to find out what happened here. Why don't you go outside and wait. The policeman will want to talk to you."

Pidge stopped dialing and led the girls outside. Coffin followed and asked the three policemen to take their statements. Faced with two weeping little girls, the men remembered who they were and what they were supposed to do.

Coffin put on his booties and gloves then pulled his hat on before returning inside.

Danny and he stood inside the interrupted routine of Thursday morning. The two girls were having cereal at a white table tucked into a corner of the kitchen. In that corner, a set of windows looked west. The lawn remained professionally green and neat before it tucked under a border of rosa rugosa and hydrangea that held the sea grass and scrub pine away. Above the rolling hills, one radio tower climbed into the feathered wisps of clouds and pointed to a Canadian blue.

"Tomorrow is Jennifer's birthday. They were going to have a party." Danny added.

"Hate to have to cancel. it." Coffin was annoyed, confused, and angry.

The two men wandered through the first floor for a few moments.

The living room had a a pit of leather sofas that opened onto a huge television and a cold fireplace. A book case sat along one wall, with a reading lamp and the usual charging cords near it. The other wall had a series of windows, now with shades drawn, that opened onto a porch, a hot tub, and a backyard.

Inside the kitchen, eight Viking gas burners sat atop two ovens, paired with two refrigerators, one of which was empty (but cold). Breakfast was scattered over the counter from a box of Cascadian Farms Purely O's and a bigger box of Captain Crunch. Next to them was a traveling mug of coffee, a half gallon of Stop and Shop Half and Half, and a dish of sugar. The coffee was half full, with a mouthful decorating an empty sink. A container of Newman's Own Mango Tango warmed on the table, between two bowls of healthy cereal. Neither man touched so much as a dishtowel.

In the bathroom, chaos arose with a grin. The rugs had flipped over, the top of the toilet had been swept clear, and the toilet paper holder had been smashed. The toilet was full of vomit, including Captain Crunch, coffee, and milk. In the trash can, a plastic bag labeled "Eternal Brutherhood" winked up.

Both men backed out, and into the entry way.

"Doesn't look like he was planning on getting high." Danny surmised.

"No needles, no spoons, no white dusted surfaces." Coffin added.

"Yet."

"The coffee in the sink and the vomit in the toilet…"

"It was more than he thought." Danny said. "He threw it up."

"You think poisoning?" Coffin added

Danny shrugged. "Or he snorted it up in the bathroom, came out to help the kids, and got overwhelmed. More than his usual bump."

Coffin looked at him. "This is what we think these days?"

"We have seen some shit." Danny looked past him. "He wouldn't be the first."

Coffin nodded. "Can you get some samples from the toilet, the sink, the coffee mug, the juice, the cereals, and the cream."

"Yahsuh."

Coffin frowned, but let it be and opened the door.

The girls were gone by now. Pidge stood on the edge of the pavement, framed by three police cars. Two of the cars still had their lights going.

"My brothers," Coffin spoke to the air. "We can turn the lights off now. Emergency is over here."

The two younger officers looked at Macy, and the lieutenant, in his white shirt, nodded.

"Are the state cops coming?" Henry demanded.

"As soon as you are finished."

Coffin squinted at the man, then decided he was hiding a truth he didn't need to know. "Good."

He nodded to Pidge.

"Let's talk."

She crossed her arms and walked. Coffin led her around the side yard into the back. Two gray Adirondack chairs were at right angles to each other, facing the scrub oak and beach grass beyond the yard.

"They wouldn't let me leave. They would't let me go to the hospital."

Coffin nodded. "I'm sorry. I told them it was a crime scene."

"That makes me a suspect."

"I am afraid so," he admitted. "But we can dispense with that. Where were you when Brian collapsed?"

"Probably coming back from the hospital. The girls called me."

Coffin wrote that down.

"They called 911?"

"Yes. I got here first."

Coffin continued to write on his legal pad.

"Look at your phone, would you?"

"Sure." She took it out.

"What time, exactly, did they call you?"

"7:06."

"You got here?"

"7:15."

"And he was in the bathroom?"

"Yeah."

"What was his condition?"

She looked at him.

"You checked him out? Yes?"

She sighed. "Shallow breathing, accelerated pulse, no response."

Coffin stopped asking for a moment. If Brian had collapsed at 7:00 with five minutes until the girls noticed and called. He was untreated for fifteen minutes. The E.M.T.s would have given him a naloxone as soon as the got here. At about 7:20.

They both considered those twenty minutes collapsed against the bathroom wall.

"So," Coffin continued. "Let me ask you some obvious questions."

"Shoot."

"To your knowledge, is Brian a habitual user of narcotics."

"No. And my knowledge is solid." She was considering the wisdom of talking to the old man.

"Do you bring him narcotics from the hospital for your own personal use?"

"Fuck, no."

Coffin nodded.

"So there are cameras?"

Pidge sat up as if she had first thought of it. From where they could see, one camera was on either side of the house, examining the front and back yard. Coffin pointed at them with his pen. "Do you know who does his security?"

'No."

"Any cameras inside?"

She felt her mind hiccup. "I don't know."

"Most of these security cameras will get saved on a server somewhere. Brian can access it from his phone. Or a computer.'

"I don't know his passwords. I can't get in. If…"

"Any idea how this happened," Coffin snapped her into a different headspace.

She shrugged.

Her hands were between her knees. She was looking into the grass.

"When you walked in, what did you see."

"The girls were crying."

"Where?"

"In the living room."

"And Brian?"

"Was slumped against the wall in the bathroom, next to the toilet."

"Did you do anything to the kitchen? Run the water, put something away?"

"No."

"Did you put anything in the trash in the bathroom?

"Nothing."

Coffin nodded.

"Has Brian had any enemies? People who would want to hurt him?"

"You think someone might have done this?"

Coffin shrugged. "Somehow he got a lot of narcotics in his system."

"I don't know," she said. "The only one who hates him is his father."

"Big Jim."

"That's the one."

"You think he could do this?"

"Sure."

Coffin had met Big Jim on many occasions. He wasn't sure if murdering his own son was possible, although Jim was capable of professional stupidity.

"How about you? Anyone you know who would do this."

She looked at Coffin. He would remember this moment distinctly.

"No," she said.

Pidge left for the hospital.

Macy put a pretend phone to his ear and the Inspector urged him to wait.

Coffin put on a new pair of booties and went looking for his partner. A line of plastic bottles, in tagged and labeled bags spread across the counter. The plastic bag labeled "Eternal Brutherhood" had pride of place.

"Henry," a voice called.

"Where are you?"

"Upstairs."

Coffin dreaded what he would have found. Needles, bags, syringes; or something more medical.

His partner stood in the master bedroom. He displayed none of Coffin's fears.

The king sized bed had been tidied. The light in his closet was still on, displaying rows of pressed pants, shirts, and jackets. On the other side of the bed, a white laundry basket sat on the floor, with folded panties, shirts, and scrubs. On that side's night table, the light stood by itself. On the other, a charging station for his phone, a book, and a jewelry box too big for a ring.

Carefully, in the grip of his blue gloves, Danny opened the box.

Coffin didn't recognize the contents, then he did. One thin wire, with two wires springing from it, like the antennae of an insect. I.U.D.

Danny spoke. "I think our girl has made a commitment."

CHAPTER TWENTY-EIGHT

In the squad car, they called into the hospital. They heard that Brian was still getting examined.

Then, as the two men approached town, Herman Lamb's name appeared on the computer screen. Attorney Lamb was calling them through the dispatcher.

"Herman?" Henry asked.

"Inspector, is that you? I asked the dispatcher…"

"It's Danny and me. How can we help?"

"Could you come down to Swain's at Whaler Lane."

"Is there a problem?"

"Getting there."

"Two minutes, Herman."

By nine o'clock, the realtors, the secretaries, and the rest of the bright eyed and bushy tailed had reported to their offices. And their phones told them the news that a part of the Swain family wanted known: "Brian had overdosed and was at the hospital. It didn't look good." And "His fiancee, the nurse, wasn't with him last night." And "I wouldn't have thought he was an addict. You never can tell, can you?"

In the center of the storm, concerned, of course, but reassuring, was Big Jim. He had the madras pants on, the red jacket, the golf shirt. As soon as one of the associates had unlocked the door, he had taken charge of his son's office.

He even cleared the desk..

Attorney Herman Lamb had been woken by the concerned buzzing of his phone. At 9:15, he stood in the driveway of Swain's Realty, wearing a gray suit, a straw hat, and his briefcase.

With nowhere to park, Danny dropped the Inspector off. Happily, he carefully drove around looking for parking. Eventually, he found a slot near the police station.

Coffin watched him go, then he turned to the counselor.

"Herman?"

"We have a situation."

"Okay,"

The attorney took a moment to silently identify, then understand, the bruises on the Inspector's face.

"How is Brian?"

"Most recent reports say that he is being examined."

"He is alive?"

"Yes."

"Can he speak?"

"Probably in a bit." Coffin hedged. "Why?"

"We have a situation."

"Herman, it has been a morning. From one old man to another, how can I help? Be brief."

"Jim Swain is trying to take control of the business. When he signed the sale agreement years ago, he agreed that he wouldn't visit the office and he wouldn't get involved in the business. And..."

He looked darkly.

"Several of the women in the office have active restraining orders."

Coffin worked through everything the lawyer did and didn't say. "We want him out?"

"Absolutely."

"Can I have the papers?"

Herman handed him a file.

Standing on the steps, in the shadow of the Whaling Museum, on the grounds where some of the earliest money in his investments accounts were squeezed and put into barrels, Coffin saw what he was right now..

He was a janitor.

He was in charge of messes, made by messy human beings, who didn't want to admit they made the mess. Everyone else was allowed to pretend that the vomit on the floor was invisible, save for the janitor. He got to clean it. Addicts who die on the sofa, mothers who disappear, murdered cabbies; all were his messes. And now, old realtors who should be telling secretary stories on a fishing boat.

He opened the door to the office and was greeted with a smile from an unknown face.

"Swain and Sons, Can I help?"

The name of the company had changed.

"Would you tell Big Jim that Henry Coffin is here for him."

"Do you have an appointment?"

"No. But Herman Lamb has sent me with papers."

"Why don't you take a seat?"

"I would rather not."

The receptionist lit up with a studied smile.

"This could be a while."

"Call Big Jim and tell him I am here."

"I am not to disturb him and you don't have an appointment."

She beamed with deep professional warmth.

Coffin began walking.

By the time he entered the main room, all six realtors stared at him. Two of Brian's siblings, his brothers, Stephen and Jamie, sat at two computers, while Jamie's very pregnant wife, Rosemary stood behind them.

As Henry strode to the closed door of the back office, their heads popped up.

"Hey!" One shouted. "You can't go in there."

Coffin kept walking and found the door unlocked. Big Jim sat at the desk. Two Erving Paper boxes sat on the floor with Brian's pictures and knick knacks in them. Big Jim was also peering at a computer.

"Jim?" Coffin asked.

He looked up.

The years had not used this old man as he had demanded. His face had evolved into something more red and swollen, his patch of white hair had migrated, and the eyes had lost the twinkle of mischief and the beg for forgiveness.

"Henry, someone has already kicked your ass today."

"I looked worse yesterday," he said. "What are you doing in here?"

"As my eldest son is now in the hospital, I came in to help run things while he was ill."

"Did he request it?"

"No, he certainly did not. But since he is going to be in detox for a while, I was needed. You can't run a shop from a hospital bed or a psych couch." He settled back in the chair and brought his hands together. "Moreover, I wouldn't want the business with my name on it to fall apart because the owner and lead realtor is a junkie."

"Do you really think Brian is a junkie?"

"He just overdosed, didn't he?" Big Jim let loose a mocking grimace. "Maybe that new wife of his. If he knows where she is, can either get him more of the good stuff or can treat his little addiction. But he can't be here." With a leer, Big Jim leaned forward. "I think I know where she is, if he needs a hint."

"Right now she is at the hospital."

"Good for her," he said. "Her meal ticket is pretty sick."

Henry sighed.

"Jim, I have a set of papers that makes clear that you cannot be here. I have the purchase and sale agreement and I have three restraining orders all of which forbid you to be here."

"I am here on an emergency."

"Doesn't matter, Jim. You have to leave."

"That lawyer is here."

"Herman Lamb is outside."

"Fuck him."

"Papers are pretty clear, Jim. And it looks like all of the computers are locked down."

"Tell you what, Inspector. You don't arrest anyone. So, unless you have the stones to lock me up, which you don't, I am going to stay here, behind my own desk, in my own building. If those girls are upset, they can go home."

Coffin sighed and turned.

Big Jim continued. "I thought you had taken one too many beatings today."

Coffin walked out of the room. The realtors in the outer office watched him. None of their computers were signed in. They flashed an image of Brant Point on a warm summer day.

As he passed the receptionist, who seemed satisfied with the proceedings, he turned. "I'll be right back."

Outside, Sergeant Danny Abraham stood next to Herman Lamb.

"Danny, would you like to some real police work today."

"Absolutely."

"Let's go and arrest Jim Swain."

Herman Lamb shifted his weight, but said nothing. Behind him, a thin white man with a Red Sox hat arranged a camera. The Inquirer and Mirror was on the case, ready to spread the news.

Henry led his partner into the office. The receptionist was attempting to lock the door when they walked through.

"Pardon me."

She stepped back and stared at the black man with the gun, the nightstick, and the handcuffs. Danny noted it and found himself rising, just a bit.

In the main room, all eyes were on both officers, including the Swain children.

The door to the inner office was locked.

Coffin raised a finger to halt his partner..

"James Swain, you are trespassing on this property and are in violation of three restraining orders. If you do not come with us willingly, we will arrest you.

"It's my building."

"Unlock this door, or we will break it down."

"I am calling my lawyer."

"Unlock this door."

"Not until I talk to my lawyer."

Coffin nodded.

Danny lurched into the door and splintered the door frame. Big Jim remained at his desk.

"Oh, so you brought your nigger in?"

With his hands cuffed behind his back and his belly swelling over his pants, Big Jim Swain was led out of the real estate office, down the stairs, into the camera of the Inquirer and Mirror, and the eyes of history.

The officers walked the swearing and bellowing patriarch two blocks into the police station.

The officers on duty, the ones who had been so helpful at Brian's house, had to clean out the old files out of one of the cells so that they could tuck Coffin's first arrest in ten years behind bars.

Chief Bramden, not in the office twenty minutes yet, sipped a cup of coffee. Lieutenant Macy feared what his Admiralty brother was going to expect from him.

Once the older realtor was safely stowed and bellowing, Danny returned to his partner.

"Brian is out of danger and he wants to talk to you.

Coffin looked at his partner. "You can do the paperwork?"

"Better than you."

"Probably."

"Take one of the day-timers." Danny gestured at the young cops.

CHAPTER TWENTY-NINE

When Coffin walked into the hospital, the news of his first arrest in years had just seeped through on social media, along with a particularly unflattering picture of a famous local businessman in full throated and handcuffed anger while being led by a large black man.

Nurse Stein addressed him.

"You look better, Henry, at least from the last time I saw you."

"I heal slowly, but surely."

"At least you can heal. Are you here for Brian?"

"Of course."

"Come with me. He asked for you."

Coffin drifted behind the counter. The waiting room was punctuated with older folks waiting to have their blood tested for the day. All of them kept their eyes on the Inspector.

Brian Swain was in one of the examining rooms. His bed was angled upward and he was sitting and smiling, garbed in a hospital johnnie and looking not a little worse for wear.

"Forgive my voice," he croaked. "Apparently, this is an aftereffect of the drugs."

Pidge sat next to him, and, although she did not cling, she looked as supportive as she could.

"I don't look my best either," Coffin answered.

"Where's your partner?"

Coffin smiled. "Well, we just arrested your father, so he is doing paperwork."

Brian's face fell. "I don't have my phone."

"Probably a good thing," Coffin answered. "But if Pidge has hers, you should contact Herman and get someone to unlock the computers."

Brian made a quick call to a realtor at the office. He gave everyone the day off and locked the door. Then he called Herman. Then he saw the picture of his father.

"Well," he croaked "Dad's been busy."

"He has a great sense of timing," Coffin responded.

Brian chewed on an ice chip.

Pidge had not spoken.

"Brian, I don't think you have too many words today, so why don't you tell me what happened briefly."

"I woke up. The girls were downstairs. Pidge was working."

"I was at the hospital with her."

He nodded. "I came downstairs and made the girls' breakfast. The I made myself coffee. I drank some and I felt sick. I spit some in the sink, then I went to the bathroom. I threw up and then I passed out."

By the time he finished speaking, his voice had faded to a hoarse whisper. He picked up some ice chips.

Pidge turned to the Inspector. "Brian is going to be under observation today, but they will probably send him to the Cape for an MRI of his lungs. They are afraid that there might be some damage."

"What was it?"

"Fentanyl.," she answered.

Brian waved and flashed a thumb's up.

"Can I have your toxicology report?"

Brian nodded vigorously.

Coffin left the room, found Nurse Stein and got the realtor to sign the form. An important thought returned to the old man's mind.

"Brian, you have security cameras."

He nodded.

"How can I watch the videos?"

He took the pen from Pidge and wrote the password on a piece of paper.

The young officer wasn't happy to chauffeuring the Inspector about, but he didn't really have anything to do until the school's closed and he had to run the lights and stand at the crosswalk. After the arrest this morning, nobody at the station was in a hurry to tell the Inspector he had to come back.

So, the two of them went off to Cliff Road.

He settled into the car while the Inspector returned to the house.

Henry didn't let the officer sit too long.

The laptop computer was in Brian's Italian leather briefcase. The Inspector set it up on a black marble coffee table in the living room. He unlocked it, then went back 24 hours and started watching.

The house had more cameras than he had thought. They weren't inside, but two more cameras were tucked into the eaves. And both doorbells, front and back, were cameras.

Most of what he watched involved deer, rabbits, at least one feral cat, and a dog that chased one of the rabbits under the porch.

Then, at one in the afternoon yesterday, the rear camera on the porch went black. Coffin rewinded the video until he came at the exact moment (12:58) when the camera blacked out.

Realizing where he was, he stood and walked to the French doors, unlocked and opened it, and found a "Paw Patrol" sticker on the rear doorbell/camera. While he considered removing it, he remembered that it was certainly evidence, as was the video he had been watching.

Coffin returned to the sofa and reviewed the tape of the rear of the house. He couldn't be sure, but it certainly seemed that the brush was moving strangely out beyond the wall.

He closed the computer and brought it back to the car. He called the State Police and asked them to try to take fingerprints off the rear door. He doubted there were any there, but it would keep them busy.

After the paperwork had been completed, Danny brought the Inspector back to his house. They sat in the car at eleven in the morning.

"You are lucky none of the women are here," he said. "You wouldn't leave un-hurt."

"I am sure Pip misses me."

"I am sure he doesn't. My daughter has been pumping cheese and crackers and anything else into him. Sherrie let him sit on the sofa with her."

"He's not supposed to sit on sofas."

"You might have to reinforce that rule."

The two officers began walking up to the door. A dog was letting loose a crescendo of barks.

"See?" Coffin said.

"He's just hungry."

And there he was. He used his front paws to bounce into a louder bark. When Henry stepped inside, the doggo led him into a sitting room and put his front paws on the Inspector's chest.

The old man put his hand on the side of the dog. "Now, down boy."

When Coffin sat on the chair, Pip rubbed one side and then the other against his knees. When Coffin stopped stroking him, he put one foot on the Inspector's leg, and then wiggled his considerable self onto the old man's lap.

"He probably needs a pee," Danny volunteered.

"Of course. What else could it be?"

"I imagine he doesn't like being left alone in a house."

"Which is why he comes with us."

"His leash is on the back of the front door."

Coffin walked to the door, followed by his loyal Pip. With his collar and leash, Pip sashayed out in front of his now rediscovered master. Both of them investigated a telephone pole. They took a lap around the neighborhood, then returned to the house.

"Well, he looks happy," Danny allowed.

"He does, doesn't he?" Coffin said.

"You noticed that we got him his shots and his registration."

Pip went to his new water bowl and slurped.

"Thank you," Coffin added. "I'll pay you back."

"Oh, you will," he said. "It won't cost money. You are going to have to share Pip."

Coffin looked at his partner.

"How are we going to do that?"

"We'll figure it out. He already has a bed in the back seat.

Pip picked up a toy gnome and squeaked it. With the his jaws occupied, Coffin put the new collar on, refashioned the leash, and followed the squeaking animal out to the car.

Danny did not want to be home when the women in his life returned. But he would.

CHAPTER THIRTY

"Well, you have had a big day," Jon-Jon pushed a cup of coffee to the Inspector. To his eye, the old man was beaten, more than just in the face.

"Well, not every day is sun beams and lollipops."

"No, indeed."

The owner of the Chicken Box moved to the registers that were spitting out long lines of paper tape. Henry considered the latest Red Sox loss in a forgettable season.

On the last Thursday in September, the Chicken Box was slowly escorting its clientele out the door. Danny and Pip had sat outside in the squad car with the lights rotating. The wedding season had grown around them, so the cabs and the vans were lining up on Dave Street to bring the valued guests back to the bed and breakfasts so as to prepare for Her Big Day. The bartenders may have ruined it, however, by over-serving.

They served Henry another cup of coffee with Jim Beam.

When Danny returned, a group of four partiers remained at a finger bar. The lights were up, the band was packing (three weddings tomorrow!!), and the bouncers stood nearby. Even their glasses were empty.

Jon-Jon glanced at the black man. Danny understood and wandered over to the group.

"Party is over, gang," he said. "You have to go."

"We're finishing up," They lifted their empty glasses.

"Finish up faster, please. Everyone here wants to go home."

"This bar won't close for another hour. We know that."

"It is, unfortunately, closed for you."

"We will go in a moment."

"You are a half an hour late."

"In a moment."

"You don't have a moment."

Henry got off his stool and walked over.

"What's the problem?" He asked the group of visitors.

"This guy wants us to go."

Coffin nodded.

"Do you know who he is?"

The four white twenty somethings examined the black man.

"No."

"His name is Sergeant Danny Abraham. Look him up."

Their phones came out. One of the women took his picture.

Then they looked at one phone. Danny was frozen in time, with an arm on a bellowing Jim Swain.

Coffin saw this.

"He enjoys locking up white people."

They looked at the old man with the beaten face.

"Isn't that right, Sergeant?" Coffin added.

"Yup."

"Jon-Jon?"

The Jamaican shouted over from the bar. "Yup."

Coffin looked at the young partiers, "Do you think we are lying?"

"Fuck, I don't need this," A young man grabbed his coat.

"We aren't hurting anyone," Another said.

"We were going to keep buying drinks," The third snarled.

"We won't come back. And we will tell all our friends," Came from the fourth.

One of the women snapped a picture of Danny, Henry, and the two bouncers for Instagram Revenge. Then both women flipped them off with their wedding manicures.

After the door closed, Jon-Jon went back to his registers. Danny looked at his partner.

"Did you just lie?"

"No."

"You said I enjoy locking up white people."

"Don't you?"

"I wouldn't say that."

"You wouldn't say it. Doesn't mean its not true."

"You people do tend to turn a really amusing shade of pink when a black man puts you behind bars."

Henry smiled and patted the shoulder of his partner. "We have to talk. Stay here."

Coffin returned to the bar, picked up his coffee and one for his partner. He walked a sloppy path back to the finger bar.

"If you want privacy, why don't we go back to the car?"

"Who said I wanted privacy?"

Danny sipped his coffee. "You are a funny man with a smashed up face."

Coffin nodded, "You have something to say to me."

"How do you know that?"

"Because you haven't said it."

"Well, we had to entertain the fine young cannibals."

"And now?"

The sergeant cleared his throat.

"We released Big Jim around two in the afternoon. Herman and someone else got him to sign something to make the trespassing go away."

"And the restraining orders?"

"No idea," he said. "But I think the old man can write checks."

"That might be the best thing we do," Coffin muttered. "Three orders?"

"That's right. Or those are the ones Lamb had. Might be more."

Coffin nodded.

"Brian has had his hands full with Dad."

"Sorry he can't spend more time in jail."

"He got punished."

"Really."

"You've seen your picture, haven't you?"

"I have. And it will be forgotten in a week."

"No, it won't. People will remember that for the rest of his life."

"Because he got arrested?"

"By a black man."

Danny shook his head. "This is one fucked up island."

"I am trying, my brother. I am trying."

Coffin finished his coffee. Jon-Jon sent over two more cups of coffee.

"You keep drinking that, you won't be able to work tonight."

Coffin nodded. He sipped it and it seemed that heavy pours were the order of the night. "So," Coffin said. "What did the state police tell you about the phone?"

"How do you know?"

"The state police hate me. Yet, they came to work a crime scene twice today."

"Twice. Tell me about the second one."

"You first."

"We can't do anything. We can't go to court."

Coffin raised his eyes to his friend and partner.

Danny hunched over the finger bar and moved in closer.

"They wanted the phone."

"Of course. With Pink and Caroline dead, they needed the phone and the girls."

"Caroline was a confidential informant?"

"Yes."

"So, the phone she had was listening and broadcasting constantly."

"Ah." Coffin did not know much about the electronic world. But he knew enough about bureaucracies and the state police to know that, if they could get a running tap on someone's life, they would. He saw a forty year old in a gray polo shirt listening at a computer terminal while he played video golf.

"The recordings that she made, and that Pink made, are with the F.B.I. now."

"Does that include our friend Mr. Christmas and his art?"

"It does."

Coffin looked into his coffee cup. He now considered that the guy in the golf shirt made copies of Mr. Christmas' art for his own personal consumption.

"So…"

Danny looked away.

"Caroline died on the Saturday night of Labor Day weekend. Apparently, she overdosed."

Coffin looked at his partner's ear. He wouldn't turn. He had to believe in someone and he believed in his job. He wouldn't look him in the eye.

"How many deaths did the staties need before they stopped it."

Danny didn't answer him.

"Where was she?"

He said nothing

"Brody." Coffin guessed.

"Yup. Overdose," The sergeant muttered. "They were talking, then they weren't."

"Then what happened?"

"The phone had fallen. They guess underneath his bed. He slept for hours. Then, they heard him moving her. Then silence. Then the phone reawakened in Pink's cab and recorded his moves for the next two days."

Coffin sipped his coffee. Danny did not return his gaze.

"So, the whole reason that phones broadcast is to protect the C.I." The old man asks.

"Supposedly."

"And the C.I.—Caroline— they allowed to be choked, beaten, and whipped, legally. She overdoses, they don't arrive with an ambulance or a cruiser. They let her die."

"Yes," Danny said. "Yes, they did."

"They let her die."

"Yup." Danny said. "And because Paul was not a target, with a warrant and a judge's signature, we can't use the phone against him. Indeed, we can't use anything from the phone. They will deny the transcripts are real."

"How many have died in September since Caroline?" Coffin looked at him.

"More than three."

"More than three." The old man repeated. "What kind of business are we in?"

"We should talk to Paul."

"We will," he said. "Later."

Coffin took several minutes to finish his coffee. Danny watched him dawdle. It was a night when he should drop him off on Main Street and complete his shift on his own. But he wouldn't because he wanted to pick him up again.

Coffin's hope was his curse. He hoped everyone would be their best selves. And they never were.

Jamie Swain, Brian's brother, walked into the Chicken Box, amid a small group of waiters and waitresses from the Club Car.

He aimed for the two officers.

"I hope you're proud," He snarled.

"Of course I am. Your father looked great." Danny returned

"He's out."

"In all sorts of ways."

"Your little stunt meant nothing."

Coffin looked at him.

"I am glad that your brother is okay."

"Yeah," Jamie said. "Yeah. He's in Boston. They are looking at his lungs."

"Well, that's good."

"You know who is not there? His little junkie whore."

"Have a good night." Danny stood in front of him.

Jamie thought about taking his shot, but even Johnny Walker wasn't that stupid.

CHAPTER THIRTY-ONE

"Now, to our darker purposes," The Inspector muttered. Danny and he were parked at the Lifesaving Museum at four in the morning. No cars had driven by for an hour, but one guy on a bike was heading out to Sconset at three. The old man has slept his coffee off and was, at this point, only slightly drunk. Pip remained asleep.

"Let's go see the English teacher."

Danny put the car in gear and headed east. The road remained empty, although the deer liked to poke out of the woods and dodge the cars. In the winter, more deer than people wandered the island, which said more about the deer than the people.

They made the turn on the Wauwinet Road and rolled through the hidden hedges of the plutocrats. At the guardhouse, he turned south.

"Shall I put the top lights on?"

"No need. He's awake. He's probably expecting us," Coffin said. "But I want you to come with me."

"Do you want me to soften him up?"

"You have a way about you."

"I am a black man with a badge. And a gun."

"Just so."

Along this dirt road, every building emerged from Architectural Digest. It might have been from six months ago or from twenty years past, but the money was stacked in historically appropriate ways that pleased the client, the neighbors, and the magazine's advertisers. Save for Brody's. It remained true to the drunken fisherman's shack that it had once been.

In front of the house, Brody's ancient Blazer was joined by a black Chevy Tahoe with a license plate that read "Swain."

"Well, that is interesting," Coffin said.

"Brian is off island."

"And his intended is right here."

"Oh, dear, dear, dear me," Danny said. "You white people sure get yourself into a mess, don't you?"

Danny parked the patrol car directly behind the Blazer. Not that Brody was going anywhere, but now he was doubly sure.

Coffin picked up an iPad and a very thick folder of transcripts from the state police. Pip hopped out of the car, and toddled over to the edge of the building. When he finished, he joined the Inspector.

Brody was on the back porch, enjoying the last breath of summer. Above him, the fog and the high level clouds were getting between him and the stars. He had his pitcher of lemonade, flip flops and a pair of swim trunks.

"Morning, Paul."

Brody straightened up and blinked. "Inspector," he nodded. "Danny."

"Nobody ever uses my title." Abraham said.

Coffin glanced back. "And I don't like mine. I think he is trying to cast us some shade. He wants us off balance. It's a lawyer trick."

Coffin sat in one of the beach chairs. Danny stood.

Pip popped up onto the porch. The young man sat up and offered his hand. The dog sniffed it. He got his scratches.

"Who is a good boy?" The teacher asked, while rubbing the dog's head.

"Not you, brother," Danny smiled.

The younger man finished with dog.

"He's a good addition to the team, Henry. He warms you up."

"How's that?" Coffin responded.

"Everyone loves a dog. When everyone sees you, they don't know what to do. But when they see this good boy…"

"Pip."

"Pip," the teacher concluded. "Of course. Great Expectations?"

"No," Coffin said. "Moby Dick."

The English teacher grinned. "That would make you Ahab, wouldn't it?"

"I'm afraid so."

Pip, drunk with attention, returned to the Quaker.

Brody spent a moment with his eye on the Labrador, then he turned to the old man. "Henry, you took a beating. What does the other guy look like?"

"He's in jail. Probably looks a little crestfallen."

"You got to use your head for something better than that."

Coffin flashed a grin, than dimmed it.

"Are you selling the house?" Danny asked.

"No."

"The realtor is here, you know."

"Just his car. Pidge is an old friend."

"Is that what you kids are calling it these days?" Danny intoned.

"Paul, I want to have a quiet conversation with you. I don't care who is on your sofa or in your bed." Henry spoke.

"Fine."

"Remind me again about your relationship with Caroline Bird."

"Inspector…". Brody sighed and looked out to sea. He sat in silence for thirty seconds.

"Would you like me to interview you at school?"

Paul sighed.

"I am thinking I should have a lawyer."

"You are a lawyer."

"The lawyer who represents himself has a fool for a client."

"If you want to call Herman, go ahead. We'll reschedule and we can meet in his office during business hours." Coffin out the folder on the glass table. "You know who I am. You know how I like to work. I would think you would prefer to have a conversation with me at four in the morning than one with Herman, his legal secretary, Ericka and the Chief…."

"She hasn't given birth yet?"

"Soon, we all hope."

Brody nodded. "I assume we are having a conversation, then. No charges will rise tonight."

"No."

"Then why is he here?" Paul gestured to Abraham.

"I am his emotional support nigger," Danny said.

Coffin glanced at his partner.

"We both thought that it would be better to be safe, than sorry. Sergeant Abraham…"

"Thank you, Henry." His partner nodded.

"…Is here to insure that everything remains civil."

Silence settled onto the deck. Brody looked at the two of them. This may be as good as it could get.

"Okay," Brody said. "We'll talk and I won't kill you."

"Thanks," Coffin smiled. "So, you told me about your relationship with Caroline Bird. You said that the two of you had been seeing each other, on and off, over the summer. Neither of you were exclusive. You had a date on Saturday evening of Labor Day weekend that ended here. You told me that she got a ride back to town with Pink on Sunday morning and she was headed to Florida. Is that basically correct?"

"Sure," he said. "Sorry to hear about Pink. I was quite broken up about it."

"Har, har." Danny grunted.

"Well, I will relay your feelings to his brother."

"Okay."

"Caroline Bird was an informant for the state police, as was Pink. They were focussed on some Russians for sex slavery, prostitution, and heroin. You may have heard of that investigation."

"Got a bit fucked up."

"It did, but it's an island. You run out of places to run, fast. They have arrested everyone," he said. "The courts will do their work."

"Okay."

"These days, when the staties have a confidential informant, they give them phones that are always broadcasting. They not only know where the informant is, they know what they say and they take pictures from the phone. We have, from Pink, pictures of you in the back of his cab that morning."

Coffin said nothing. He saw it coming.

"And, of course, we have the last 72 hours of Caroline Bird's life."

Brody felt the trap spring and he felt himself fall off a cliff. He knew that he was not in danger right now, but the panic was rising. Danny was here for a reason.

He had wondered where she got her stuff from.

He took three deep breaths.

"Fine."

"Fine?"

"Fine, Inspector," he said. "It's embarrassing, but you don't have Caroline. And you don't have Pink. I didn't kill either of them."

"Nice to know that you are innocent," Danny spoke from over Coffin's shoulder.

"We're not in court." Coffin said.

"No. I didn't murder her." Brody reiterated.

"Didn't say you did?" Coffin chuckled. "Danny, did I accuse him of murder?"

"Nope."

"I heard the recording. You can, too. I have it on the iPad. It's pretty clear that you are passed out when Caroline has her death rattle."

"You didn't stir."

"Not that the phone caught."

"Not a peep." Danny added.

"Danny was thinking we could charge you with negligent homicide, because we earlier heard her asking for you to inject her." Coffin said. "But I think we would need a body for that."

"I think we could make it stick." The black man added.

The silence rose up.

"You think this is appropriate to joke about?" Brody said.

Danny stared at him. In the star light and illumination off the ocean, his face closed and set. Coffin smiled, but the shadows crossed his face as well.

"Sergeant Abraham and I are talking to the man who was there when she died. The man who slept through it, then woke up. Then went to town with Pink. And her phone."

"You don't know she died."

"When you hear a death rattle, you know," Coffin said. "You were clearly asleep. You were surprised when you woke up."

"You said 'Oh, Fuck.'" Danny added.

Brody shifted on the lounge chair. "I don't know why you are here right now."

"Would you like to meet downtown tomorrow. Lawyers and reporters and all?"

Brody looked at the two of them.

Sergeant Abraham resumed his watch. He trusted the old man, but there were times that stretched the patience. Coffin enjoyed drawing this out; he claimed to have his reasons, but Danny assumed it all began and ended with an old man's vanity.

Brody was right. If they were going to press charges, they should do it in daylight.

"Now that I know that Caroline is actually dead, even if we don't have her body, I have to go and tell her sister. I have to tell her son. He is eight years old and seems to be upset. I have to bring him peace."

Brody looked uncomfortable. "I didn't know she had a son."

"You didn't ask about the tattoo?"

"No," he said. "When I met her, it wasn't an issue."

"How did you meet?"

"She was performing."

"You were with Christmas?"

Brody looked uncomfortable.

Danny found something burning in his gut. "Were you there for the beating or for the whipping? Or for the Wheel?"

" The Catherine wheel," Coffin added.

"That must have been a treat," Danny felt the smoke rise in him. "Don't get to see that everyday."

"We saw the pictures." Coffin added

"I bet you were the nice guy who was going to get her out of all of this. I bet you weren't like those other guys. You cared." Sergeant Abraham sneered. "Although in the midst of all of that entertainment, you missed her tattoo."

"Michael." Coffin added.

Brody stiffened. "I didn't kill her."

Coffin let the silence slip. He heard two waves roll in. "Where is the body?"

"No idea," he said. "She left with Pink."

"So, I suppose we could bring that audio and video into a grand jury. Let them marinate." Coffin said.

"Again, I am sorry that Pink passed away. Pity."

Danny saw the beginning of a smirk.

"So, we bring you in front of a grand jury and tell the story of the mother and her son, then we play the tape of her death and 'Oh, Fuck." and then we bring you in and you and your lawyer can explain where dead Caroline is in Pink's car." Danny was trying to prevent the fire in his chest from catching further.

"You're here," Brody said.

"I am," said Coffin.

"You know that your chance in front of the grand jury will be thin. And Cam Christmas will walk in with an excited legal team."

"I know that," Coffin said. "I know the mess it will make."

"So, what are you thinking, Inspector?"

Coffin looked out over the open Atlantic, expelling and inhaling in the grave.

"I have another idea," Coffin said. "Aside from arresting you for negligent homicide."

"What do you want?" Brody moved from the chaise lounge.

"Let me finish," he said. "And we don't need to wake anyone up."

"I don't think she would much care."

Coffin raised his hand as the Sergeant started to clear his throat.

"My idea was to charge you with possession of a Class A drug. We have evidence of you using heroin. So, we search the house with dogs and find some residue. Then, with that, we search through your medical records and find the people who prescribed it to you. Then we look at how much and what for. That loose thread can unravel a lot."

"You might have brought some to school? That would be another charge." Danny added.

"Now, I really enjoyed Pidge's company in the hospital, but she can write prescriptions and works in the opioid clinic at the hospital. With a warrant, we could find out if you are a patient."

"So you are threatening Pidge."

"No," Coffin sighed. "We would be saving her from a drug addict who killed—Pardon, me—allowed another girlfriend to die in his bed."

Brody stood up suddenly and turned to the ocean side of the deck, where the rod holders remained from his father's last days.

Pip rose to a sitting position and became ready

Again, Brody felt himself falling in the winds of panic. He reached inside himself, found something cool and hard, then gripped it. He turned and looked at them.

"You haven't charged me or searched my house."

"No," Coffin nodded.

"So, what do you want."

"How much are you worth, Paul?"

"This house and about four hundred dollars in a checking account."

"Never lie, brother," Coffin almost sneered. "Never lie, because then you tell the world what your secret is. I know where the probate court is. I know how to read files. I saw the records."

"So."

"Two years ago, when your Dad died, you were worth about twenty million dollars."

Brody crossed his arms. He wasn't wrong.

"Seems silly to lie about being a multi-millionaire," Coffin stated.

"My father's money."

Danny snarled, "Is he using it?"

Brody felt something old and dark start to slip.

Coffin stood and dug in the file. In that moment, Brody noted how pathetic the beaten old man looked. Henry took two limping steps, and handed him a picture. In it, a boy about eight smiled in front of a backdrop. The print still had the photographers print across the bottom; it had been picture day somewhere.

"Paul, let me introduce you to Michael. Michael is the only son of Caroline Bird."

Coffin continued. "Michael has been in three foster homes this year, and he currently is in a hospital. Two weeks ago, his mother had a court date to get her son back."

"Good luck with that."

Coffin grew cold. "Well, she died next to you before that could happen."

The silence rolled in off the ocean and settled around the three men. Coffin, alone among them, felt at home in the still dark. He continued.

"The state police had sent a message to the state's attorney to allow mother and son to reunite. Everything that happened this summer. Everything that she allowed to happen to her." He let the word frame a world of silk underwear, a boat, and a bucket to shit in. "She did in order to get her son back."

"She must not have…"

"Don't." Danny said.

Coffin turned to his partner, but said nothing to him. He returned to Paul Brody.

"Her lawyer was Jay Thomas." Coffin had dropped his volume, but remained speaking in matter of fact tones. "You are going to call him up and ask him to set up a trust for young Michael. You are going to put one million dollars…"

"Two," Danny said, guttural and angry.

"Of course," Coffin continued. "Two million dollars into a trust for him. College, school, treatment, whatever he needs."

Paul remained leaning against the railing with his hands folded.

"What do I get?"

Through the darkness, Coffin settled into his eyes. He let the moment grow astronomical, as if he could see and measure the tick of the stars as they rose over the horizon. A gust slipped on a breaking wave, darted over the dunes, and brushed over the porch.

"You get the barest chance to help someone you have mortally wounded. You get a chance to mend the world."

"Best not let it slip," Danny intoned.

Pidge watched them drive away.
Paul did not come to bed.

CHAPTER THIRTY-TWO

It was a party. We knew it would be.

The bouncy house was rocking when the second car came up. Then, when all of the kids had arrived, one of their teachers painted the little ones into dragons and lions and tigers and even sharks. Once they were decorated, they made special bracelets, played wiffleball in the street, and made Tik Tok dances and selfies in a special birthday stage constructed at the last minute. We wanted to do our best for those poor little girls.

Wendy's house had been built with children's parties in the design. And so it happened. We were there. Gramma and Big Jim. Brian's brothers and sisters. Their children. Everyone in the class and at least one parent per child. Everyone knew why. Everyone wanted to know more.

We wanted to ask Danny. He was out of uniform, smiling, and letting the open ended questions sail on by him. His little girl was painted to be a black panther, which was acceptable.

The mother of the birthday girl, Wendy surveyed it all. We hugged her and wrapped an arm around her waist and let her know that they were going to be there for her.

That was true of the kids. That was true of the parents.

We were there to represent.

We were there to support.

Jennifer was a good girl. She didn't cry.

If this has to be borne, it has to borne by the whole clan.

Including Danny and Hadley.

The children ate cupcakes.

Jennifer opened presents. Which were more than generous.

The children hit the piñata.

And when the time came, a big basket of parting gifts came out. Husbands took the kids home. The mothers stayed and cleaned.

Whatever we could do. We said.

We were there for her. For anything.

One person was not there.

Pidge.

Moira was sitting on a park bench. She had one paper shopping bag with her.

Coffin had only just woken up and had stepped outside with a demanding Pip. The old man was having trouble putting all of the clues together.

"Good morning."

"Good morning, Inspector."

He paused.

"How can I help?"

She fumbled. She thought he was going to say something else. Coffin let her sit.

She was in jeans and an Atlantic Cafe sweatshirt. Her white tennis sneakers had turned gray and, if you looked for it, had worn most of the tread off the bottom.

"Inspector," she said.

"Call me Henry."

"Henry, they forced us off of the boat. Our housing has run out."

"I'm not surprised."

"The restaurant doesn't want to house us. They are having….troubles."

"Also, not surprised," Coffin said. "Wait."

She waited.

"You need a place to stay?" Light, he realized, was dawning on Marblehead.

"Yes," she flashed a begging smile.

"Sure," he turned around and opened the front door. "Why don't you go upstairs and pick a bedroom. We'll talk about it later."

"I have money."

"We'll talk."

"I can leave you first and last, then…"

"We'll talk later. There is some barbecue in the refrigerator. Take what you want."

"Oh, I can't," she was crying.

"You're welcome." He beamed, then turned, angled his hat, and headed across the street.

The funeral director, Dickie Lewis, was sitting in his office.

As was true also to the Swains' Real Estate office, Dickie had converted the kitchen at the back into an office. He lived next door in a house built in the forties by a prior funeral director who had the hope and the wealth to expand.

Later, that man sold the business lock, stock, and barrel to Dickie's Dad and moved off island while he could.

Henry knocked on the side door. Dickie stood up, unlocked it, and returned to his chair.

"Afternoon, Inspector. Are you here for business?"

"I'm fine, Dickie."

"Your face isn't ...It's killing me."

Coffin smiled, "Two days and that is the first someone used that joke on me."

"You need to be of a certain age."

The funeral director scratched the black Labrador. Pip acquiesced to it and bore the scratching as best he could. His tail thumped the floor.

The two men smiled at each other.

"Let me ask you a question," Coffin spoke.

Dickie, conscious of all of the news around the old man, nodded.

"What is going on with Pink's body?"

"Nothing."

"Nothing?"

"Well, not here, at least," Dickie said. "His brother lives up in Winthrop and has some big time bank job. When the state coroner released the body, they sent it there."

Coffin nodded.

Dickie turned his computer and searched.

"No death announcement yet. Nothing in the paper or online."

"What does that mean?"

"They are going to be private."

"Don't they need an official death certificate?'

"I am sure the family has that. He got hit with the steamship propeller. Crabs were involved"

Henry stared at him.

Dickie continued, "I was there when they pulled him from the water. They stored him here, then they took him away."

Dickie stopped smiling and examined the old man.

"Did you want to say goodbye?"

"I guess I did."

"You thought he would come back here?"

"I did."

"Brother was next of kin. His call. Probably a cremation. I'll tell you something else that I heard."

"What's that?"

"The brother is getting ready to sell those ten acres. He is on-island right now, getting ready for the yard sale. He may have the ashes with him. You can talk to him, if you want."

CHAPTER THIRTY-THREE

That night, Henry and Danny parked their cruiser on the opposite side of the street from the Brian Swain's home. At two in the morning, no light seeped from the house, nor did any in from any nearby house.

"We shouldn't be here," Danny said.

"No," Coffin agreed. "You're right."

"There's no one here. The girls are with their mother. And Pidge isn't here."

"No," he agreed.

"She might be out in Quaise."

"She might be at the hospital."

"She's not in Boston with Brian."

Henry sighed, "No."

Danny settled back into his seat and let the silence build its cobwebs.

"Poor bastard."

Coffin looked at him.

Danny continued, "His father is a piece of work. Pidge seems to be…questionable. She runs to Brody when Brian needs her."

"It's a tough island."

"It can get tougher. Spotlight is on everyone." Danny added.

"Time will solve that." Henry added.

"Still sucks."

"Nice kids, nice house," Coffin challenged him. "Seems to be on good terms with the ex."

"Money will do that."

"Not always."

Danny had to allow that Henry might know more about that then he did.

"Henry, what happened here?"

The old man sighed.

"Don't do that," The sergeant responded.

"Don't do what?"

"Get all silent and moody. You brought me here for a reason. Let's hear it."

Coffin looked at him. Then he reached into the back seat and scratched the black dog. The day had been long. "Fair enough. Bring a flashlight."

Pip was put on his leash. Coffin led the way into the backyard, with Danny one step behind. The old man stepped up on the back porch, by the hot tub.

"See this?" The Paw Patrol sticker, of the German Shepherd in the police uniform, was still on the doorbell.

"Swain has cameras all around the house. I don't lock my door, but he has cameras."

Because he has kids, Danny silently noted.

"See the sticker?"

"Sure. It's Chase."

"Who?"

"The name of the dog, on Paw Patrol."

"The things you know," the old man commented. "That sticker is covering the camera that looks straight in back of the house. I watched video from the last three days. This camera blacked out in the afternoon before he overdosed. And his daughters didn't do it."

"You've seen the video."

"I have."

"The cameras didn't happen to catch a sneak-thief."

"They did not. They have blind spots and someone was clever."

"Okay."

Pip was sniffing around on the deck. The sergeant looked at the dog.

"Do you suppose someone dropped a hot dog?"

"Possible."

The dog was walking in tight circles.

"The reports aren't back yet."

"Your friends on the state police may not prioritize this."

"No, but…"

"But."

"Someone snuck in the house, in the afternoon, dosed up the cream for the coffee, then left."

"Someone."

"Yeah."

"His Dad?"

"Did he seem capable of being this sneaky"

"Probably not."

"Walk with me."

Pip was on the case. He continued to sniff his way across the back yard.

Coffin walked straight out into the darkness. Danny lit the way for him, all the way to the edge of the yard. Then Pip began picking his way through the beach grasses and bushes. The two of them stepped in about ten paces, behind three scrub pines. Coffin squatted down.

Pip continued sniffing in the grass.

"Are you going to be able to get up, old man?"

"With your help," Coffin allowed. "When I was watching the videos, these trees didn't move in the wind. When I came out here, the grass was worn down. Someone was watching."

"Pip thinks so."

"Unless they throw hot dogs out here."

"I think that's unlikely."

The dog did not stop.

"Brody?" Danny suggested. Henry was looking with warmth at his dog.

"The spurned lover? He goes up to Boston to sweep Pidge away, she sends him off, he comes down and takes aim at Brian. And he hits. Brian overdoses in the bathroom."

"Next to the 'Eternal Brutherhood' wrapper," he said. "Kind of clumsy."

"Would have worked. A heavy does of Fentanyl was in him for twenty minutes. If he had been dead, right after everything that had happened, it could have worked. Overdose victim, drug package, bathroom. Who is going to check the cream for the coffee."

"Sure." Danny nodded. "Can you prove any of this?"

"Not unless he was very clumsy with anything inside. I don't think he was."

"Brody," he concluded. "What about Pidge?"

"I don't know."

The two men stood in the high grass. Pip had another trail to follow, but Henry pulled him back. The dog sat.

Danny clicked off his flashlight. The night filled in around them. Their eyes opened to the stars. The Milky Way streaked a stream across the sky. The crickets continued to chirp and the ocean moved and sighed against the far off sand.

Then a car came up Cliff Road and the moment suspended. Both men walked back to the squad car.

CHAPTER THIRTY-FOUR

They got the call at six in the morning.

Without a word, Danny put the big car in gear and drove out of the Lifesaving parking lot. The rain had held off for Jennifer's birthday party, but it had slipped in early in the morning and was dropping in a wet monotony.

They knew where they were going. They did not hurry. Ronnie would be waiting.

They arrived before the E.M.T.'s. Pip did not leave the car.

Nancy held the door open for them. She was in sweatpants and a purple Disney sweatshirt. Both children had been tucked away upstairs.

Ronnie lay on the kitchen floor. Coffin squatted down and felt his pulse.

Nothing.

He looked up at Nancy.

She had her arms crossed.

The dishwasher was open and half full. They went through a lot of bowls and not many plates. "God Bless this Mess" was affixed to the window over the kitchen.

"He's gone, Nancy."

"Well, I'm sorry for it. He was a good man."

Coffin looked up at her.

"You took the phones from the kids, didn't you?"

"No."

"You waited to call us until you were sure he was dead."

"That is a horrible thing to say," she sniffed. "To me, especially."

"But it's not untrue."

The E.M.T.'s walked in the front door. Danny looked at her. "How long had he been down?"

"Ten minutes."

"Okay."

He presented the Naloxone spray and shot it up his nose. Ronnie's body shook.

The E.M.T.'s immediately began unpacking the defibrillator.

Coffin steered her into the living room.

"He shot the last two mortgage checks into his arm."

Henry was quiet. In the breakfront, wine glasses, dishes, and china bells. Behind it all was a set of silver spoons.

"Nancy, he just needs treatment."

"We're going to my mother's. She lives up in Skowhegan, in Maine."

"Nancy..."

"He's gone, Henry," she said. "He's been gone for a long time."

"Nobody's gone."

But the E.M.T.'s had put him on the gurney and were taking him out the front door. He appeared to be a little pink. Danny stood by the stairs watching his partner in the dining room. The two kids appeared at the top of the stairs.

Say goodbye to Daddy, kids.

Both officers followed the ambulance to the hospital. Both cars ran the lights and sirens through the wet morning. The cars and trucks along Old South Road pulled aside.

The ambulance backed into the special parking bay with the doors open. As soon as it stopped, the personnel began the process of reviving Ronnie.

Pidge pushed this gurney from the head. She, the team, and Ronnie disappeared into the hospital.

Danny parked and Coffin left the car.

The sergeant remained with the puppo and was glad to be among the living

Nurse Stein stood behind the administrative desk. She signed a series of papers on an aluminum clipboard. She handed the clipboard back to the E.M.T. and he headed back to the ambulance. She loomed half a head taller than the Inspector, and about six inches broader in the chest. She had worked the Emergency Room for ten years and had, in that time, exhausted her supply of smiles.

"Morning, Henry."

"Ellen."

"I don't know anything you don't know about our most recent admit," she said.

"His name is Ronnie Folger. He was a mason. He lived out on Daffodil. Two kids."

"I'm sorry to hear."

"Me, too."

"Nancy waited before she called us."

Ellen nodded, "I can't imagine."

She was looking at papers on her desk.

"How can I help you, Henry?"

"Is Pidge working in the emergency room?"

"Just for this admit. She picked up a shift upstairs on the floor with Gabby. The two of them are thick as thieves. When we have an emergency like this, we pull someone down."

"She's been here all night?"

"At the hospital? I assume so. I've been here all night. She s driving the fiancee's big SUV around. Getting a feel for it. I haven't seen it move."

"Okay."

"If you wait a few minutes, she can tell you the bad news herself."

At seven-thirty, the medical team felt they had done as much as they could. Dr. Tupper called it. Ronnie Folger had left us.

When Pidge came downstairs to the emergency room with the papers, Henry Coffin remained in the waiting room. Pidge remembered what Ellen Stein had told her about the old man a month ago.

He had the right last name.

When they returned to Daffodil Lane, the door was still open. The rain was caught in the wind and blew over the house, leaving the doorway dry. At this hour of the morning, after the long feast of death, Coffin did not particularly want to go in and engage Nancy.

Danny thought they could just flash a thumbs-up.

Instead the old man, without his rain poncho, slumped up the walkway with the news.

While he was inside, the high school called the police switchboard. Paul Brody hadn't come to school for two days and he didn't answer his phone. Would they check?

When they pulled into the dirt driveway in Quaise, a cloud of seagulls rose from the side of the house. They called out, screaming and squawking, and then spun about and landed on a nearby roof.

Pip was up and ready and barking at the birds. His yelps filled the car.

"Call the ambulance." Henry said.

"Do you want help?"

Coffin sighed. "Not right now."

He did not open the dog for Pip to come out, even though Pip was throwing himself at it.

Coffin walked around the house. Three brave seagulls perched on the railing of the porch. One stood on one of the PVC fishing pole holder Paul had installed for his sick father.

And there he was. Free from the gulls. Free from the crows that sat in the trees on the other side of the road. Paul Brody, son of Elliot, graduate of Groton and Connecticut College, U.S. Army Ranger, member of the Massachusetts Bar, and English teacher at Nantucket High School.

The pitcher had been knocked over, as had the glass. Its contents had spilled and all but washed away in the rain. Blood had dripped under his body.

Danny left the car and joined the Inspector on the deck.

He had nothing to say.

For their own sakes, they kept the birds away until the ambulance arrived. They took their pictures, bagged their evidence, and stood watch, alive, in the driving rain.

Coffin had no eulogy for the man. It was another loss in a month of losses.

With the body wrapped in plastic, the ambulance drove away. Danny and Henry left the porch to the wind, the rain, and the birds.

CHAPTER THIRTY-FIVE

The two men did their best to sleep through Friday. They took two routes to that. Danny, for his part, had some CBD gummies that Sherrie had picked up off island. For some quirk of the law, marijuana products could be legal in Massachusetts, but they couldn't cross the federal waters to Nantucket. Either way, in the pleasant float of a cherry flavored CBD jelly duck, Danny drifted off to sleep.

Henry had to bear witness, but he didn't need to do it sober. Moira was working the lunch shift. So, Henry and his ancestor Zenas, lined up the three wise men: Johnny Walker, Jim Beam, and Jack Daniels. They reviewed the butcher's bill. The recent ones appeared before him, as if Hermes was leading them in a last walk down to Hades: Palmer, Caroline, Meaghan, Pink, the Russian, Ronnie, and, with pride of place, Paul Brody. He drank to all of them.

Pip slept easily.

"No more," Henry asked. "No more."

Zenas wouldn't promise anything.

Coffin climbed the ancient stairs, lay down fully clothed, and let the bed spin him to sleep.

"Henry, you don't look good."

Coffin sat in the passenger seat of the old police cruiser.

"It was a tough afternoon."

"I slept through it." Danny responded/

"Me, too."

Pip had a good afternoon. He was ready for the night. Both men were glad for the dog's presence.

Coffin nodded. Danny started to back out of the spot. As the calendar inched closer to Columbus Day, the weekends became busier. Apparently, the inns and restaurants had a sliding scale for weddings that kept increasing as soon as you broke into the month of October. At eleven in the evening, the cars and cabs were bringing the happy parents home from the rehearsal dinner at Lola and sending the younger ones out to the Chicken Box. We love that they have a good time, and are happy to write the check. Sometimes, however, we would love the quiet of fog and the peace of the dark.

"We have some water and some Tylenol," Danny suggested.

"No thanks."

"It wasn't a suggestion. It was an order."

"An order?"

"A request from Hadley's Dad."

"Wow. You want to pull rank like that?"

"Your beat-to-shit, hungover face is a little much even for me."

Danny began to head out east to their spot by the Shipwreck Museum. Coffin had just opened the glove compartment. "Nope," he interrupted the drive. "We have to go to Cliff Road."

Danny adjusted his thoughts while the old man swallowed three pills and drank some water.

"Drink all of that water, old man."

"Why?"

"Your breath is a problem," he said. "Who are we bothering tonight?"

"Pidge."

"You don't think she has enough on her mind."

"She killed Brody."

Danny didn't say anything, because the old man was right.

Although he had ridden with the old man for years, Danny hadn't really figured out what Coffin did that was so special. On island, Henry Coffin was as famous as the lighthouses and as regular as the ferry; the old man might miss a few trips, but generally he was right. He knew all of the year-rounders, they knew him. And they all owed him a favor.

But that wasn't all of it. People who should know better gave Henry their story, and he gave them his forgiveness. When he walked into a room, it fell quiet. Then people listened. Danny didn't really know why.

In his time—in this time—you could say that Henry had white man's privilege. And he did. He was old, he was rich, he was limited to that view. Coffin would answer the charge, were it ever brought to him, that to whom much is given, much is expected. It was true, but it wasn't the whole answer.

Perhaps, the reasoning was simple. Coffin didn't lie, either by omission or by commission. He wasn't going to say something untrue and he wasn't going to let the truth go and hide behind a look, a sheet, or the grave. How often do you find an honest man? Perhaps his privilege allowed that, the money, the community, the times. But he lived the truth: He walked the path. He was going to show up, knock on the door, and speak truth.

That's what they were doing.

The Swain house had lost the police tape. The "Swain" car was parked in the driveway, right next to the path to the front door. One set of lights was on on the ground floor, including the flashing green light of the big TV screen.

Coffin rubbed the scruff of the dog's neck. He slowly rose. Coffin leashed him and led him outside of the car. The dog shook himself awake.

Coffin knocked the softly at the door. Danny stood behind him, and Pip was before him.

After a moment, he knocked again.

Eventually, the door opened.

"Inspector? Danny?"

Sergeant Abraham sighed at the slight. No one would use is title. He should call himself "Tonto."

Pip looked up.

"And who are you?" She exclaimed.

"This is Pip," Danny introduced.

"Pip!" She bloomed. "What a wonderful name."

"He tries to be a good dog."

"I bet he is a good dog. Bring him into the kitchen."

She was wearing sweatpants and a t-shirt. Both men watched her, then followed the dog.

She opened the refrigerator, found a piece of ham, and turned to the dog.

"Sit."

Pip, who was a Good Boy, sat.

The ham arced. He leapt up and grabbed it.

"Pidge, do you have a moment?" Coffin asked.

"Of course."

Danny and Coffin looked around the crime scene. All remnants of the crime scene were gone. The kitchen gleamed.

"Actually, I was hoping we could sit out back. Danny and I very much enjoy your back yard. I think Pip would like it."

"O-kay," She questioned. "Can I get you anything?"

Before Danny could refuse, Henry spoke. 'Two coffees would be great, if you have them."

She smirked. "It will take a few minutes to get the pot going. When I am not working, I don't drink coffee at night. Do you want some cookies or a piece of cheesecake?"

"Some cookies would be very nice," Coffin said.

Pidge eyed him. As did Danny. This seemed odd.

"Why don't you make your way out there?'

"Of course."

Coffin led his partner through the hallway, the living room, and out the sliding glass doors to the back porch. Pip remained alert for another fallen hot dog.

"Henry, you could have asked her for some time in the hot tub?"

"I didn't bring my suit."

"Maybe tomorrow."

"Perhaps."

He turned and saw that Chase remained stuck to the button/camera. Coffin thought about peeling it off with his thumb, but this seemed unnecessary.

Instead, the two men crossed the patio to the Adirondack chairs. Coffin found a third one and a small table. He set together a small gathering at the edge of a very well-maintained yard. The table was between all three chairs, but they angled themselves so you looked out over the grass. Even in late October, the Hydrangea swung their heavy blue heads.

Coffin sat in the middle, with his partner on his right.

"Henry, she isn't going to drug us, is she?"

"The staties took the cream."

"Well, why wouldn't she drug us?"

"Why would she?"

Because she was a murderer, Danny thought.

The night remained as still and as quiet. The rain had passed to the northeast, leaving only the starless dark. Two of the neighbors had returned for the weekend. Out over the sound, the lights of a deep sea fishing boat made its way through the channel, out to George's Bank.

They heard the doors slide open and shut. Pidge had put on a pink polar fleece jacket and a pair of white crocs. She was holding a tray with two hands. It had a pitcher of coffee, three mugs, and a selection of Nilla Wafers. She walked carefully across the grass and then, with relief, set the tray down.

Henry made himself some coffee. He poured some cream into it.

Danny remained confused, but made his as well. Pidge waited for the two of them to finish before she finished the pot.

"Pidge, my partner is afraid that you have slipped some fentanyl into his cream. I told him that you wouldn't do that to us, would you?'

"Your both too big for me to move."

"That's true," Danny allowed.

"Do you want the lights on?" she asked.

"No," Coffin spoke over the lip of his mug.

"No?"

"No. Why should we wake up Brian?"

"Suit yourself," she said.

"I'm pretty sure you don't want Brian to hear this. But if you want us to tell him…"

"No," she allowed. "That's fine." She was starting to appreciate how difficult this was going to be.

Pip wandered over to the soon-to-be bride and sat at her feet. It had been good ham. She reached out and scratched him under the ears.

"Pidge, I am going to tell you what I think. Unless you have been really sloppy, there is no way I can prove any of this," Henry said. "After I speak, you can decide what you want to do, if anything."

"Okay," she drew that out. "I haven't done…"

"Pidge, let's speak truth out here, okay? No lawyers, no recordings, no statements, no witnesses. Just us. It's all I ask."

The night filled the quiet.

"Fine," she said. "Go ahead. Say what you want."

"Let me ask you a question. Why did you come to Nantucket?"

"A good paying job popped up. I grabbed it."

Coffin bowed his head. He started wrong. He asked her a question when he knew that answer. Now she was defensive because he thought he was smart.

"Pidge, I'm sorry."

"Okay."

"Pidge, after J.T. Palmer died, I asked questions. I found out that you came to Nantucket from the Neonatal Intensive Care Unit at Brigham and Women's Hospital in Boston. You were a surgical nurse…"

"Physician's Assistant."

"Thank you. You were very, very high on the totem pole at that hospital. All of your references sing about you. You are qualified to work in the top hospitals in the world. You came here."

"I did. For my reasons."

"I am coming to that," Coffin smiled.

Pidge settled back.

"You had a doctor who you worked with. The head of pediatric surgery. Ted Driscoll. The two of you were professionally close. The rumors are you were having an affair. Not a surprise. You are young, he is a doctor with a history And he and his wife have a house out here on Meadowbrook Road."

She nodded.

"Then, he transferred to Mary Hitchcock in New Hampshire last May."

"Last January," she corrected him. "I've been on island for about nine months."

"I'm sorry. That's right." Coffin made a note on his yellow legal pad. "Right around the same time he left, one of the younger nurses, Peter Wright, also disappeared. You and Peter volunteered together in some clinics in Chelsea. The two of you worked with addicts."

She nodded again.

"I have a picture of Doctor Driscoll and you at the memorial service they had for Peter." Coffin turned and faced his partner. "Peter committed suicide and overdosed. His body was found in the Charles River. His mother thought that Peter had proposed to you and you refused him."

"Can I talk?" Pidge interrupted.

"Sure," Coffin leaned back.

"All true," she admitted. "Peter loved me, I liked him. We worked together. Ted and I were together at the time. Ted wasn't going to leave his wife and I didn't want him to. But that doesn't mean that Peter was right."

"He did commit suicide?"

"He died, Inspector. Had I been there, I would have stopped him."

"The autopsy suggested he died before he hit the water."

"He died. I am sorry he is gone. He was more than a good man. Poor addicts in Boston have missed him. And I miss him."

"I'm sure."

Pip heard the note in her voice. He looked at her and cocked his head. She returned to scratching him.

Someone else, Danny thought, would have a pinch of sarcasm in that comment, but not Henry. He was sorry that Peter had died many months ago.

"So, you left your job and your history in Boston. Dr. Driscoll wrote you a glowing recommendation, made a few calls, and you moved down here."

"Correct."

"You rented Driscoll's house?"

"Yeah. Big mistake."

Coffin looked over.

"Ted and I were done. As long as I was in one of his houses, we weren't."

"You started dating Brian over the summer?"

"I would like to change that to Brian started dating me."

"Whats's the difference?"

"One way, it sounds like I was a siren drawing him in, the other sounds as if he was seeking me out. I didn't entrap him."

"Sure."

"Really."

Coffin put his notes aside, took a moment, and looked at her. "Yes, of course, you didn't entrap him. Brian came to you."

"We met in the hospital. Big Jim was having heart problems and Brian brought him in. Little blue pills brought hurt the Jim's heart. Brian kept coming by. Then he asked for my phone number."

"You moved in about six months ago."

"I did."

Coffin looked up.

"A girl needs a place to live. I couldn't very well stay at Driscoll's and date another man," she said. "I am told that many relationships get fast-forwarded like that out here. Trust me, if I could have bought a little condo so we could have some time and privacy, that would have been great. I wouldn't have to live with all the shit his family has thrown."

Henry paused. Danny nodded. "We are familiar with the family you are marrying into."

"Dad's the worst, but not the only, problem."

Coffin chose his words. "Brian Swain is not an easy man to marry. First, there is the bright spotlight that he travels in on the island, then there are his daughters and their mother, and then," he looked at his partner. "There is Big Jim."

"Don't forget Gramma. And the rest of the women. And Rosemary."

"Okay," Coffin felt his narrative slip in his hands. "This fall, I met you in the Emergency Room with J.T. Palmer. You were on the night shift."

"Yes."

"I assume you were on the night shift, as an engaged women, because you were unsure of your marriage."

"You're being very delicate, Henry." Pidge smiled.

"Then you killed Miss Palmer."

Pidge didn't move.

Pip kept looking into her face.

Coffin let the moment sit. He was sure she wouldn't confirm nor deny.

Coffin elaborated,"Miss Palmer, although beloved on the island, had had a catastrophic stroke. She would have died, shrunken and alone, off island. She is not the first old person not to survive the night before their trip to a rest home."

Pidge did not speak.

The dog re-shifted his weight and waited for the Nice Lady to keep scratching.

"Sometime in there, you started seeing Paul Brody. Post-Langueduc?"

She nodded.

"Paul Brody was an addict, of course. He got Oramorph prescribed to him from the V.A. although he may not have needed it as much as he used it. You were still engaged to Brian but something happened downtown. Then we met the two of you on Polpis Road."

"The Swains happened," she said.

"Of course."

"Then we met you again when we went out to talk to Paul about Caroline."

"I don't know anything about her."

Henry glanced at his partner.

Pidge repeated herself. "I don't know anything about her."

"Sure." Coffin said. "Paul must have been a hard bargain."

She looked at her ringed hand.

"Paul was an addict. That way only ends one way, Henry, as you know well. I will say this for Paul, he wasn't the Swains. When I was with him, nobody was sizing me up and waiting for the moment to knife me. That's what I learned at the Langueduc. Even a blowjob couldn't get Brian off that stage."

Henry looked uncomfortable.

"Paul had no stage. I could hide there. It was great."

"Except he was an addict. Was he trying to quit?"

"Sure."

"That's why you poured the lemonade out."

"He mixed it with Oramorph. He said he was trying to stop. They are always trying to stop."

"Getting them to stop is your new job."

"It is."

"And you were in a familiar position. Between two men."

Pidge was quiet for a moment.

Pip was feeling abandoned. He returned to the Inspector and lay at his feet.

"I suppose so," she said. "The situations are different."

"One man is a secret that you have to maintain, the other is a public pillar. Not all that different."

She paused for a moment.

"I don't think of it like that."

"Okay."

She flashed. "What do you mean 'Okay?' You weren't there. You don't know."

Coffin finished his coffee. He dropped his tone.

"At least twice in your life, you've been in relationships with two men at the same time. One of those men lived a very public life—Brian, Ted, the other lived a very private one—

Paul, Peter. For the man in public life, you could be a secret sin. For the man in private life, you could hide with him."

He settled himself.

"And in each case, you killed the one that would have made your life uncomfortable."

Still riding her adrenaline and anger, she gazed in wonder at the old man. And his dog.

"I didn't kill Peter. He killed himself."

"He overdosed."

"Yes."

"And you didn't kill Paul? He overdosed as well."

"He's an addict. It's different."

"A lot of people around you overdose."

"I am a nurse. I work with addicts and sick people."

Danny leaned in.

"We got to Paul a day after he overdosed. He was on the porch. Crows. Seagulls. Morning. Afternoon. Night. Morning. Then we came. It won't be an open casket"

She put a ringed hand on her face.

Coffin added to his partner. "So you know, I would also like to believe that Brody tried to kill your fiancee. When I watched the videos, I see some motion in the woods right in front of us, there is a sticker on the outdoor camera, and there were traces of Fentanyl in the half and half. Brody, I assume, snuck in, dumped something in the carton, and snuck out. My operating theory is that Paul went to Boston to ask you to marry him, or run away with him, or whatever. You bounced him out, and he came here to eliminate the competition."

"Seems to make sense," Danny said. "Although we never saw him on the videos. And there are no fingerprints on the creamer. Yours were there, of course."

"She lives here now." Coffin responded.

"Yup. To be expected. Not a surprise."

"A lot of people around Pidge overdose." The old man added.

"Not a surprise, either."

"You think I tried to kill Brian?" She barked.

"No, I just told you," Coffin said. "We think your friend, Brody did it."

"Even though he isn't on camera and has no fingerprints."

"He used gloves," she insisted.

"Of course." Henry looked at her over his notes. "That's why there were no fingerprints, at all, on the drug package we found in the trash. No drugs on the wrapper, either. You'd think there would be traces on that."

"Nothing. No traces, no drugs," Danny agreed.

They were out of coffee and cookies.

The crickets has returned to their song. Out in the sound, the fishing boat had passed out of sight, on its way to Great Point, and the dark Atlantic.

"What do you want?" she asked.

"Did you talk to Paul after I left the other night?"

"A little."

"How did he explain our arrival?"

"He said you guys were trying to pin Caroline's death on him."

"You have heard of her." Coffin noted. "Earlier, you said you didn't."

"What does it matter?" she said. "Caroline is dead. You two think Paul killed her. She's dead. Paul is dead." Her voice sizzled and crackled. "What do you want?"

Danny looked at Henry. He remained as calm as the night. Pip also looked at Henry and not at the woman who gave him ham.

"Pidge," he said. "We are just about done."

"I should have a lawyer."

"Probably not," Danny added. "If I know anything…"

She looked to the black man with some interest.

"Pidge," Henry said. "Danny and I had a similar conversation with Paul that we are having here with you. We know that Paul did not kill Caroline, yet she overdosed in his house. He did lie to us and he did hide her body, so there is that. Paul and I had come to an understanding. He was going to fund a generous trust fund for Caroline's son, Michael. In acknowledgement of the role he played in her death. He was a very rich man, thanks to his Dad. The money would have been easy for him."

Coffin was whispering.

"I assume he died before he made those arrangements. His death may have been in him as we spoke."

The Inspector let the bugs and the ocean make their noises.

Two seagulls took up position on a neighbor's roof. Danny made a point of looking at them, so Pidge turned and followed his eyes. She shuddered.

"You have a choice," Coffin continued. "You can pretend we never visited, keep up your life, and hope your luck holds when we send the state and hospital people in to discreetly check to make sure the pharmacology logs are spic and span."

"We just had a drug bust out here. Makes sense to check the supply." Danny mentioned.

Coffin nodded to his partner.

"Or, you could write a confession, go, and sin no more."

"You didn't kill anyone. The court would have a hard time doing much. Perhaps they could take your licenses," Danny suggested. "Just a slap on the wrist. Brian would understand."

Coffin left those two suggestions out there. Both cases would result in headlines, Facebook threads, and whispers in the grocery store for the rest of her life on Nantucket. And she couldn't leave if she lost her license. Unless she wanted to live in her car and work for Amazon warehouses in Utah.

"Or," Coffin added. "You could resign your position at the hospital in…let's say….six weeks. Send them a letter tomorrow with a date certain. I am sure it would be taken with great reluctance, but understanding. You are marrying a very busy man, with two little girls right now."

She nodded.

"You need to be sure—very sure—that nobody close to you overdoses in the future. We are going to be very interested in preventing that."

"Do you know how hard I had to work, what I had to do in order to get my ticket?" Pidge demanded.

"No," Danny said. "But I know what your boyfriend looked like with his eyes pecked out."

She shuddered.

Coffin looked at her. He remembered Brody's cheeks.

"I think your choice is pretty clear. I think you have made it already." Coffin said.

"It will be a lot easier when you're pregnant." Danny mentioned

"I'm not pregnant."

"You had to give Brian a sign of commitment, didn't you?" Coffin added. "You came back to him after Boston, didn't you? You live here now, you are wearing his ring, but you had to give him a token. Something to tell him that you were his."

"Until the morning, at least." Danny commented.

"She didn't poison him, remember?"

"Oh. Right. Sorry."

Pidge looked at the black man with an edge of fury and anger.

Coffin spoke and took her attention. "We searched the house after Brian overdosed. It was a crime scene. So we found the IUD."

"And we made a reasonable conclusion."

"Then, you and I met in the hospital. I am glad I was awake to talk to you. You are as well." Coffin allowed.

The meaning was not lost on her.

"Then, while your love and the possible father of your baby was in the hospital off-island, you shared a bed with Paul Brody," Coffin said.

"We made a reasonable conclusion there as well."

"Then he died. Overdose."

"But there is a reasonable question…" Danny suggested.

Coffin let the moment run.

"Time will tell." Henry summarized.

"It always does." Danny echoed.

She put her hand on her stomach.

Coffin stood and Danny and Pip followed. Henry collected the empty dishes and mugs, put them on the serving tray and carried it inside. Pidge remained outside, considering the gulls.

CHAPTER THIRTY-SIX

Paul Brody had no will, no last instructions, no bequests.

Out there in the world, he may have a cousin or an aunt who could, in the end, claim him, his investment portfolio, and his house. The realtors were already interested, they circled the property like seagulls. Brian Swain had sent his lawyer, Herman Lamb, to make discreet inquiries. We weren't surprised; it was a phenomenal piece of property.

Nonetheless, Paul Brody was a public school teacher. True, his death was one of despair. The last thing the island wants is for its children to absorb the suicide, then think of it as an option. It would be far better to just announce that Brody had died alone or a heart attack or an aneurysm and let his body get shipped off island. But, he hadn't been thinking of the kids when he died.

So, his death become a teachable moment. He died of a stroke, we decided. The appropriate rumors popped up. Someone found Narcan in his desk. He had been a soldier and had gone to war. He was sick. He was addicted. We saw him at the hospital.

As a teachable moment, Brody couldn't be waked at Dickie's Funeral Home, so they put the closed casket in St. Mary's Church. The faculty, the school committee, the superintendent, and the P.T.A. sent flowers. The Opioid Crisis Clinic at the hospital also sent flowers. We admired them.

We declared a half day off on Tuesday. We taught the kids appropriate behavior on Monday, then walked with them after school down to the church. Many cried. Some had written poems. Some had made paper flowers.

On Tuesday, Father Nunes led a mass and a funeral at noon with most of the school. Coffin, Jon-Jon, and Danny sat in their usual seats at St. Mary's. Father Nunes kept looking at the Inspector as the old man ignored the instructions to stand, sit, and kneel. After the mass, they drove in front of the hearse up to the St. Paul's burial ground. They buried Paul next to his father, Elliot. We all walked up to the graveyard and watched him get lowered into the ground. The VFW played Taps and folded a flag. They gave it to the principal.

Pidge stayed away.

It was a good lesson for the kids. We knew they would need it.

The school was somber until Friday. Then it was just school again.

.

After the burial, the three men sat in a dark Chicken Box. Without the weight of duty or anyone to hide from, Henry drank his whiskey neat. Danny carried that public weight, so he had a cup of coffee. Jon-Jon stood on the other side of the bar and waited for the other two to speak.

"We have seen our share of death." Jon-Jon observed.

"Probably not yet," Danny allowed.

Coffin looked at him.

"We have an island full of heroin addicts," the sergeant explained. "Addicts die," he said. "Often."

Jon-Jon nodded. He had heard the rumors about the teacher.

"Ronnie had people. Meaghan. Caroline. They all had people." Coffin said.

"Victims," Danny replied.

"They kept Ronnie alive."

"Or did he try to kill them. Or harm them," Danny added, with a share of anger. "Think of those two kids. Calling every time Dad falls down. Then, Mom keeps their phones and Daddy dies in a pile of shit on the kitchen floor. How do you live with that? Or what about the two Swain girls. Dad collapses on Thursday. Happy Birthday Friday." Danny felt the darkness roll.

"He wasn't an addict."

"What do the girls know?" Danny snarled. "Do you think they are going to keep looking for Dad's stash? What do they think every time he goes to the bathroom? Should Ronnie's kid show them how it is done?"

Coffin cast his eyes on his partner. Jon-Jon refilled his glass. The Inspector looked at his bartender. "Did you want kids?"

"Sure."

"What happened?"

"Life. Biology. Now, we are too old."

Coffin nodded. "I miss him."

Both of the other men fell to silence. The knew who he referred to.

The old man continued. "He would have been with all those kids today. He would have been in Brody's class, maybe. I would have been looking for him at the funeral, or on the walk. He would have friends or a girlfriend."

"Or a boyfriend," Danny chipped in.

"Wouldn't have mattered" Coffin sipped. "We measure time in children. When you don't have children, you don't have time."

"Or you have too much time." Jon-Jon added.

"You two are full of shit."Danny said.

That night Coffin did not need to patrol. Danny had dropped him off after the Chicken Box and he settled into his house.

He read.

He puttered.

He scratched his dog.

He poured himself three whiskeys.

He read the paper.

Full of whiskey, he drifted off to sleep in his king-sized and ancient bed.

Then, at two in the morning, he heard his front door open. After a confused moment, he identified the footsteps. Moira.

Pip woke up and the old man shushed him.

She put something in the refrigerator, then climbed the stairs. She went to the bathroom. When she sat on her bed, she sighed. Her shoes came off in two thuds.

Then, in a long moment, she was asleep and snoring.

The silence had retreated.

CHAPTER THIRTY-SEVEN

Danny drove to Duxbury. They could have borrowed a squad car from the Hyannis Police, but that wasn't the Inspector's way. Instead, they rented a a white Ford with black interior, bluetooth, and a small dent in the rear quarter. Danny felt like they should stop at McDonald's, and then go to the mall to see what they had on sale at the Gap. Perhaps they could get a Cinnabon. We know that s what the kids do when they go off island.

It was the last little bit of work. Neither man much relished it. The Inspector could have avoided it, but it wasn't his way and he wasn't wrong about that. For Danny, it meant a return to the mainland, Dunkin Donuts, and bringing back Chinese food from Hyannis.

Henry did not have much to say. Instead, the old man watched the traffic pass. Eventually they came to a twelve story cement block a half mile from Plymouth. Danny had made the old man call ahead. It wasn't Nantucket, he said. You just didn't show up and see if they are home.

Colonial Corners was neither colonial, nor a corner. But the parking lot was full of recently built cars, the lobby was clean, and the elevator didn't moan.

Apartment 225 was down the hall from 223, where grandma was getting ready for Halloween. She had a Halloween floor mat, a black cat on the door, and a witch statue that cackled when you walked past. Duxbury must be different, Danny thought. In Boston, that wouldn't have lasted the night.

Henry was carrying what he had of Caroline's in the same paper bag that it had been handed to him. It even still had Moira's phone number on it. With Danny behind him (and in uniform), he pressed the bell.

When Susan answered, she was in sweatpants and a "Barnacle Bill Clam Bar" work shirt. She examined both of them.

"Inspector," she said to Henry.

Coffin paused, "You remember Sergeant Danny Abraham."

"Of course. Your name slipped"

"No problem," he nodded.

"Can we come in?"

"Of course. I don't have to go to work until four."

"Is Michael...?"

"No," she said. "He is still in a hospital. But as soon as they stabilize his meds, I have a room for him."

"How sick is he?" Coffin asked, still standing.

"I don't know. He has a lot of anxiety. Naturally."

She gestured to a longish white sofa. Her living room had a large television opposite the sofa and a chair, but the sliding glass doors of the porch looked out over the parking lot, several tree-lined streets and, in the distance, Massachusetts Bay.

"You're here about Caroline."

"Yes," Coffin answered.

"She's dead."

"To the best of our knowledge, yes."

"What the fuck does that mean?"

"We don't have her body."

Susan opened a pack of Marlboros and lit one.

"What do you know?" She asked from a cloud.

"We think that…"

"What do you know? Don't treat me like some fucking idiot."

Coffin sighed.

"We have heard a recording that seems to include your sister's last words. On the recording, she was shooting up with a guy, then they both pass out. She dies afterwards. Overdose."

"How do you know?"

Danny leaned forward. "Ma'am, when people die, their last breath tends to some out like a cough. We heard that."

Susan looked at the black man as if he was a particularly large bug.

"Did you know that your sister was a Confidential Informant?" Coffin added.

"It doesn't surprise me."

Coffin nodded.

"She had a recording device. It recorded her all of the time."

"All the time?"

"As long as she had her phone."

She nodded.

"So, who killed her?"

"She overdosed."

"Okay, but who killed her?"

"The man she was with has also died."

"Did he kill her?"

"I don't know," Coffin said. "It doesn't matter."

"It matters to me."

"Somebody put the needle into your sister and pushed the plunger. Could have been him. Could have been her. They are both dead."

"You found him."

"He was lying on his porch, also overdosed." Coffin added.

"But he got rid of her body?"

Coffin nodded.

"Where?"

"He didn't tell us."

"Have you looked?" Her tears wet her cheeks.

Coffin let her sit for a moment.

After she recovered her breath, she asked him again.

"Where is she?"

"We don't know. The guy she was with had a boat."

"Have you looked on it!" She barked.

"Yes."

Coffin let the silence answer her.

Susan got up after a moment and walked into her bathroom. When she came out, she had a packet of folded toilet paper in her hand as well as more tears on her cheek.

"What about that spoiled fuck?"

"He didn't have anything to do with it."

"Bullshit."

"The State Police might contact your lawyer on that."

"Probably won't."

Coffin let the silence answer that as well.

"The bitch suffered." she finally said.

Coffin nodded. "It must have been hard."

"You don't know the half of it."

"I'm sure," he said. "In the end, she would've gotten what she wanted."

Susan hung her head. "What?"

"You. Michael," Coffin said. "Everything that happened this summer got her her money. It got the state to give her her kid back."

"Well, she can't get him. She's dead."

"You're not."

She didn't look up.

"You're an asshole, aren't you?" she said. "I thought it was the big black bastard, but it's you."

Coffin sat back.

"My sister is dead, but she left me this great fucking apartment and her deeply damaged son."

"She paid."

"She paid a fuck of a lot."

"She did."

"What the fuck am I supposed to do now?"

"Help. Help him."

The pad of toilet paper had fallen apart.

"Well, fuck you and fuck him and fuck your island and fuck the staties and fuck Christmas and fuck the boat and fuck the sluts who lived with her. Fuck you and fuck everybody. Get the fuck out."

Coffin left the bag on the coffee table and walked out with Danny.

CHAPTER THIRTY EIGHT

At seven in the evening, Coffin heard a knock at the door. During the summer, occasionally, a tourist would stop and want a tour of his house. Most recently, it had been a charming woman in blue sweat pants, a matching sweater, and a straw hat. She was with an older man with some sort of protective black glasses. They had been confused of course, but Coffin was amused and gave them a tour of his dirty kitchen. They seemed nice.

Pip had trotted to the door and was barking at it.

Tonight, Brian Swain stood in his doorway. He seemed to be coming home from work, with a blue blazer, pink pants, and cuff links. In spite of his polish, he looked a bit anxious.

"Brian. Nice to see you."

"Thanks, Inspector. Can we talk?"

"Sure."

Pip ducked around the younger man's legs, then placed himself halfway through. Brian had more important things on his mind, but he stopped, bent over, and scratched Pip with energy and vigor. The dog walked out of the hold between his legs, came around and re-entered the space between his legs.

"Your dog likes the five hole."

"The five hole?"

"A goalie has five places where the puck can come through, each hand, each leg, and the space between his legs; the five hole."

Brian gave him three more scratches and then walked on. Pip followed him.

The old man led both guest and dog through the kitchen into the formal sitting room.

The kitchen had taken on a new look. The sinks was clean, the counters were clean, and somehow a teapot waited on the back burner of the stove. Moira had been putting beer in the refrigerator.

Coffin rarely visited the sitting room, but he suspected the realtor would want to see the original moldings, gilt wallpaper, and the glass paintings. His grand parents hadn't changed it, his wife hadn't changed it, and as far as he knew, it still had Zenas' touch.

Brian, for his part, did not consider the moldings.

Coffin took the moment to return some hospitality and pour him something brown, then return to the sitting room.

In that quiet and reflective moment, as Brian considered his reasons for consulting the Inspector, Pip hopped up on the sofa. He sat next to Brian and leaned into him.

"Oh, Pip." The dog recognized his name and looked at Coffin. Perhaps he was being a Good Boy.

"Get off the sofa."

"Henry, Its fine for me."

Pip looked between Guest and Master. He remained where he was.

"It's Moira. She always lets him sit with her on the sofa." Coffin admitted.

"Moira?"

"She was one of the girls from the boat," Henry pointed to the bruises on his face. "She needed a place to stay."

"So, she's here?"

"Sure," Coffin said. "If I'm not going to sell it, I might as well use it."

"Is she a tenant?"

"A guest."

Brian smiled. "Well, Henry. Look at you. A dog and a housemate."

"Am I improving?"

"A dog makes everyone better."

Pip, still sitting on the sofa, still leaning against Brian, still spreading his black hair, seemed to smile and pant.

Brian wrapped the arm that did not have scotch in it around the dog.

"So, my brother, how can I help?" Coffin asked.

"Inspector?" he began.

"Henry." Coffin corrected.

"Henry, I am on some odd footing right now."

"How so?"

"Well, I just left the hospital."

Coffin smiled. "You have had your share of drama recently."

"Glad you think so."

Coffin caught an edge of anger. He resettled.

"Brian, a lot has gone on," he said. "Someone tried to poison you."

"To kill me."

"Maybe," Coffin said. "There were enough drugs in the cream to kill you if you drank the whole container. But, sure, it was an attempt."

Brian nodded and sipped the whiskey.

"Here is what I think," Coffin continued. "I think someone had been spying on you from beyond your backyard for a few days. They knew about the cameras. They crept up to your house in a blind spot, then put the sticker on the rear doorbell camera. Then, sometime later, they snuck in and dumped an opioid in the creamer, then they snuck out."

"And in the trash?"

"Yes."

"I looked on the cameras."

"Did you see anything we missed?"

He shrugged.

"Henry, I know something about you."

"Sure."

"You don't lie."

"I try not to."

Brian leaned forward. "Who did it?"

"I don't know."

"That's clever, Henry. Clever," he said. "I would like to remain in my house. I would like my daughters to be safe."

Henry noted who didn't get mentioned.

"So, here is the thing about being a Quaker and speaking the truth," Coffin sighed. "Not everyone wants to know the truth."

"I would like to know the truth."

Coffin sipped the whiskey.

"Have you asked your wife?"

"She's not my wife. Not yet."

"If you haven't asked her, why are you asking me?"

Swain brought one of his long legs up and rested an ankle on his knee. Pip regarded it as a possible intruder on his territory.

"I will," he said. "But, as you said, I have had my share of drama."

"You are on odd footing."

"My words."

"Yes," Coffin said. "I will tell you what I think, not what I can prove. If you want that."

"I do."

Coffin had another sip.

"Your fiancee has spent some nights with Paul Brody, the teacher. After the Langueduc, it seems, that she was rethinking her future and her relationship to the island. We pulled her over on Polpis Road with Paul Brody."

"I knew that."

"It can be a tough island."

"I know that, too, Inspector," he said. "I grew up around Big Jim."

"Well, Pidge flew to Boston to pull a few shifts in the NICU, her old employer. To take a break. Brody, apparently, flew up to give her an offer of off-island living. She refused. I believe she came back to you."

"She did."

"I believe she…recommitted to you."

Brian eyed him. They both were remembered of the jewelry case on the bed side table.

"Yes. She was welcome."

"Well, I think…" Henry paused to emphasize the word, "That Paul Brody wanted to change that. He was a former soldier and an addict, so he had access to opioids and the skills to surveil your home. I think he snuck in, poisoned your cream, and left."

"You can't prove that."

"Not completely, and not now."

'Because he is dead."

"Yes."

"Do you think anyone else could have poisoned me?"

Coffin finished his drink.

"Yes," he drew the word out. "But I don't think it is likely, do you?"

"Other people do."

"They don't matter ,do they?" Coffin took the moment to walk into his kitchen, get the bottle of Johnny Walker, refresh his glass, then refresh his guest.

Brian had returned to both feet on the floor, with his head hanging. Pip was eyeing him.

"She didn't come up to Boston when I was sick."

"No."

"She stayed here," he said. "Why did she do that?"

"You would have to ask her."

Brian remained with his head hanging. Coffin could see the rest of the Swain family pecking at him in the emptiness of the sitting room.

"Did you see her while I was in Boston?"

Henry saw the glint of Zenas in the shiny painting.

"Yes. I saw her out at Brody's house. She had taken that big car out there."

"And now he is dead."

"Yes."

Swain looked up.

"Did she kill him?"

Henry sighed. "Paul Brody was a heroin addict. He overdosed. There is no evidence that anything else happened out there."

"You talk like Herman Lamb," he said. "You didn't say no."

Henry sought out the glint of his rich and devout predecessor. It hung at the edge of sight.

"Brian, you have to make a decision. You have to take that lonely walk, away from everyone else, and reflect. You have to listen to yourself. In the end, you have to have faith in yourself."

"What about the girls?"

"What is good for you will be good for the girls."

Swain sat back and looked directly at the old man.

"Was this what you talked to Pidge about when you came to the house?"

"Yes."

"Do you know why she wants to quit her job? She had been intent on keeping it. Now, she has decided to give up her career."

"You need to talk to her."

He nodded. "Not an answer, Henry."

Coffin swirled the bottom of his second glass.

"Brian, you and I have been divorced. We have seen marriage for good and bad."

The younger man nodded.

"How much do you want to know about your wife? How many secrets do you want her to give up? How many do you want to give up? I would like to believe that two people marry for the future, not for the past."

Coffin paused.

"The two of you are going to get married. The girls come along outside of that, as does Wendy. Then Big Jim and the rest of your family. Then, the island and all its people. There will always be talk outside your window. But, I would hope, the two of you will always be inside your window." Coffin finished, "If that's what you want."

At that moment, Moira clattered through the front door and saw the two of them sitting. She waved, and then hurried upstairs.

Pip was sorry to give up Brian. After he left, Henry shooed him off the sofa.

CHAPTER THIRTY-NINE

October faded slowly during its final days. The unofficial start of winter comes at Halloween. Both of the winter bars, the Chicken Box and the Muse, throw big parties and all of the drunks come out as their favorite fantasy. Time and sexual energy gets invested into the costumes until they become a tapestry of art and desperation.

We love Halloween. We celebrate children, and candy, and the end of a long summer season. By the end of October, the tourist numbers have dwindled to nothing. The foliage, such as it is, has turned and fallen in these last few weeks, the sky turned to slate, and the white caps regain their winter look of gray, implacable permanence.

On Halloween, Main Street closes at four o'clock and all of the ghosts, superheroes, and princesses with attending parents, parade up to the Methodist Church. Almost all of the shops, even those closed for the winter, open their front doors for witches, Elmo, and goblins.

Coffin and Abraham drew the crowd control duty and stood by a yellow saw horse near the opening to Orange Street. Both men watched the hundreds of parents and children proceed slowly up the cobblestones to the Methodist Church and candy.

Somewhere in the crowd, Danny's wife and his daughter Hadley moved. Hadley had decided to be a princess this year, which was absolutely no surprise to either of her parents.

Pidge and Brian had come with his two girls. She and her fiancé were dressed as a nurses, and his two little girls were doctors. Wendy and the rest of the Swains said it was cute (and they were relieved that Pidge had resigned. It would have been too much.) The Swains walked in the crowd, amid several other families.

Pidge saw Coffin. He stood on the other side of the street, hands in his pockets, watching the families walk up the cobblestones. He didn't look at her. But her eyes found him.

For his part, Henry watched everyone who wasn't there.

Made in the USA
Middletown, DE
09 August 2024